Who's Looking After Who?

A COMEDY SERIES

Who's Looking After Who?

JAMIE C MCNEISH

T

Troubador Publishing Ltd
Unit E2 Airfield Business Park,
Harrison Road, Market Harborough,
Leicestershire LE16 7UL
Tel: 0116 279 2299
Email: books@troubador.co.uk
Web: www.troubador.co.uk

ISBN 978-1-80514-451-9

British Library Cataloguing in Publication Data.
A catalogue record for this book is available from the British Library.

Printed and bound by CPI Group (UK) Ltd, Croydon, CR0 4YY
Typeset in 11pt Minion Pro by Troubador Publishing Ltd, Leicester, UK

MIX
Paper | Supporting
responsible forestry
FSC
www.fsc.org   FSC® C013604

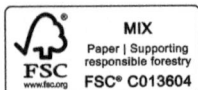

For Jim and Helen, two tremendous parents who lived their lives to the full.

Chapter 1

A tsunami of water evacuated the area where I was. Suddenly, I awakened, feeling suffocated and claustrophobic. I was unusually warm, wet, gooey and squelchy. Where on earth was I? I felt like I was upside down. I lightly felt around and my hand became lost in what seemed like the texture of a whale or something from the sea. It smelt a bit fishy too – like those crab sticks I used to eat down the pier. Finally, a memory, but I couldn't picture who I was. I had no recollection of how I got there and little idea of how to escape. I felt weak, like I had no physical power. I felt like a sad sack of potatoes. I tried to look around with the poor vision that I had – something or somewhere felt similar, like I'd been there before, many years ago and not just once. I was shitting myself, but I was so unbelievably comfortable, the most snuggled I'd ever been. Then, I realised I was naked! Oh, for the love of Gawd… I was absolutely starkers. Please don't make this some crazy sex cult, I begged.

I tried my hardest to escape, kicking as much as I could, but there wasn't much leeway. There was a horrific background noise, like a wailing that seemed far in the distance – this reignited my sex cult suspicions. Perhaps there were others trapped, being raped or tortured. I really needed to get out. This was way darker than anything I could remember. I used every bit of strength I could conjure up, every limb in my pathetic lifeless body to move around as much as I could. The distant wails turned into caterwauling screams – someone was being tortured. I was sure of it. That will be me next, I thought. Where was I? Hell? This had to be hell.

Suddenly, there was an opening and my head was vacuum-sucked into a different area. I was splatted with blood that covered my face and I could taste the saltiness of it in my mouth. It was disgusting. I tried to spit some out, but my lips could barely move. There was blood in my eyes and I couldn't clear them as my body was stuck behind me. I kicked with my legs and punched with my fists. The screams became even clearer and unpleasantly louder. The more I heard it, the more I moved. I just wanted this torture to end. Please, please stop! I couldn't bear it anymore. What had I done to send me to this purgatory? Was I such a bad bastard? I tried to think back… back to my very last memory. I could have been an old man, lying peacefully in my bed. Was this just my psychosis?

The soft fleshy walls lightly touching the side of my forehead, ears and cheeks began to move and convulse, as my nimble body flopped behind me. My head began gyrating forwards and backwards in sudden swooping motions. Think back, think back, think back. Was I, perhaps, a fisherman or did I go skinny-dipping in the sea and was swallowed whole by a whale? How terribly unfortunate that would have been. If I was lucky, maybe I was about to be coughed out into the ocean. Though, knowing my luck, I'd be ravaged by a great white shark. What had I done to deserve such a harsh punishment?

The outside noises became unbearable, then my head suddenly moved through some very red, soft, smelly, bloody flesh and black bristles. A tremendous amount of light completely blinded me, causing me unexpected shock, and I passed out.

Chapter 2

Ye Olde Tea Shoppe, Isle of Cumbrae, Scotland, late 1970s.

Helen had long peroxide blonde hair, which was tied back in a ponytail. She was heavily pregnant and wearing an old kaftan and strappy sandals. She was frantically frying fish in two skillets and chips in an old chip pan, while trying to avoid dipping her oversized breasts into the hot, sizzling oil. Her red-raw face was beaded with sweat from the heat and steam. She had marks over her hands and arms, which were historical kitchen burns. Gasping for breath, she slurped through a plastic straw, guzzling as much Diet Coke as possible from her glass.

'It's like the Sahara Desert in here. Jim, you need to sort out some extraction,' she shouted to her husband, who was wearing a navy-blue Adidas tracksuit and had a whistle hanging from his neck. He'd rushed back from Glasgow, where he worked as a PE teacher in Maryhill High School. He was standing behind a servery between the open-plan kitchen and the busy, bustling tea shop. He had a shaggy mop haircut and a very distinctive black moustache – the kind associated with the porn stars of the 1970s.

Helen finished plating four breaded fish and chips onto two plates under the hot lights and Jim cleverly arranged them on his hands so he could carry them all at once.

'Table four,' Helen shouted.

Jim rushed away, balancing the plates in his hands.

Helen threw another four fish into the hot oil in the pans. Nearby, Helen and Jim's smaller-than-average four-year-old boy, Frank, was washing dishes. He stood at the top of a small stepladder, allowing him to reach inside the stainless-steel sink and wash the crockery and cutlery from the tea shop. He kept rolling his eyes when the staff brought more plates, which kept piling up beside him. To a small boy, it must have felt like he had Mount Everest to climb before he'd reap some kind of reward for all his hard work. He imagined himself eating an ice cream from the Ritz Cafe while watching Glen Michael's *Cartoon Cavalcade* on the TV later on in the afternoon.

The old fossil waitress (who had worked in the tea shop before Helen and Jim bought it the year before) approached the sink. Norma the Grump (Frank's nickname for her) carried two plates, both of which still had food on them. She barged in front of Frank and threw them into the sink, splashing water and Fairy Liquid bubbles all over his face. He stared at her with a murderous glare, looking like a bearded elf. He was so angry he almost launched himself onto her saggy boobs so he could pull her to the floor and wrestle with her. As she barged out of the way, her hip grazed the precarious pile of plates, which then began to wobble. Frank's eyes bulged from his head as he watched in horror as a few of them fell from the pile and smashed onto the tiled kitchen floor – right next to his heavily pregnant mother.

'Frank!' Helen screamed.

Frank was livid and shouted, 'It wisnae me! It was her!' He pointed and shook his fist at Norma the Grump, who was oblivious to the bother she'd caused – that or she didn't care.

Helen shouted, 'Get the brush!' while lifting another four fish and chips onto hot plates. Jim swiftly whisked them away.

Frank climbed down from his stepladder, shaking his head and tutting loudly. He went to the corner and grabbed a large broom that was almost twice the size of him and tried his best to sweep the broken crockery into a small pile. His mother waddled around him, working away. It was a miracle that she could still work, as she should have been sitting down with her swollen feet up on a pouffe. All the colour suddenly drained from Helen's face and she began to feel queasy, but she kept soldiering on, continuing to cook for the abundance of customers.

Frank, with dustpan and brush in hand, was now lying on the floor like he was about to scramble under a muddy net on an assault course. He'd spotted a large sharp piece of crockery and was determined to sweep it up before his mother cut herself – knowing he would be blamed if that happened. He began moving across the chequered tiles, pretending to be a toy action man, until he managed to situate himself underneath Helen's kaftan to reach for the piece of crockery.

Helen wobbled a little and looked like she was about to faint. She grabbed onto the work surface with both of her hands only centimetres away from the sizzling pans.

Jim was standing opposite her in the dining area and shouted across, 'You okay, dear?'

Frank had almost managed to climb through her legs towards his destination, when, suddenly, a bucketful of pale yellow fluid came out of Helen's vagina, gushing all over Frank's head. He was completely soaked and, unfortunately, his mouth had been wide open, which meant he ended up swallowing almost a mouthful. The rest he spat out in little spurts like a fish in a comical cartoon. He couldn't believe or really understand what had just happened, as he stared up his mother's kaftan, wondering where the liquid had come from. He questioned whether she was starting a water fight with him, but this wasn't water – he was sure of that. This liquid had a much sweeter taste and he wondered if she had a juice carton in her pants. He screwed his little face as the rancid aftertaste continued in his mouth. Helen let go of the work surface and continued to cook the fish. Jim stood there in disbelief as his wife quite matter-of-factly plated another four fish and chips, knowing that her waters had just broken all over their son.

'We need to call an ambulance. It could take hours for them to come over from the mainland,' Jim shouted across to Helen.

'Quit causing a fuss and take the bloody fish out!' she shouted back.

He looked at her like she was madder than Tommy Cooper and reluctantly took the fish out to the customers.

Frank was now standing next to Helen, still covered in the amniotic fluid from his little brother's or sister's sac. She looked down at him and he shrugged his tiny shoulders.

'Goin' clean yourself in the sink, Frank,' she barked at him, before letting out a wailing sound. Frank looked genuinely scared and slipped over to the sink, climbed up the stepladder and sank his entire head into the dirty soapy water.

Jim quickly returned to Helen after hearing her wail loudly, knowing the whole restaurant must have heard her. His piercing blue eyes looked intense as he spoke to her calmly, 'I'm going across the road to call an ambulance—'

Helen quickly butted in, 'Don't be ridiculous, Jim.' She turned around and pointed at Frank, who was kicking his legs with his head still under the mucky sink water. 'When I had Frank, it took forty-eight hours before the little shit came out!'

Jim looked frustrated.

'Do you really want to be hanging around a hospital, wait—' Helen screamed out mid-sentence for at least thirty seconds while trying to talk to her husband. 'Ca... ca... call,' she was panting between words, 'Do... Do... Doctor... Gr... Gr... Grayson! The baby's coming, you bastard! Why did you do this to me again?!'

Jim ran around the tea shop floor, shouting to all the customers while whistling in between words with his PE whistle. 'Everybody out! Out! My wife's having a baby!'

The staff began gathering the customers and escorting them out. Jim ran out the front door and across the street towards the red phone box that sat at the edge of the Millport jetty. He was almost run down by a car, who had to do a sudden emergency stop. Jim breathed a quick sigh of relief, placing his hands on the bonnet while the angry car driver stuck his middle finger up at him and beeped his horn loudly. Jim reached the phone box and swiftly opened the door. There was an old, blue-rinsed, short woman gabbing away to someone on the other line. He quickly leaned over, grabbed the phone off her and abruptly hung it up.

'Sorry, dear, it's an emergency. My wife's having a baby!' he said, ushering her out of the phone box and quickly dialing for the doctor.

***

Inside the tea shop, Helen was sitting on the cold tiled floor with her legs far apart. All the staff had already disappeared, except for Norma the Grump who was gathering up her bag and coat from the rickety old coat stand. Helen was screaming loudly, then panting several times before wailing out once again. At one point, she shouted, 'Norma, help me!'

Norma rushed down the tea shop floor and said to herself, 'I'm not paid enough to be her bloody midwife.' She then bolted out the front door, moving faster than she'd ever in her life.

Now, the only people left in the tea shop were Helen and Frank (who had his back to his mother). He hoped she wouldn't ask him to help her. She shrieked at him, 'Frank!'

He reluctantly turned around and got the shock of his life when he saw the top of the baby's head coming out his mother's vagina. A lot of "firsts" were happening for Frank that day. He meekly spoke out, 'Mum, are you dying?'

Her next shriek was the worst. It was the largest yet as more of the baby's head popped out. 'You need to help, Frank. Get clean dishcloths!'

He continued to look at her with a scared expression on his face.

This time, she screamed and spoke at the same time, 'Quickly!'

Frank slid on the slippery floor towards the pile of dishcloths underneath the sink and picked up some of them, then ran across to his mother. She was now holding onto the lifeless baby's head, which was held over a pool of blood that had spilt onto the kitchen floor. She continued to pant, 'Put the cloths underneath the baby.'

Frank repeated the word, 'Baby?' And at this point, he clicked at what was actually happening. He placed the cloths on top of the blood splatter on the floor. The baby's shoulder was now out of her vagina and Helen seemed a little calmer.

'Hold onto the shoulder, Frank, and help pull him… or her out of Mum.' He calmly did as he was told and together they pulled the baby. She let out an ear-deafening scream as she pushed with all her strength and the baby flopped all the way out, apart from the tiny little feet.

Frank looked up at his mother and said, matter-of-factly, 'Think it's a boy, Mum.'

She looked down at his wee body and smiled. 'So it is.'

Jim's whistle oscillated between each shoulder as he bounded across the tea shop floor, eventually reaching the kitchen.

Helen pulled the baby's feet out of her vagina and looked across at him. 'Where the fuck have you been?' she said to her husband, scornfully.

Frank dotted his eyes from left to right, shocked by her language. 'Mum, you said "fuck".'

They both ignored their son's first swear word, pretending it didn't happen. Jim instinctively walked over to the cutlery drawer and grabbed a pair of kitchen scissors. He picked up a clean dishcloth - giving them an extra wipe. In front of Helen and the baby, he knelt down and gingerly cut the umbilical cord.

Helen, who now had the baby in her arms, began to panic. 'Jim, I don't think he's breathing.'

Jim unexpectedly grabbed the baby and harshly rubbed his back. 'I saw a doctor do this on TV. You need to rub the back until they cry.'

Awl... awl... get the fuck off me. It's like the Blackpool illuminations in here and it's bloody freezing. Where are my clothes? Why is that woman looking so sad? Oh geez... she's covered in blood and looks like she's about to pass out. Hoi you... peroxide blondie with the massive tits. What's your problem? And who's this Wee Shrimp staring at me, soaking from head to toe? Why're his tiny hands covered in blood? What have I just arrived into? A brutal massacre? And someone keeps pounding on my back!

Jim lifted the baby around to face him to see if he was breathing.

For fuck's sake. He's lifting me around like I'm on a forklift truck. Gawd, look at the state of this guy. Is he some kind of Woolworths catalogue model? Wi' his tracksuit and big, bristly moustache. Hey, look, he's got a whistle. If I could laugh, I would.

Jim turned the baby around to face Helen, who was both physically and emotionally exhausted, and carried on rubbing his back harshly.

Holy fuck! I'm a baby! A new born baby! Cheer up, Blondie! I know I've just burst through your fanny, but I thought you'd be pleased to see me. What will it take for this dude to stop rubbing my back like I'm a pipe band drum. It's really irritating.

Helen whispered repeatedly, 'Please cry, please cry, I just need to know you're okay.'

Why does she want me to cry so much? Is she no wise? Alright, alright, I'll cry if it'll stop Woolworths from manhandling me and to cheer you up, Blondie. It's no nice seeing a pretty lady cry.

The baby cried loudly, which caused a great deal of relief for his parents.

I hope you're satisfied 'cause I'm giving myself a headache.

Helen picked him up, wrapped him in some dishcloths and cradled him on top of her hanging breasts.

Oh, sweet love… now, this is paradise, resting between these two big bouncy bosoms. They're like fucking mountains. Maybe Blondie isn't so bad after all. I'll just close my eyes for a wee second and have a wee kip.

The baby fell asleep on his mother's bosoms. Jim and Frank gathered around and stared at the new addition to their family. Helen looked down at her newborn son and smiled.

'You're already my favourite,' she said as Jim snorted and glanced at Frank, who looked like he was chewing a wasp. Helen winked at Frank. 'It's just his birth lasted five minutes – yours was forty-eight hours and you had the umbilical cord wrapped around your neck. But, to be fair, Frank, if you hadn't annihilated me when you came out, this little devil wouldn't have slipped out so easily.' Helen looked back down at the baby. 'No more difficult than a morning jobby!'

Jim laughed while Frank seemed confused and scratched his head. He'd had enough of the palaver and just wanted TV and ice cream.

'Right, Jim, take the baby, gently, 'cause we don't want to wake him,' said Helen.

Jim carefully took the baby off her and cradled him in his arms, looking all proud. The baby opened his eyes.

Oh, come on, Woolworths. Give me back to Blondie. I don't want to see your ugly moustached mug. I want to lie on her giant exotic bazookas.

The baby looked up at his father and scowled, then cried. Helen stood up awkwardly and had to grab onto the work surface to steady herself. She signalled to Jim to hand over the baby.

'Are you sure you'll manage, Helen?' She nodded, took the baby and returned him to her breasts.

Here we fucking go. Only room for one in the inn tonight and that ain't you, Woolworths!

Helen had a mischievous look in her eyes. 'Do you think we should open the doors? Let some customers in to make up for this afternoon's takings going down the pan,' she asked.

Frank's eyes dotted around in their sockets and he grabbed his head with his hands.

'Dear, you're being ridiculous.' Jim shook his head at Helen.

'Yes. I'm going to the Ritz for a marshmallow ice cream!' Frank blurted out, shaking his two fists.

Jim ushered Helen away from the kitchen as she held onto her sleeping baby. 'Upstairs, dear. Doctor Grayson is on his way and we need to show him we are sensible, normal parents.'

Helen looked up at her husband and laughed. 'Good luck with that!'

Chapter 3

Helen was cradling her sleeping baby in her arms in their small cream-papered living room. She was sitting on an old tattered yellow floral couch, which had been discovered in a skip on a street in Glasgow. Jim thought it would be a good idea to transport the couch on the roof of their yellow 360 Volvo. After all the hard work attaching it onto the roof, just as the family were ready to leave for Millport, the car roof caved in due to the weight of the couch and just missed crushing the entire Coyle family. The cost of fixing the car was much more than if they'd bought a brand-new couch.

They'd spent all their money on buying the tea shop and had a huge loan from the bank, so had to scrape around for furniture to fill the upstairs flat, which was small and basic. They did have a small TV that Frank was glued to while watching a new cartoon, *Jamie and the Magic Torch*. He loved his time in front of the telly and despised working in the tea shop, especially with that old bag, Norma the Grump.

The family's two red setter dogs (Tana and Brochan) were lying lethargically in the middle of the floor. They were both pregnant and had recently been deliberately bred. Helen thought it would be a good idea to sell the puppies when they were born to make some extra cash for the tea shop. The rest of the family thought she was bonkers, as she already had so much on her plate, but she wasn't one to listen to their advice. She was a pioneer with a clear-minded vision of what she wanted in life and that included money.

Jim came into the living room, slurping loudly as he drank a mug of coffee, which was dribbling off his moustache onto his chin. He proudly held up a large celebration Cuban cigar that he'd kept for a special occasion – he was delighted at being a dad again. He was wearing his tracksuit for school and needed to leave for his teaching job in Glasgow.

Helen looked up at him. 'Make sure you register the birth. The name we agreed. James McNeish Coyle.'

Jim rolled his eyes; he didn't like her choice of names. He felt the old tradition (of naming the baby after its father and taking the mother's maiden name as his middle name) was quite dated and left a bad taste in his mouth. He decided to keep quiet on the matter and lit his cigar, then went to leave. The end credits for the cartoon on the television began to play, 'Jamie, Jamie, Jamie and his magic torch.'

Helen had a sudden light-bulb moment and screamed out, 'Jim, hold on!'

Jim came rushing back into the room in a panic. 'What's happened? Are you okay? Is the baby okay?'

Helen stood up and the baby woke at the same time. 'We're not calling the baby James.' She pointed to the TV.

'We need to call him Jamie. Just like the boy in the cartoon with the magic torch,' said Helen.

Frank turned around and glared at his mother, before whispering to himself angrily with his famous scowl, 'How come he gets such a cool name?'

The baby looked up at his mother. *Oh for fuck's sake. Could you not call me something normal, Blondie?*

Jim seemed like he was coming round to the idea, as he didn't really want another James. His own birth name was James, and his father and father-in-law were both called James. His firstborn was Frank James. The name wasn't much different, but at least it wasn't identical.

Helen nodded her head and became animated. 'Yes. I like it. Jamie… Jamie… Jamie… Lee Coyle.'

Jim almost choked on the cigar he was puffing and coughed out smoke. 'Lee?' he asked.

Helen continued to talk and was quite excited by what she was saying, 'After that actress, the one with the famous parents, Janet Lee and Tony Curtis.' Jim looked puzzled as Helen kept rabbiting on. 'You know, the one from that awful horror film we watched at the Town Hall last week to try and induce the baby.'

Jim laughed, then spoke. 'No baby that night, just a wringing pair of knickers.'

Jamie looked up at his mother, wishing he could speak. *You have got to be fucking kidding me. Why can't you name me James Bond or something masculine? Not after an actress! And one from a horror film where a bunch of stupid Americans run up the stairs instead of out the front door to get away from some crazy creepy psycho. Blondie – you need your head read.*

17

Jim shook his head, sighed and left to go out for his work. Helen sat down, pleased with herself. Jamie started crying, so she opened her dressing gown, revealing one of her bare boobs.

Oh, sweet pups! Now we're talking, Blondie! I'll forgive you for the name because you provide me with two of my favourite things – milk and titties! Jamie began to suck on her nipple, slurping in the milk like a creepy wee pervert. He stopped for a second and smiled. *Now, this is fucking heaven.* He nuzzled back into the boob with his mouth open, feeling delighted. No better way to spend a relaxing morning.

The doorbell rang and heavy footsteps came down the corridor. Before long, Helen's father, Jimmy, opened the door. He was wearing a pair of white overalls with paint splattered all over them, glasses with thick lenses and dark rims, and his thinning grey hair was swept back by a thick layer of Brylcreem. He was closely followed by his youngest son, Grant (who was Helen's baby brother and was only fourteen) – he had a pair of flairs on and a flannel shirt. He was vigorously chewing gum, trying to disguise the fact he'd just smoked a cigarette round the back of the tea shop. Helen's mother, May, was the last to come into the overcrowded living room. She was very much a socialite and was dressed to the nines in a smart blue dress-suit and a matching pair of high heels. She looked like she was about to go to a posh function, but she was actually just going down the street to gab with her acquaintances. There was a bowl in her hands, which was covered over by a dishcloth.

Jimmy glanced over at Helen, who was still breastfeeding the baby, then quickly looked down. 'For fuck's sake. Put that away, Helen,' he said, as May rushed over to Helen and took the dishcloth off a glass bowl of orange jelly and tinned mandarins.

'Dad! What have I told you about swearing in front of Frank?' said Helen.

Frank looked up from his cartoon as May placed the dishcloth over Helen's chest. 'Mum, you said "fuck" after *he* was born,' exclaimed Frank as he pointed at his baby brother.

Helen sighed, exhausted at the fact she was still having to explain that swearing was bad. She pointed at her son. 'Frank! I warned you! I'll ban you from cartoons for a week.'

'Papa said it, too,' replied Frank.

Helen glared at her father, who was now sitting down at the window. 'Papa is very naughty!' said Helen.

Gran May knelt down next to Frank with the bowl of orange jelly and mandarins and smiled as she spoke, 'I brought you your favourite, Franko.'

He looked at her in a funny way, confused at why she'd just called him Franko. He then became quite excited and looked inside the bowl. 'That's not a Mars bar,' he said, but May ignored his comment and went to the kitchen to fetch a bowl and spoon.

Grant was sitting on the couch next to Helen. The baby had stopped feeding and had fallen asleep. May came back into the room with a bowl, spoon and a carton of cream.

Jimmy, who was staring out of the window towards the Millport pier, turned around and said, 'The front of the tea shop is a fuc—' Helen stared angrily at her father, just as he was about to swear. He tried to control himself. 'The salt has damaged the exterior. It's peeling and chipped. It looks a bloody mess. I'll make a start on it today.'

Frank looked up at his papa as he scooped a spoonful of jelly and cream into his mouth. 'Can I help you, Papa?' he asked while spitting out jelly onto the carpet.

Jimmy looked at Helen and she shrugged her shoulders. 'You can help me with the ground windowsills and hold the ladder for me when I'm painting high up. But no fucking about, it's really danger—'

He stopped mid-sentence when Helen screamed at him, 'Dad! No swearing!'

Jimmy ignored her and took a dig at Grant, who was cockily lying back on the couch with both his hands behind his head and his legs crossed. 'It's good that one of the boys in this family wants to learn about painting. I wish I could say the same about my lazy son.'

Grant smartly spoke back. 'Jimmy, I'm clever. I think painting is a bit out of my range. I'm going to be an entrepreneur and make real money.'

Jimmy angrily stood up, waving his hand at his son. 'And I'm gonna slap you across your heid. We'll see how clever you are then.'

May went to sit next to Helen on the yellow floral settee and patted the baby's head while she smiled at her daughter. 'Helen, our Grant has been exploited from school.'

Grant snorted cheekily and spoke in a patronising tone, 'Mother, I think the word you're looking for is "expelled".'

Jimmy was still angry and shaking his fist at his son. 'I don't care what the fu… u… the word is. The little shit has been chucked out of school.'

Helen rolled her eyes at her baby brother, 'Grant! What have you done?'

May placed her hand on her daughter's arm, looking disappointed. 'He's been caught selling cigarettes and sweets in an abandoned shed in the school playground.'

Helen seemed quite proud of him. 'They expelled him for that? He does sound like an entrepreneur.' Grant sat back on the seat, pleased with himself.

Jimmy aimed his anger at Helen: 'Trust you to support his bad behaviour. We were never out of the headmaster's office when you were at school.'

May continued, 'He's also been insulting to some of the teach—'

Grant cut her off, 'The word you're looking for is "insulant", Mother.'

Jimmy's face became redder the angrier he got, listening to his son's cheek.

'Helen, we thought that perhaps you could give him a job in the tea shop,' May softly asked Helen.

'How's that going to work? We don't finish until late… how will he manage to get back to Glasgow?'

May kept smiling at her daughter. 'Could he not live with you? In Frank's spare bed?' asked May.

Frank turned around with a wide-open mouth and bulging eyes – shocked at what he was hearing.

Helen scratched her head. 'We do need the staff and we won't have to pay him as much as everyone else.'

Grant scoffed, 'I don't think so. I'll be making major

profits for your business, therefore I expect to be paid more for my efforts.'

Helen ignored him and turned to May, 'What about his exams?'

Grant laughed cockily. 'Are you kidding me, sis? One of the reasons I was expelled was because I had to teach the other kids. The teachers were entirely incompetent and intimidated by my intellect.' Helen chuckled out loud as Grant continued, attempting to condescend her, 'You worry about your little café, which you know I'm going to be a huge asset for.'

'Oh brilliant... I can see the top headline in the *Largs & Millport News*. "Grant, the tea shop saviour", retorted Helen, sarcastically. She then leaned forwards and became all serious. 'Okay. You can stay in Frank's room.' Frank couldn't disguise his disappointment and grunted very loudly, wondering when he would actually be able to have an opinion on anything. Helen addressed Grant seriously, 'But there are rules: no drugs, no girls, definitely no sex or alcohol, and you still need to study for your exams.'

Grant reacted in a conceited manner, still chuckling arrogantly, 'Sis, you know I have a photographic memory. I already know everything.'

Helen retorted, 'Yeah, everything about being a cocky dick!' She looked down at her baby and stroked his head.

Jimmy shot Grant the dirtiest of looks, before he exited the room, swearing under his breath. An uninvited Frank followed his Papa, mimicking his actions. Grant stood up while yawning and raised his arms in the air, satisfied with himself.

Baby Jamie caught a glimpse of his uncle as he left the room to view his new palace – his nephew's bedroom. *Who's this joker? The Artful Dodger?*

May smiled at her daughter and new grandson, proud as punch, before checking the boys had all left the room. 'How's everything downstairs?' she asked.

Helen sighed. 'To be honest, Mum, I'm dying to get back to the tea shop. We could really do with the cash.'

Jamie tried to move his face in disgust. *Brilliant, Blondie, you ready to abandon me already. You going to get Old Dear to look after me? I'm pretty sure there isn't any water in the well.*

May nodded to Helen's nether region, 'Helen, I meant down… stairs… after the birth.'

Helen thought for a minute. 'Oh, it's like a car crash has occurred and the car has to be taken to the scrapyard and sold for parts.' May looked horrified. 'But nobody is ever going to buy those parts.'

That's right, Blondie… this gorgeous wee baby messed you up real good.

'Except for one man, who will have to keep the old banger because it was him who crashed it in the first place.'

May and Helen laughed out loud, then Helen gave her mother a pleading look. 'In all seriousness, Mum, we really need to re-open the tea shop.'

May looked disappointed. 'Already? It's only been a week.'

Helen became defensive. 'Aye, but we're haemorrhaging money every day.'

May smiled and seemed pleased. 'Oh, that's good, so you'll be able to stay shut for a wee while longer.'

Helen became a little agitated. 'No, Mum. We're losing money every day and if we don't open soon, we'll need to close the tea shop indefinitely. Jim's teaching wage just isn't cutting it.'

May looked a little worried. 'Who's going to look after the baby?' she asked.

Helen smiled through gritted teeth and spoke nicely, 'I was hoping you might be able to help with the childcare?'

May looked delighted. 'Yes, of course, Helen. I'll help when I can, when we're staying at The Wee Hoose in Millport.'

Helen seemed relieved. 'Tonight?'

'Oh, Helen, I've got an Eastern Star meeting tonight. The girls would never forgive me if I missed it.'

'Wednesday? Thursday?' Helen looked at her mother in a desperate manner.

'Wednesday is bowling and Thursday, there's a Whist drive on, then we're back up to Glasgow for a dinner dance on Friday,' said May.

Helen sighed, while she put her hand on her forehead. Then, she stroked Jamie, who almost looked like he rolled his eyes. *Fucking lot of good she is! Not even one night she can look after her gorgeous wee grand-baby!* Helen began to shake her head with disappointment.

May smiled at her daughter and spoke, 'I could take him out in the afternoons for a walk.'

Helen forced a smile, even though she was bitterly disappointed. Thoughts were racing through her head, determined that she wouldn't be beaten. There were options – perhaps not always ethical. When Frank was born, she didn't have the extra responsibility and when they bought the tea shop, she managed to persuade him that washing dishes was a really fun game – with soapy bubbles and splashing about in water, pretending to be a pirate. He was actually a natural worker and much better than some of the other staff. Frank doing dishes in the tea shop became a normal occurrence. During the day, he was allowed to play in the mud patch in the garden and hang out with the dogs – while building mud castles with his bucket and spade. He seemed happy enough in the kitchen at night time. She'd convinced herself it would be good for his future work-ethic and that he could go on to do extraordinary things when he was older – that, or he would be completely burned out.

Brochan, the Irish Setter, slowly stood up from the middle of the floor in the living room. She was the skinnier of the two pregnant dogs and the one who would more likely be a pedigree dog – one that could have entered Crufts. She mooched around Helen and baby Jamie. The other dog, Tana, still lay on the floor, with no energy whatsoever. She was a much larger dog and was really struggling with the pregnancy.

Grant appeared at the door and stood as Helen clapped the dog.

May stroked her grandson's head. *Hey, Old Dear. It's a bit fucking late to make amends.*

'Have you thought of a name for this little sausage?' asked May.

Who are you calling a sausage? I'm a real human boy!

Helen came out of her glum state, becoming excitable. 'Yes, and sorry, Mum, I've decided not to use your maiden name or Dad's name. His name is Jamie.' Helen decided not to reveal the middle name yet as she didn't want to explain herself again.

May repeated the name. 'Jamie… Jamie. Yes, I like it. I mean, I would have liked James… but every Tom, Dick and Harry is called James these days,' said May and Grant snorted out loud.

'Well, no, Mother. Every Tom, Dick and Harry is called Tom, Dick and Harry.'

May tutted and shook her head. 'Oh, Grant, you know what I mean.' May was fed up with his wise cracks.

Helen was deep in thought, then addressed her brother. 'Right, Grant, you've got another fifteen minutes to settle in, then you can start your new job. We're opening tonight! Mum, you can take Jamie in his pram and show him off to all your pals. You're in charge afternoons.'

May looked a bit flustered, but nodded her head and picked up her grandson.

Oh gawd! Give me fucking strength. This is my life.

Helen jumped up from the sofa, regretting her decision immediately as she felt pain down below, however, she had made a commitment that she would honour. She proudly shouted out, 'Open for business.'

Chapter 4

Grant was standing shiftily next to a black front door on Ritchie Street, around the corner from the tea shop. He was heavily puffing on a cigarette, trying to inhale as much nicotine as possible before he had to start his first shift. He threw the cigarette on the ground and stubbed it harshly with his fancy Adidas trainers, which he'd bought himself from his entrepreneurial business takings. This was before his operation had been busted by the school headmaster. He'd already made a bad name for himself as a troublemaker with his smart-arsed ways, before the entire teaching force at the school had worked together to snare him in a teacher sting operation – mainly to prove that he wasn't actually as smart as he thought he was.

Grant opened his mouth and threw in a piece of chewing gum to disguise his rotten fag breath. He gazed towards two girls who walked past him – one tall and one quite small. They were giggling to one another when they spotted Grant, who was standing cockily in front of them. They had a soft punk look, dressed almost identically with torn tights and headbands that helped make their sprayed-blonde hair stand on end. They were also chewing gum. His eyes met with the smaller girl as she walked past him and they held gazes for a few seconds before she turned to her friend and giggled quietly. Grant watched them walk away, rubbing his hands together and feeling pleased – knowing he was going to enjoy his time in Millport. There would be work, but hopefully some play as well. The smaller girl glanced back just before going around the corner and Grant smiled and raised his eyebrows at her.

He walked around to the outside of the tea shop (which was a black-and-white painted stone building that looked a little tattered). He looked up at Jimmy, who was on the top of a ladder (relieved he didn't have to help him) and scraping paint off the outside wall. Frank was standing next to the windowsill, feebly rubbing the paint with a piece of sandpaper. Helen and May were lifting the old Silver Cross pram out of the back door – which was separate from the entrance to the shop.

Helen shouted over to her brother, 'Come on, Grant, give us a hand.'

Jimmy looked down from his ladder. 'Boy. Help your fuc… your mother and sister, you lazy…'

Grant sighed loudly, peeved off that he had been shouted at by two people before he'd even had the chance to help. He marched over, shuffling next to his mother and grabbing the back end of the Silver Cross pram, before helping Helen place it on the outside pavement.

The pram had been bought for Grant, who was a much later, accidental baby. May had sold the old pram she'd used for Helen (who was the oldest of four) and her other two children – Mary and Danny. She'd had grand social plans for when her children had grown up, but Grant's birth had deterred her for an extra ten years. Helen was already sixteen when Grant was born and so she helped her mother, as did Mary and Danny until they all left home. May was a gregarious lady – very popular and social. She did, however, have parental burnout, which allowed Grant early independence. May and Jimmy weren't entirely aware of their youngest's rebellious nature and sometimes even turned a blind eye to his mischievous school misdemeanours for an easy life. They'd already brought up Helen, who was also very forthright and sometimes confrontational, especially with figures of authority. The nature of both siblings stemmed from their father, who would always speak his mind.

Helen put her leadership skills into practice now, happily bossing her family around. 'Grant, inside now! You've got work to do.'

He stared at her for a few seconds, trying to impose some authority of his own before he went inside.

'Mum, take Jamie for a walk – show him off to all your gal pals and be a proud granny.'

May smiled at her daughter, as she was super excited about showing off her new grandson and was ready to lap up attention from the entire town. She placed her hands on the pram proudly.

'And Mum. Let me know when you're off to your Eastern Star meeting. I'll need to try and figure out where to put him next.'

Jamie was awake in the pram. *Where to put me next? Why don't you just shove me in a cupboard, Blondie, with all the rest of your fucking knick-knacks!* May pushed the pram. *Hey! Hold up, Old Dear. You're pushing me away from ma milk and ma titties!*

Helen stared up at Jimmy on the ladder and shouted at him. 'Dad, I need the ladder away by five. We need to let customers know that we're open for business.'

Jimmy swore to himself. 'For fuck's sake!'

'Frank. You can finish that window, then come in for your tea. We need you on dishes tonight.' Helen marched inside the tea shop in an authoritative manner (even though, deep inside, she was feeling physical pain).

Anger built up on Frank's face, which reddened very quickly. He stamped his feet and threw the sandpaper on the ground and shouted out, 'For fuck's sake!'

Jimmy heard him and looked down (unable to hide the grin on his face) feeling a little proud of the clone he'd created.

***

May walked past Newton's Amusement Arcade with her head held high, while pushing her latest grandchild in his pram. She'd only managed about fifty yards before being stopped outside the Ritz Cafe by two of her chums – Isa and Betty. They were both smartly dressed with similar brown skirt-suits and bright-coloured blouses, which matched their blue-rinsed hair. They looked like they'd taken fashion tips from Mollie Sugden's character – Mrs Slocombe – from the TV show *Are You Being Served?* Isa even had her own pussy, who was called Becca.

May gingerly pulled down the hood from the pram and smiled at her friends. Her accent changed as she became much posher than normal, 'Here he is. Little baby Jamie.'

The two ladies gasped, then cooed into the pram with excitable smiles.

Jamie opened his eyes to two new pairs of curious eyes staring back at him. *What are you two old bags staring at? Have you no got the bingo to go to?*

May addressed her two chums in her put-on posh accent, 'Helen said that the birth only lasted five minutes…'

Whoa! Hold on a second, Old Dear. You weren't talking like that earlier. Who do you think you are? Queen Elizabeth?

'She's put me in charge of all the daytime babysitting, but he has a nanny for the evenings,' exclaimed May. Isa and Betty raised their eyebrows in unison and seemed very impressed.

A nanny! Is Mary Poppins going to appear from around the corner singing 'A Spoonful of Sugar' at any minute and whisk me over the fucking rooftops?

'Our Helen and her wonderful husband, James, who's also a higher education teacher, own "Ye Olde Tea-shoppe".' May knew that Isa and Betty knew this information, however, she enjoyed a boast whenever she saw them. 'She's had to go straight back to work.'

The blue-rinse brigade seemed rather unimpressed by this statement and clucked to one another in their own secret clucking code.

I've no idea what these old hens are muttering on about, but it's a disgrace that she's back at work – 'cause I'm thirsty and the saggy paps in front of me look dryer than their leather handbags!

May became a little defensive. 'Our Helen has a mind of her own. I certainly wouldn't have gone to work when my baby was so small, but, of course, he will be well looked after.' She quickly shut the hood of the pram.

At last! I thought those two old birds were gonna peck my eyes out.

'I must go. I need to go to MacFarlane's butchers before he shuts for the afternoon. I'll see you at the Eastern Star meeting tonight, girls.'

Isa and Betty rolled their eyes and spoke over one another as May pushed the pram away from them. She walked another fifty yards before she stopped off next to a woman who was sitting on a large metal bucket like she was Oor Wullie. She was a larger lady with a stout build – her hair was greasy, grey and swept back on her head. On her face was a giant mole, which had thick black hairs sticking from it, and her lip had an infected cold sore that looked red and raw. A grey skirt covered her legs, which were wide open as she sat forwards, holding onto two large walking sticks – these stopped her from toppling over. Stood behind her was her husband, who had a golf polo shirt on, which clashed with his red tartan trews. His hair was also greasy and he had a smarmy look on his face. He spotted May first and looked towards her chest before he raised his eyes to look at her face.

The lady waved one of her sticks and was surprisingly friendly, shouting out, 'May... over here, May. I've been dying to meet your new grandson.'

May smiled and waved. 'Hello, Muriel and Tam.' She put the brake on the pram and pulled down the hood.

Tam helped Muriel stand up slowly from her bucket with the help of her two sticks – by the time she had stood up, she was completely out of breath. 'Oh, May, he's gorgeous.' She leaned in for a closer look, as did creepy Tam.

Jamie opened his eyes to see Muriel and Tam peering down – frightening the life out of him. *Oh Gawd. Please don't hurt me – I beg ya! I've been kidnapped by those inbred folk from* The Hills Have Eyes.

May popped her head back into Jamie's view.

What a relief. I've never been so happy to see someone in my life. Now, say your goodbyes to these… these… fuck knows what they are. Jamie stared towards the couple, lost for words.

Muriel smiled at May. 'Isn't he gorgeous?'

May put her posh accent on again. 'Oh yes! Baby Jamie is absolutely delightful. I've not heard a peep from him all day.' She turned around when tapped on the shoulder by another lady and Tam creepily began to stare at her boobs. Muriel tickled the baby's chest with her finger.

Jamie moved his face as much as he could to try and deter her. *Stop it, ye hairy mole. You're making me itchy.*

She started to move her mouth towards his and this gave him a close-up of her face. 'I'm going to steal a cheeky wee kiss while your gran isn't looking.' She spat a load of spit over Jamie as she spoke.

Naw. Naw. That's child abuse. And you've got fucking herpes. I'm only a week old. Give me a chance. Help, help, Old Dear! Look what she's doing to me.

Muriel reached Jamie's face with her big, hairy, infected lips and kissed him on the mouth and nose, slobbering all over his face. Jamie was screaming inside, feeling completely violated. He closed his eyes in the hope that when he re-opened them, she would be gone. The shock had hindered his ability to cry. He could feel her wet saliva all over his face and was horrified, but couldn't do anything to stop her. *Please be gone. Take your herpes and go kiss your perverted husband-brother. I'm just an innocent wee baby.*

Jamie finally managed to cry out loud and Muriel reluctantly backed away, as May leaned in and tickled him lightly on the chest.

Well, Old Dear. That's me ruined already. I'll have nightmares for the rest of my life... and herpes. I've only been in this body for a week. You didn't see it, but when my little mouth breaks out in scabs – it will be your fault 'cause you took your eye off the ball and let that monster swallow me up! Jamie cried even louder in the hope that the noise would be too unbearable and May would push him away from these ghastly folk.

Muriel placed her hand on May's arm. 'Tell Helen if she ever needs a babysitter, Tam and I would love to oblige.'

Nooo!

May smiled at Muriel, pleased with the offer. 'Oh Muriel. How kind. I'll let Helen know.'

You'd be as well to shoot me now or drown me in the sea. 'Cause my life is fucking over!

Creepy Tam leaned in and smiled, revealing a set of rotten teeth and awful foul-smelling breath. He reached his hand inside the pram and Jamie, terrified, closed his eyes and could only hope. *I promise I'll be a good wee boy from now on, if you take me away from this awful nightmare.* The pram felt like it was moving.

Jamie opened his eyes and could thankfully only see his gran in front of him and the buildings that lined the shore rolling back behind her.

Chapter 5

There were many hungry tourists on the jetty, across the road from the tea shop. They were watching fishing boats in the harbour while hanging around, waiting for all the bars and restaurants to open. Jimmy was clearing up all his painting equipment, putting it away into his old banger as May walked back from her jaunt on the high street with baby Jamie in his pram. She hadn't actually managed to go very far as she'd met so many people who were desperate to see her new grandson - and this pleased her greatly. She kissed her husband on the cheek, leaving a bright-red lipstick mark, knowing he was about to go into the Kelburne Bar for his early evening pints of Tartan Special.

'Jimmy, can you get something off Helen for your dinner tonight?'

He nodded, but didn't speak, as he was still thinking about the outside of the building, unhappy about the progress he'd made.

May picked up the baby from the pram and roused him from his sleep as she carried him into the tea shop.

Jamie opened his eyes and then his mouth, like he was

a goldfish in a fish tank. He was hoping there would be a plentiful supply of warm breast milk waiting for him, but was disappointed when he eyed the actual boob his head was rested on. *Gawd. Not that dusty sack again. Where's Blondie?*

He fell back asleep on May as she walked past the main dining area, passing Grant who was rolling cutlery into napkins at a vigorous rate. This surprised May, as she'd always deemed him as being lazy; never offering to help her around the house. She smiled as she passed him, feeling a little proud. She finally reached the kitchen, where Helen was spooning tablespoons of spices from a large black bin liner into an enormous pot. She'd sent Jim to the Indian spice shop in Glasgow the year before, hoping he'd come back with enough spices to last for six months. Typical of Helen and Jim crossing their wires - Jim had spent over a hundred pounds and brought back six large black bin liners of spices that would last for about thirty years! This amused Helen as she sometimes thought of the poor wee village in India that had to eat bland mince and tatties, because Jim had stolen all their spices. The tea shop was the only place in Millport that did a curry night. It had become very popular in Scotland – particularly in Glasgow. Helen liked to think she was bringing exotic cuisine to Millport, which was very much an ice-cream-and-fish-and-chips town.

Helen stirred her pot of chicken curry, as May approached the counter with sleeping Jamie in her arms.

'We had a lovely wee trip down the street,' said May, beaming. 'Think he might be hungry, though.'

Helen looked a little stressed. 'Pass him over, Mum.'

May passed Jamie to Helen and he woke up and saw her. *Where have you been, Blondie? I'm famished.* She lifted up her T-shirt and bra, exposing her right boob. *Now we're talking.*

May flustered around her – embarrassed that Helen was showing her flesh – and grabbed a dishcloth.

Jamie eyed up her boob. *Oh, how I've missed you, Laverne.* He glanced at the other one. *You'll just need to wait your turn, Shirley.* He began to suck, all pleased with himself.

May placed the dishcloth over Helen's breast. 'Wouldn't want Grant or any of the other staff to see your private lady parts, Helen.'

Helen rolled her eyes. 'Mum, it's just a bit of flesh.' There was a tray full of cut fruit; apples, tinned peaches and pears. Helen added it to a second metal pot and began to ladle the cooked chicken curry in with the fruit, as she breastfed her child.

'Helen, I saw Muriel and Tam down the street.' Helen took an angry deep breath inwards, insinuating that she didn't like to hear those names. Jamie moved his head from the milky nipple as his tiny ears pricked up. 'Muriel said she would be delighted to babysit wee baby Jamie while you're at work.'

No, Blondie! Please, I beg you.

Helen thought about it for a second. 'Would he be there?' Helen asked bluntly, as May looked at her, confused.

'Who?' she asked meekly.

'Her pervert of a husband,' Helen said brusquely.

You're worried about him? What about her? She tried to eat my face off and she gave me fucking herpes.

'Helen, that's not fair. He's a lovely man,' May said defensively.

'Well, if you call groping women's private parts and gawping at their chests nice, then he's a "lovely man",' Helen said sarcastically.

You tell her, Blondie.

'He doesn't do that,' May continued to defend him.

'Your dad and I have been aqua… consequences with them for many years.' May muddled her words.

Helen eyed her like she was crazy. 'Do you mean acquaintances?' she asked, pouring Tabasco sauce into the pot of curry.

'Yes, Helen. That's what I said,' replied May.

'Look, Mum, you must have your head in the clouds if you can't see it, but he's been groping your daughters for years and there is no way, over my dead body, that creepy Tam is coming anywhere near my baby!' said Helen, forthrightly.

That's right, Blondie. The Hills Have Eyes*: 1 – Baby Jamie: 1!*

Grant walked over, holding a large tray of wrapped cutlery, and placed it on top of the servery. 'Right, sis. What's next?' he asked.

Helen had to do a double take, shocked at her little brother's positive energy. She was used to working with Norma the Grump, who had zero enthusiasm and did the bare minimum. Helen picked up a bowl from a pile and a takeaway container.

'Curry night, Grant. We have hot and mild. Both served with rice. Eat in or takeaway,' she said. 'What's the difference between them?', Grant asked. 'Well the mild one has fruit and the hot one has Tabasco sauce in it',

Helen retorted. 'Is that ok with you Fanny Cradock?!' May knew it was time to make her exit – her nose out of joint after Helen's assassination of her friends. Deep down, she knew what Tam was like, but didn't wish to face up to it or admit that he was a predator, as that would have been too awkward. She smiled and patted her grandson on the head. 'See you tomorrow, Jamie.'

Jamie temporarily removed his mouth from Helen's nipple. *Old Dear, what have you got in store for me tomorrow? Are you going to stick me in a cement mixer and roll me onto the pavement?*

May waved bye to Helen and Grant, who were concentrating on their work.

'Grant, why don't you write a "curry night" sign and staple it to the board on the jetty?' suggested Helen. 'Then try and round up some customers.'

Grant saluted back at her. 'Aye, aye, captain.' He marched down the restaurant and passed Jim, who had just arrived back from Glasgow; in his tracksuit as usual.

Jim stopped briefly and spoke to Grant, confused why he had tea shop overalls on over his clothes. He then approached his wife and his baby, kissed Helen on the cheek and rubbed Jamie's head – who took his mouth off the boob temporarily, milk dripping down his face.

Wish people would stop patting me like I'm a fucking dog. He looked at Jim directly. *Surprise, surprise… it's you, Woolworths. Woofie-fucking-woof.*

'What's Grant doing with the uniform on?' asked Jim, curiously.

'He's working here now. And staying in Frank's room,' Helen told him, matter-of-factly.

'Would have been nice to have been asked, dear.' Jim glared at her.

'You weren't here and, besides, we need the staff – desperately!' Helen lifted a bowl of curry.

'That's another point. We're opening tonight? This also wasn't discussed. You only gave birth a week ago,' Jim said, seeming displeased.

'Look, Jim, I'm fine. Do you want to be a teacher for the rest of your life? Or do you want to be a successful businessman?' Helen asked firmly.

Jim raised his eyebrows. 'Yes, dear.' His voice deepened as she handed him a bowl of the hotter curry. He picked up a spoon, took a massive mouthful, slurped loudly and spilt half of it over his face, before a chunk of chicken and yellow sauce covered his tracksuit top. Helen rolled her eyes, unsurprised – Jim was famous for eating in his own special way.

'Jim, where's the birth certificate?' Helen remembered to ask. His response was sheepish and she knew something was up. She put out her hand. 'What have you done? I want to see it.'

Jim pulled out a crumpled piece of paper, which he'd placed underneath his tracksuit top, and reluctantly handed it to Helen.

She grabbed it off him and her eyes went straight to the name. 'Jamie… Coyle,' she said and Jamie's ears pricked up in hope. Helen looked at Jim, absolutely livid. 'Where's the middle name?'

Jim pretended he didn't know what she was talking about. 'Middle name? We didn't discuss a middle name. We agreed to change James to Jamie,' he said.

41

Ye wee beauty, Woolworths! If I could high five you…

'Lee! Lee!' shouted Helen.

Jim came round and kissed his baby son on the cheek, covering his face in curry.

That's fucking rank, Woolworths.

'He doesn't need a middle name. Just Jamie Coyle,' said Jim as he wiped the curry off Jamie's face with a napkin. 'We're not naming our son after an American horror actress. That's quite frankly – absurd.'

Yes, Woolworths.

Helen was a little taken aback.

'What about McNeish?' Helen said defensively.

'Dear, this isn't the 1920s. Why does everyone have to have a middle name? We can make our own decisions and not care what others think,' said Jim.

Woolworths, I'm actually beginning to like you.

Helen sighed and then smiled. 'I suppose you're right. At least you kept the name Jamie – I would have killed you if you changed that.'

Jim kissed Helen on the lips.

Ew… yuck… get a room.

The tea shop front door was opened by Grant and a plethora of hungry customers came bounding in – instantly creating a bustling atmosphere.

Helen (who was still holding and breastfeeding Jamie) grabbed an apron from a neatly folded pile. 'Jim, take off your tracksuit top and put this on. The boy's done good,' she said, throwing the apron at Jim, who caught it and turned around to see that all the tables were almost full.

Norma the Grump appeared from her hiding spot in the pantry cupboard and sighed deeply.

Frank had been sitting quietly in the small back area where the staff ate their dinner. He'd just finished off his fish fingers, chips and beans, which had made him gag. He hated beans so much that he'd placed all the fish fingers and chips onto the dirty table. The prospect of eating old crumbs and dirt appealed to him more than beans. In his mind, they were the absolute worst – beans and any kind of eggs. Every time he thought of them he'd vomit in his mouth.

'Frank, prepare yourself. It's going to be a busy night,' shouted Helen, as she stirred her large pot of curry while still holding the baby. Her nether-regions had gone from feeling like someone had punched her repeatedly there; to a milder, sweaty, multiple nettle sting - and Helen could cope with that.

Norma was staring at all the guests while she stood next to the servery.

'Norma, will you take some orders, please? Mild and spicy curry served with rice. Sixty pence a portion. A pound for two,' said Helen, urgently.

Norma grunted loudly, so Helen would know she wasn't happy. She walked at the speed of a tortoise to the nearest table, snarling as she went.

Helen was desperate to sack her for having a bad attitude, but she'd come as part of the tea shop package and she didn't want to rock the boat in Millport as Norma was a local – born and bred. Helen lifted the lid on a pot of boiling rice and steam flew at her and baby Jamie.

Oh, you fucking bastard! Blondie, what you doing? My skin's only a week old.

Jamie started to cry and this panicked Helen, as she knew she had to serve the food but make sure her baby was okay as well.

'Oh shit,' Helen swore. She stood back from the cooking area, knowing she'd almost burnt her baby.

Frank was standing behind her and wasn't going to let her get away with swearing. 'Mum, that's a bad word,' he said smartly as he waved his finger at her in a disapproving manner.

'Frank, not now.' Helen was flustered.

Grant came up to the servery. 'Sis, you may as well just start lifting the curries and...' Grant bowed down at her, 'you're welcome. Bet this is the first time this place has been filled to the brim and bustling all year. And all because of *moi*—'

'Grant, shut up! I need to figure out where to put the baby while I lift the food. It's not safe,' said Helen in a panic.

Fucking right, Blondie. My skin's still red raw!

Jamie continued to cry as Helen splashed some cold water gently over his face.

Grant hunted around in the kitchen and managed to find a wicker picnic basket. 'What about in here with some dishcloths? That'll keep him cosy.'

What? You're gonna stick me in there? What am I? A boiled ham sandwich for a fucking teddy bears' picnic?

'Yes, Grant. Good idea. Frank, gather up some clean dishcloths. It will only be for an hour or so. Just until we serve all the customers,' said Helen, happy with the solution.

Why don't you just stick me in the pram, you knobs! Who are these people?

Helen organised the cloths inside the picnic basket and placed Jamie inside, next to the sink on a work surface. Frank sniggered and stared towards his baby brother, deciding he was going to enjoy this evening.

What are you staring at, Wee Shrimp? See, when I'm bigger than you, which will probably be in about six months, I'm gonna batter the fuck out o' you. Wipe that smart grin off your face.

Frank scooped some Fairy Liquid bubbles from the sink with a mischievous look and rubbed some onto his brother's chin.

Piss off, you wee prick!

Helen picked up a ladle, then spooned curry and rice into some bowls. Grant and Jim swiftly took them out to the satisfied customers at three times the speed of Norma the Grump. Baby Jamie started to cry to taunt his mother and also because Frank kept teasing him. This made Helen work at a much faster pace, as she couldn't bear hearing her baby cry – it made her feel so guilty for opening the tea shop. She felt like she was stuck between a rock and a hard place with the situation. Her heart was in the right place, as she wanted her children to have a great life and she knew hard work was the only way to achieve this. She went over to the sink and caught Frank hitting the picnic basket with a wooden spoon. There were soapy bubbles everywhere.

This wee guy thinks he's such a smart-ass. He thinks I'm just a wee baby he can pick on. Well, let me tell you something, Wee Shrimp. I'm one of the biggest manipulators you will ever meet and revenge is a dish served cold.

Helen was totally fuming. 'Frank! You're meant to be looking out for him, not taunting him.' She picked up the basket and rocked it back and forth using the handle. 'There, there, Jamie. Be good for Mum.'

Frank's face looked like thunder. He started to wash the dishes with a pouted lip.

Ha ha… told you, Wee Shrimp. Don't mess with big baby baws!

Now Jamie had stopped crying, Helen placed him back on the work surface. She sighed and wiped her sweaty brow with a dishcloth. The heat of the kitchen was making her hot, along with the spicy curry. The busyness of the restaurant had temporarily made her forget about her lady pains, but she now felt the agony down below and had to take some deep breaths before lifting more bowls of curry.

Frank death-stared his baby brother and shook his fist at him.

I'm way wiser than you, Wee Shrimp. When I can finally move this body, you better watch out! 'Cause I'll be coming for you!

***

At the end of the evening shift, the family sat around the largest table in the tea shop. They were all eating bowls of leftover curry. Grant wolfed his down, as he was absolutely famished after a hard day's shift. He smiled smartly at Helen, who held onto Jamie. They were next to Frank, who was playing with a "mega" rainbow Slinky, which he'd bought in Mapes toy shop with his hard-earned cash. Jim counted that night's takings at the same time as he characteristically slurped his curry loudly.

'Sis, you going to call the *Largs & Millport News* tomorrow and let them know that Grant is the tea shop saviour?' asked Grant.

Helen nodded at him, half disapproving and a wee bit proud at the same time. 'It's just your first night and Millport is heaving at the moment,' she said, unable to give him full praise.

'Aye, but I was the shepherd and rounded them up like a flock of sheep. They were putty in my hand,' said Grant.

Helen rolled her eyes.

The Artful Dodger is so up his own arse. He's even worse than that Wee Shrimp dick.

Jim looked up at Grant. 'How many people did you count coming in tonight?' he asked.

'One hundred and twenty,' said Grant, pleased with himself.

'The money doesn't add up. There should be about a hundred quid with the sales of all the curry and the drinks,' said Jim, looking confused. 'There's only sixty quid here.'

Helen looked at Jim, concerned.

Grant instantly stood up and pulled out his trouser pockets. 'I know I'm the new guy, but it wasn't me,' said Grant, defensively.

'No one's blaming you, Grant,' said Jim, calmly.

'It's not the first time this has happened,' Helen said agitatedly.

Frank looked up with a suspicious look on his face.

It's hardly a big fucking mystery and shouldn't take Sherlock Holmes to work out who the thief is.

Chapter 6

Helen lay down in her bed, late at night, with her mind racing. She was still trying to figure out how to run her business and look after her baby at the same time. Jamie was two months old now. He had become much more physical and was demanding when it came to being fed. Time was also running out on him being able to lie in an old picnic basket next to the kitchen sink, where she could keep an eye out for him while working. Till now, they'd had a reasonably good routine. She'd tend to him in the mornings and watch some TV with Frank, then someone would take him out for a walk in the pram for an hour – usually her mum or she'd call on a friend for a favour. During this time, Helen would attend to her kitchen prep for the evening and serve out lunches.

Surprisingly, Grant was proving to be a massive asset and seemed to be putting his money where his mouth was – mostly when it came down to the hard grafting work and the extra marketing that was required. She knew that Jamie would eventually sleep in the other bed in Frank's room, though, so she'd need to figure out somewhere for Grant to sleep as she didn't want to lose him, especially with Jim teaching during the days – except for the school holidays, of course. The summer was fast approaching and, if last year's takings were anything to go by, they'd make eighty per cent of their yearly earnings in six weeks. Six weeks of absolute hell – if she couldn't find a babysitter. Helen blamed Jim for her stressful life because if he hadn't been so horny, they wouldn't be in this predicament. Helen had known that buying a small business would be hard work, but she hadn't banked on them having a baby at the same time.

Jim came into the bedroom from the bathroom, scratching his genitals over his white Y-fronts. Helen looked up at him and smirked. He passed the cot where Jamie was asleep and tiptoed to the bed, trying not to wake him. There had been a drought in the lovemaking department for obvious reasons and Jim thought that, perhaps, tonight could be his lucky night. Helen had an anxious look on her face, while thinking deeply about all her woes. Jim shuffled into the bed and cosied into Helen, who ignored him. He kissed her on the cheek gently, then put his arm around her shoulder.

'Jim, how much money did we make tonight?' asked Helen, the tea shop on her mind.

Jim had something completely different on his mind and ignored her question. He gently rubbed her shoulder and this made her look directly at him. He raised both his eyebrows, which was his way of trying to be sexy. She put her hand on her forehead, stressed. He kissed her on the mouth and she batted him off, then made a loud noise that woke Jamie.

'Jim, what are you doing?' she said, baffled, as sex was the furthest thing from her mind.

'It's been almost a year... since we... well, since anything happened in here,' he said, a little peeved.

'I'd like to see you try shooting a ten-pound baby out of your fanny. We'd see how much sex you'd want after that,' said Helen, frankly.

Jim seemed quite understanding, but kissed her on the neck anyway and made little grunting noises that Helen seemed to quite like. Jamie, lying in his cot, looked through the bars. He could see the beginning of a horror show play out in front of him.

That's disgusting! Wi' your own bairn in the room. I think I'm gonna puke.

Jim rolled on top of Helen and she put her hand out firmly. 'No, Jim, no. I am not having another baby. No way,' she said, without any doubt.

'Cause the next one might turn out like the first one. A wee dick – not like this little superstar. You lucky bastards!

Jim sighed while still on top of her and felt a bit deflated.

Helen became all matter-of-fact. 'I tell you what, if you book yourself in for a vasectomy next week, then we could discuss doing the business in the near future,' said Helen, like she was organising an office meeting.

'I'll make sure I write it in my diary, Helen,' said Jim, sarcastically.

Sounds like a good plan, Woolworths. Maybe you could have a wee suck on Laverne to keep you going in the meantime, but don't make any of those creepy noises.

50

Jim rolled over and opened the bedside cabinet. He soon pulled out a questionable condom with a shrivelled old wrapper.

Woolworths, no!

Jim waved the condom in Helen's face. 'What about now?' he asked with a smile.

Helen grabbed the condom off him and looked at it, which gave Jim a second's worth of hope. She soon screwed her face at him, though. 'You've probably had that since you were a horny teenager.' She examined the condom even closer. 'Is that the condom you used to keep in your wallet? I don't think they make this brand anymore.' She threw the condom on the floor. 'Think we'll just stick to the vasectomy plan for next week.' Helen rolled onto her side.

Woolworths has been turned down. I might cry and get a wee suck on Shirley to make him jealous. See how he likes it then.

Jim sighed and switched off the bedside lamp, feeling a little disappointed as he lay down to sleep.

The lights had only been out for five minutes when a sharp, squealing noise came from the living room. Helen sat up in the bed suddenly. Jim was already sound asleep and snoring loudly. He was one of the lucky people who could sleep through anything – he'd probably sleep through an earthquake if there was one in Millport. Helen questioned if she had imagined the noise or if it was perhaps just a dream. She was so tired at the moment that her mind could be playing tricks. She lay back down on the bed and tried to fall asleep again.

Jamie was awake in his cot and knew exactly what was going on. *You two are always so slow to pick up on things. If only I could talk, I'd have this place running like clockwork.*

Soon after, another enormous squeal unexpectedly came from the living room and, seconds later, another one. Helen sat up and wobbled on the bed – almost falling back down again. Jim was still asleep, snoring even louder. She nudged him really hard.

'Jim! Jim! There's someone in the flat,' she said in a very loud whisper.

In a split second, Jim went from being fast asleep to standing by the side of the bed in his Y-fronts with his fists in front of him. Helen was shaking with anxiety. The door of their bedroom creaked open and Jim was ready to pounce on the intruder by punching him on the nose.

Frank's eyes almost popped out of his head – his dad was only a metre away from hitting him on the face!

'No, Jim! It's Frank!' screamed Helen.

Go on, Woolworths! Lamp the wee prick.

Jim placed his fists down and looked a little stunned himself.

Helen addressed her son, 'Frank, you scared the life out of us. Why were you screaming?'

Frank was a wee bit angry now and almost on the brink of tears. 'Mum, it's the dogs. I think they're dying,' he said.

Helen's face collapsed and she felt devastated, but then she suddenly remembered and jumped out of bed. 'Oh shit! Jim! The puppies! They must be having the puppies!' She ran towards the bedroom door and almost tripped over the bed, but instead stubbed her bare foot on the wooden leg and the pain hurt like hell. She winced on the spot for a few seconds, but braved the agony and hobbled out of the room to find the dogs.

Jim scratched his Y-fronts in a daze before slowly following her.

Hey, Woolworths. Oh, come on… the one interesting thing that's happening here and you're leaving me in my cell!

Jamie cried as loud as he could as he didn't want to miss out on the entertainment. Jim went back and lifted him out of his cot, placing him against his hairy bare chest.

Woolworths, I appreciate the sentiment of you taking me there, but you're a bit prickly and you don't smell half as good as Blondie. He let out a little sneeze as some of the hairs on Jim's chest tickled his tiny nose, then he screwed up his face and rubbed it with his small hands.

There was absolute chaos in the living room. Helen paced from left to right on the only bit of floor that wasn't occupied by a dog, a newly born puppy or doggy afterbirth. Frank was standing up on the couch and looked stunned – he didn't seem to understand what was happening. Grant was lurking beside the hallway door – half asleep while wearing a pair of black Y-fronts and a tattered "Sex Pistols" T-shirt. He was half asleep and had been woken up by the noise. Jim held Jamie against his chest as he came through the bedroom door, which opened onto the living room. Everyone in the flat had been woken by the intense situation that had been thrust upon them.

Tana and Brochan – the two Irish Setters – had already given birth, as there were three puppies lying on the soiled floor. Helen was momentarily glad that they were skint and hadn't been able to afford to buy a new carpet when they moved in. She continued to pace and seemed stressed.

Jim spotted this and calmly spoke to her, 'Helen, calm down.'

She looked at him with panicked eyes. 'But we don't know which puppy goes with which dog. Are they Tana's? Are they Brochan's? We already have pedigree buyers for Brochan's pups,' Helen said agitatedly.

Jim slowly walked over to Helen. 'The dogs need a stress-free environment. It's traumatic enough for them.' He looked around the room and spoke to Frank and Grant, 'We can all watch them, but we have to be quiet.' He handed Jamie to Helen and sat them both down on the couch.

He's right, Blondie. Stop making a mountain out of a molehill. Get your tit out and enjoy the show.

Frank was still standing on the couch, holding his willy over his pyjamas, looking like he needed to go for a pee. 'Dad, are the dogs going to die?'

Jim laughed quietly. 'No, Frank. They're both becoming mums for the first time. Dog mums.'

Frank screwed his little face at his dad. 'What? Dogs can become mums? Eh?' Frank was having none of it.

Jamie looked at his brother. *Seriously, was the Wee Shrimp brought up on a banana boat?*

Helen had calmed down and put her hand on Frank's shoulder. 'Tana and Brochan are both bitches.'

Frank gasped. 'Mum, you said another bad word!'

Helen rolled her eyes at him. 'It means that they're both girls. Remember when Jamie came out of Mum's privates in the kitchen downstairs?'

Frank threw dagger eyes at his baby brother as he replied, 'How could I forget.'

Helen nodded at him. 'Well, the same thing is happening with Tana and Brochan.'

Frank pointed at the three puppies on the floor. 'So that's their babies.'

Finally! Sherlock has solved the case. Are you sure we're blood-related? He's an absolute spoon.

Helen nodded at Frank. 'Yes!' she said. Frank was still holding onto his willy and suddenly squeezed his face. 'Go to the toilet, Frank. We don't want your pee on the couch. There's already enough muck on the carpet.'

Frank ran to the toilet and Grant sat down on the couch, gagging at what his sister had just said. Frank had almost made it out the door, but couldn't hold his pee anymore and weed in his pyjama bottoms.

'Mum, the pee's dribbling down my leg!' shouted Frank as he rushed out of the door.

Has the Wee Shrimp got no self-control? Blondie gonna put a nappy on him… he's obviously not ready for his big boy pants.

Helen, who was mesmerised by the dogs and puppies, spoke to Grant while turned away from him. She tapped him on the shoulder with her free hand. 'Grant, go and sort out your nephew, will you? He's pissed himself with all the excitement.'

Grant, still half asleep, stood up without any questions and left the room. He knew if he was allowed to continue to live in the flat, he had to help in some ways. He liked Frank – seeing him as a smaller version of himself. There was definitely a "gene" connection.

Jim had been standing in the corner while staring at the two dogs and their puppies. All had been quiet on the western front for a little while now. Tana had two pups beside her and Brochan had one.

Helen stared at Jim and spoke to him in a very loud whisper, 'Jim, how are we going to tell which puppy is whose? We'll need to mark them in some way.'

Jim shrugged his shoulders.

'Do we have marker pens?' asked Helen.

From the door, Grant said, 'What about paint? I'm sure Jimmy left some in the cupboard. Think there's some avocado – the kind that was used for the bathroom – and white?'

'Go and get it,' Helen said enthusiastically and he left the room. She was so anxious about not mixing the puppies up, as she'd personally contacted Crufts and blagged access to their contacts list. She'd managed to secure some sales for Brochan's pups, who would be bred specifically for dog shows.

During all the chatting, Brochan had moved herself into the kitchen and appeared to be embarrassed about giving birth while all eyes were on her. Her poor lone pup, who had a white stripe on the top of its head, was wriggling around on the floor helplessly.

Helen became agitated. 'We have to help it. She's left the pup on its own. It desperately needs its mum,' she said.

Jim sat down beside her. 'Keep calm, dear, and all will be well,' he said as he placed his hand on her shoulder.

Woolworths has a point. Blondie's pretty neurotic.

There was a massive dog scream from the kitchen and Helen once again began to panic. Jim stood and quietly went to check Brochan was alright. Two new pups had been born and were now lying beside her. One was still attached to the umbilical cord, still in the sac. The other pup was cuddled up to its mother. Helen stood at the door and held onto Jamie. Brochan started to eat away at the umbilical cord and sac that enclosed her puppy.

That dog is eating her own baby. Sick bitch!

'Do you think she's alright? The puppy?' Helen asked Jim.

He rubbed her back. 'Yeah, should be fine. Why don't I gently move the puppy in the middle of the floor into the kitchen next to Brochan? It seems to be shivering and needs some warmth.' He picked up the tiny striped puppy with extra precision and care, moving it into the kitchen and gently placing it next to Brochan.

The other puppy was now free from the sac and the umbilical cord had been entirely eaten.

A scream came from within the living room and sounded different from the previous ones. Jim and Helen turned around and Frank was standing in front of Tana with his jaw open, in total shock. Along with the two original puppies, there was a new lifeless and slightly deformed one lying on the floor. This pup was a greyish colour and looked different from all the other red ones that had already been born. There was also another pup attached to the umbilical cord, which Tana was chewing on.

Helen went over to Frank and grabbed his hand, as she held Jamie in her other arm. 'It's okay, Frank. Tana is just caring for her,' she said, gently.

Tell him the truth, Blondie. No wonder precious wee Frank is such a fucking baby. She's eating her own offspring 'cause she's a sick bitch!

Frank pointed at the grey puppy and was almost crying. 'It's that one. Look! It's dead, Mum,' he said.

Helen turned to Jim, concerned, and he knelt down and examined the pup. 'Think it's breathing, but it does look quite poorly,' Jim said, shrugging his shoulders at Helen.

Tana had freed her third healthy pup from its umbilical cord, which she'd finished off by eating it. She moved her nose towards the poor grey pup and pushed it away – dismissing it from her litter.

Helen looked at Jim, not knowing what to do, and whispered, 'Is she rejecting the pup?'

He once again shrugged his shoulders in confusion. Frank started to sob loudly.

Grant came through the door into the living room, holding two pots of paint. 'Right, let's mark these pups and make lots of money,' he said as he stared at the rest of the family, then looked confused. 'Why the sombre mood?'

Artful Dodger, can you not see one of the pups is dead and precious Wee Shrimp can't handle it? And it's really early for Blondie and Woolworths to explain about life and fucking death.

Tana stood up and moved closer to the grey pup. Helen became instantly relieved and hopeful as she gently rubbed Frank's shoulder. 'Look, Frank, she's going to bring her pup closer to all the others and care for it.'

A look of hope took over Frank's face, then instant horror as Tana roughly picked up the grey pup with her teeth. The poor soul was hanging from her mouth by the skin on its back. Frank's eyes bulged from their sockets and Helen had to stop herself from neurotically shouting out at her cruel dog. Tana slowly walked to the other side of the living room and dumped the pup behind the television.

Frank was anxious and panicked. 'Where's she taking the pup now?' he whined.

Helen patted him on the shoulder. 'Just to watch some TV, Frank.'

Stop sugar-coating it, Blondie. The Wee Shrimp has to find out sometime about death. You'd be as well explaining it to him now – before some of those old folk cark it!

Tana came back over to tend to her three healthy puppies.

Jim knelt down beside Frank and placed his hands on his arms. 'Frank, that wee puppy wasn't strong enough to survive in this world and is probably going to die,' he said.

Helen rubbed his arm. 'Yes, Frank. Everything is born and then they die.'

Very wise, Blondie! Sure you're not Yoda from Star Wars?

Frank seemed concerned and looked up at his parents. 'Does that mean you're going to die?'

Jim stared at Helen – she'd opened another can of worms in an already stressful situation. He rubbed his son's head. 'Yes… one day… but a long, long time away.'

Frank seemed a little bit relieved, but then had another alarming thought. 'What about Gran and Papa? Will they die soon?'

Good Gawd… probably – they're old. Grumpy Old Painter fought in the war, for fuck's sake!

Helen looked down at Frank. 'You don't have to worry about that. They're both healthy at the moment,' she said as Jim eyed her, then nodded. 'Come on, Frank. Think it's time you went to bed. You can meet the rest of the pups tomorrow.' Helen passed the baby to Jim and took Frank's hand, leading him off to the bedroom.

Grant squatted down and carefully splashed enough avocado paint onto Tana's puppies with a small paintbrush. Another huge dog scream came from the kitchen. Jim rushed to the door with Jamie in his arms. Brochan was lying on the floor on her side with her back legs wide open, howling loudly. She was unaware that Jim and Jamie were watching her. A new pup's head popped out of her. The sac had already broken; the pup's eyes were closed and looked like they were covered over by some slime.

Wow, that's a bit graphic, Woolworths. Why did you bring me to this revolting scene?

Jim watched the birth with fascinated eyes as the body of the pup slowly came out of its mother, before gently plopping onto the kitchen linoleum – still attached to the umbilical cord.

Grant rushed past Jim and Jamie into the kitchen. He had a tin of white paint hanging from his hand by the handle. The paint splashed onto the floor as he knelt down. He had a small paint brush in his hand, which he dipped into the paint and lightly marked six of Brochan's pups with a splash of white paint. He'd previously marked Tana's six pups with the avocado paint. Jim nodded his head at Grant in approval of his quick thinking.

Helen came back from Frank's room and stared towards the helpless wee grey pup. Jim turned to face her and smiled slightly, with a small tear in his eye. He walked towards her and put his arm around her shoulder, holding Jamie (who had fallen asleep on his chest).

Helen sighed. 'Poor wee thing. Didn't get a chance to live.' She looked at Jim with a worrisome look. 'Do you think he's still alive?'

Jim handed Jamie to Helen, then knelt down on the ground and gently placed his finger on the inside of the pup's rear leg, checking for a pulse. He'd learnt how to do this when Tana and Brochan were puppies themselves. Jim kept his finger on the pup for a few minutes, but couldn't feel a pulse. He shook his head at Helen, feeling helpless and disappointed, before he picked up the tiny puppy with both hands. 'We'll bury him tomorrow,' Jim said, solemnly, to Helen, who was now cradling baby Jamie on her chest. A tear ran down her cheek and she felt nervous deep within her stomach. She drew Jamie further into her chest for her own comfort, which woke him up.

Good Gawd! Where the hell am I? Jamie turned his head a little to the left. *Phew! Laverne.* Then, to the right. *Oh Shirley… thank Gawd it's my two favourite girls.*

Helen patted the deceased puppy. 'I think the funeral will be good for Frank, Jim.'

That's right, Blondie. Protect the precious Wee Shrimp.

Jim took the pup away.

Grant came out of the kitchen, paint splattered over his "Sex Pistols" T-shirt and bare legs. 'Sis, why don't you go and get some sleep? I'll stay up until I think all the pups are born. Surely there can't be too many more,' he said.

Helen smiled at her brother, impressed by his kind gesture. 'You have a lie-in tomorrow, Grant. Jim and I will do the early shift,' she said.

Grant saluted her, 'Aye, aye, captain. See you in the morning.'

Helen had one last look at Tana, who had six healthy-looking, avocado-painted puppies snuggling into her. At that moment, she understood the difference between dogs and humans: it was how pragmatic a dog could be – able to discard their own flesh and blood as if they never existed. Her own motherly love and instinct seemed to, somehow, have been switched on whenever Frank was born. She wondered how a mother (any mother) could abandon one of their offspring. She went to bed that night appreciating the love she had for her children even more.

Chapter 7

In the back garden of the tea shop, the sun was shining brightly. There was a concreted area that housed a kennel for the dogs and their recently born puppies. A door led into a small but cosy room where they slept at night while nursing their pups. They lay outside, huddled next to one another – still sporting the allocated paint to tell them apart. The kennel area was enclosed with chicken wire, so there was little chance the dogs could escape. There was a large muddy patch next to the kennel, which would have been ideal for growing vegetables for the tea shop.

When Helen and Jim moved in there were carrots, turnips and even some lettuce – unfortunately, gardening was neither Jim's nor Helen's forte and they'd somehow managed to kill all the good root vegetables with some questionable weedkiller they'd found in a cupboard. The previous vegetable patch was now a pile of mushy mud – to the delight of Frank, who liked to get down and dirty. It was the only place he could find some peace and quiet... well, that was until those previously subdued Irish

Setters had fourteen puppies between them. Fifteen, if you included the poor wee soul who died.

Jim and Helen thought it would be a good idea to teach Frank about death early on to prepare him for the future. They'd arranged a small funeral at the bottom of the garden for the dead puppy, who he had been allowed to name. After a lot of deliberation, he'd decided on Scooby-Doo – the main character from one of his favourite cartoons. The two contenders had been Scooby-Doo and Keith Chegwin from *Multi-Coloured Swap Shop* – his favourite Saturday morning show. There was something about Keith Chegwin's enthusiastic energy that reminded him of a dog – the way he bounded about. He wanted to remember the dead puppy in a happy way and would have been content with either decision. As he was four years old, it made sense for him to name the puppy after a cartoon dog.

The burying of the puppy was to take place in the main garden, which was a much prettier area. Jimmy had taken over the gardening when he was in Millport, leaving strict watering instructions when he wasn't there. Helen usually forgot, but, fortunately for her, rain was common all year round in Millport and the garden looked nice. There was a greenhouse where he grew tomatoes and other colourful plants. A slabbed pathway went up the middle of the garden with two sides of flower beds, which had an array of flowers – different ones for alternative seasons. As it was springtime, there were crocuses and daffodils in all their glory. There was a grassy patch that had a clothes line across it, which had a combination of dishcloths and nappies flapping around in the wind. The other side of the garden had a shed for all of Jimmy's tools and in the far right corner, there was an old birch tree. The garden had stone walling all the way around, allowing some privacy for the occasional, optimistic sunbather.

The puppy had been wrapped in an old T-shirt of Jim's, which Helen was desperate to throw out as it was full of holes and had permanent sweat marks under the armpits – any excuse to try and improve his dress sense. The pup had been put into a Kellogg's Coco Pops box to (literally) sugar-coat the funeral for Frank and to make it less sad. Helen had kept the pup in the tea shop's chest freezer to save it from rotting and had hoped that Frank would forget about what happened. Every day, he'd ask her where it was and she'd dodge the question. Then, one day, while he was having his dinner in the staff room of the tea shop, he'd gone into the freezer and pulled out the Coco Pops box. His tea had been chicken pie and vegetables that night, which he didn't really like, so he opened the box and pulled out the wrapped-up dead puppy. He then unravelled the T-shirt and the frozen dead pup plopped out onto the dinner table. Frank screamed blue murder. He was traumatised for a second time. This is when Helen knew she had to have the funeral. She'd asked May, Jimmy and Grant to attend as official mourners - in order to support.

The family all stood under the birch tree, where Jim had dug a fairly large hole in the hope that one of the dogs wouldn't dig up the pup and eat it when they were running around in the garden. Helen had little hope that they wouldn't after witnessing Tana's brutal act of disregarding her own offspring when it had been born deformed. She'd surely have no qualms, then, about chewing into the dead carcass.

The clouds were beginning to move over the sun, seeming like rain was on the way. Helen was holding onto baby Jamie. She thought it was as well that he should be here – maybe it was good for his future, too.

Jimmy looked agitated, like something was bothering him, and he made this very clear by tutting loudly. He only managed to contain himself for a few seconds before blurting out, 'Who ran over the fucking flower bed?'

Helen eyed him and harshly said, 'Dad!'

May stroked Jimmy's arm.

Grumpy Old Painter's my favourite 'cause he swears even more than me and he's always so pissed off. No fucking wonder with this shower of lunatics.

Jim held onto the Coco Pops box with the dead puppy inside. He looked down at his son. 'Frank, would you like to put Keith Chegwin in the ground?'

Frank looked up and screwed his face. Helen jumped in, 'Jim, he decided the puppy was called Scooby-Doo.'

Trust the Wee Shrimp to come up with such an original fucking name.

Jimmy tutted loudly, disapproving of the chosen name.

May looked down at her grandson. 'What a lovely name for him. Goodbye, scabby dog. Rest in peace,' she said.

Grant grunted loudly over his Mum's *faux pas*.

Frank looked a bit upset with her. 'Gran, he wasn't a scabby dog.'

May looked at Helen. 'I thought that was his name?'

Grant quickly chipped in, 'Mother, it's *Scooby-Doo*! The coolest cartoon dog.'

Seriously, let's just bury the corpse. The fucking thing was barely alive.

Jim realised it was all taking too long and bent down, then placed the Coco-Pops-puppy inside the deep hole and stood up again.

Frank stared up at his dad. 'Dad, why do we have to put Scooby-Doo in the ground? Can he not go on top of the mantelpiece in the flat? Then we can see him every day.'

Jimmy shouted to his grandson, 'He'll stink the fucking house out.'

Helen eyeballed her dad as she tried to think how she would explain to her son about burying.

Grant had a smart smirk on his face. 'We could always take him to a taxidermist, then Frank could see him every day.'

Think that's the funniest thing the Artful Dodger has ever said!

Helen huffed at Grant. 'Grant, don't you dare open that can of worms.'

May looked at Helen and spoke, 'Helen, you know there will be worms with wee spotty-dob, deep down in the ground.'

Helen could only sigh in despair at how badly things were being explained to Frank, who was already confused. She took a few seconds to think, then let rip at the family. 'Mum! The puppy in the box is called Scooby-Doo.' She then turned her attention to Grant. 'No, Grant, we will not be stuffing him. Stop stirring the pot.' Jimmy was next as she glared at him. 'Dad! No swearing! This is meant to be a funeral.' Helen then knelt down next to Frank with Jamie still in her arms, placing her free hand on his shoulder. 'The best place for him is the ground. When something dies, we bury them and we will always know where they are. But the most important place to remember them is…' – she rubbed the top of Frank's head – 'in here.'

Frank looked at her in a puzzled way. 'How did Scooby-Doo get inside my head? Will he be there forever?'

What a fucking idiot. I despair of the Wee Shrimp.

Jim intervened and also knelt down. 'What Mum means is you will always remember Scooby-Doo through your memories.'

Can you not explain this shit to him when the rest of us are asleep?

Little spots of rain were now coming down and Jimmy was beginning to get agitated. 'Would you just hurry up? It's gonna piss it doon in a minute!'

'Frank, do you want to say a good memory about Scooby-Doo? And then we can all go inside,' Helen said.

Gawd! It's just a dead dog. There's another fourteen of the wee bastards over there.

Frank seemed like he was thinking hard and the rain started to pound down. He eventually shook his head. 'No, I don't think so.'

As soon as Jimmy heard these words, he stormed off and shouted as he marched away, 'I'll be fucked if I'm getting soaked. I'm off to the fucking pub!'

Grumpy Old Painter is definitely my favourite. He's got a right good way wi' words.

The rest of the family were almost soaked to the skin. Jim went to the wee grave and picked up the garden trowel; that had been used to dig the hole earlier.

'Does anyone else have anything they'd like to say?' Helen asked. She glanced quickly at them all individually and shook her head to insinuate "no". 'Does anyone have anything they'd like to put in the grave with Scooby-Doo?'

May ruffled inside her handbag and pulled out a Mars bar and threw it into the hole with the dead puppy.

Frank looked at his gran curiously. 'Can a dead puppy eat, Gran?'

May smiled at him and nodded. 'Yes, of course,' she replied.

Helen rolled her eyes at her mother. Frank went to the edge of the grave and stuck his finger up his nose, wiggled it about for a minute, then pulled out the biggest bogie he could find. The rest of the family looked at him, astonished. He bent down next to the grave and flicked the bogie on top of the Coco Pops box. 'Just in case you're hungry later, Scooby-Doo,' he said seriously.

What a little creep!

Grant started to laugh and couldn't help being loud. The laughter became infectious as Helen, May and Jim were also soon laughing. They were all drenched, looking like they'd been in for a swim in the sea. Frank watched his relatives laughing and also burst out into giggles.

Jim quickly shovelled mud into the hole to fill it as quickly as he could manage. Helen began to run back to the house with the baby in her arms and was slowly followed by May, who waddled fast but carefully, trying not to trip. Grant also made a run for it and all the way over Jimmy's flower bed, deliberately damaging a few more daffodils because he knew it would wind the old man up.

Frank stood and stared at the wee puppy's grave as Jim continued to fill the hole. He was feeling weird – there was a new kind of sensation in his stomach. Perhaps a new understanding of all the possible heartache that was ahead. He enjoyed the water splashing over him as they only had a bath in the flat. It was like each drop of warm rain made him feel energised; refreshed.

Jimmy had made a tiny wee memorial cross in his garden shed. It was just two thin bits of kindling nailed together, but it did the job and would help Frank remember about his wee pal Scooby-Doo, who he'd seen more as a corpse than a live puppy. Jim stuck the cross into the wet mud and hoped it would remain there for a while. He stood next to his oldest son, put his arm around him and felt a little bit emotional himself – it reminded him that life could be short and that he sure as hell would live every day to the fullest.

He rubbed Frank's soaking wet head, 'Come on, son. We better go inside before we catch a cold.' He grabbed Frank's hand and led him out of the garden. There was no point in running - they couldn't get any wetter.

**

Inside the tea shop, Jim dried himself with a towel and Gran May helped Frank dry himself and change into dry clothes. Helen finished putting previously prepared sandwiches onto a platter, along with some scones. Grant was filling up a large pot of tea using the kitchen's hot-water urn. The rain was battering off the kitchen window and it was Biblical. Baby Jamie had already been dried and changed, and was now lying in the pram next to a set-up table. Helen placed the sandwiches on the table and the family sat down and dug in. They were famished. The funeral had been a bit of an ordeal and now it was time to relax. It was a Monday and they'd chosen to close the tea shop as the previous Monday's takings had been zero.

Helen, who was still fussing around the sandwiches, finally sat down. 'And relax,' she said.

The only sounds that filled the room were the loud rain against the window panes and the noises of chewing and swallowing, particularly from Jim, who'd managed to cover his moustache with mayonnaise by forcefully stuffing a ham sandwich through his thin lips; like a parcel through a letter box.

Helen looked towards Jim, feeling relieved that the dead dog was buried... but then she stood up and slapped the table hard with both hands, frightening the life out of everyone else. May spilt her tea over her plate of cheese and tomato sandwiches. Frank nearly fell off the chair he was sitting on as he'd been swinging back. Luckily, Jim's reflexes were good from his PE job and he managed to catch the chair and push it back onto the ground.

'What is it?!', he spurted out, sounding both angry and shocked.

She addressed them all, 'Did anyone let Tana, Brochan and the new pups back inside?'

Grant shook his head. Helen bypassed May, because she knew she wouldn't have done it. She looked desperately at Jim, who said, 'No!' Then she ran like a lightning bolt towards the side door, followed swiftly by Jim and Grant.

Helen flew through the door into the inside sleeping area, where the dogs were kept at night, and noticed that it was empty. The door that allowed them to wander outside into the enclosed area was shut. The battering rain could still be heard. She quickly opened it up – on the outside, the dogs were lively and drenched to their skin with very wet hair. There was some avocado and whitewashed paint on the tarmac.

Jim and Grant had already entered the kennel from the outside. They each took a soaked puppy and ran with them into the inside area.

Helen shouted to her mum, who was standing beside her with Frank holding onto her legs. 'Mum, take Frank and gather up as many towels as you can find. Oh, and my hairdryer... that's upstairs in my bedroom.'

Jim and Grant had now taken six of the shivering puppies inside. Helen bent down and picked up an old dirty towel that was lying on the floor. A little spider crawled from underneath the towel and Helen let out an involuntary yelp (as if she didn't have time for a full scream) then hit it hard with the towel, making it fly out the door like Spider-Man as the insect shot a web. She then wrapped one of the puppies inside the towel and began to gently dry it. After a few minutes, she grabbed a second puppy and did the same with that one. Jim lifted a puppy inside the room.

Helen spoke to him and Grant. 'We'll need to take them all into the main tea shop to properly dry them. It's too crowded in here.'

A while later, all the puppies, Tana and Brochan were all in the main tea shop. There were two calor gas heaters with all three of their bars switched on full. The puppies were nearly dried off and were huddled together. Helen finished blow-drying the last of the puppies with an old orange electric hairdryer. She picked up the small cute red Setter and lifted him to her eye level, desperately trying to find the paint mark that Grant had applied when the pup was born.

'Jim, there's no mark on this one.' Helen sighed, deeply frustrated. 'It must have washed off in the rain.'

Grant knelt down and examined another. 'Nor this one.'

Helen looked at Jim. 'The rain's washed the paint off all of them. How the hell are we supposed to know which ones are the pedigree ones? There's going to be a Crufts nightmare,' she said, glaring at Jim. 'It's your fault. Why didn't you let them in when you came in?'

Jim raised his eyebrows at her. 'Dear, I could say the same for you.'

May came over with Jamie in her arms. She'd just lifted him from his pram.

Woolworths, Blondie and this shower o' useless pricks, youse are all to blame. You couldn't organise a piss-up in a brewery.

May intervened, 'They're all cute. It shouldn't matter. I'm sure the Crofts sheep people won't notice.'

Grant rolled his eyes at his mother and spoke to Helen. 'Does she think that they're sheep dogs?' He then looked at his mother. 'They're not *sheep* dogs. They're *show* dogs, Mother.'

May rocked her grandson. 'Grant, I'm perfectly aware that the dogs do shows with the sheep,' said May.

Helen was almost pulling her peroxide blonde hair out in despair. 'Nothing ever runs smoothly around here. I promised the Crufts people pedigree dogs and now they could end up with chunky rejects.' She looked at poor Tana. 'I'm sorry, Tana, but you definitely wouldn't win any competitions... unless they were for eating.' Tana, on hearing her name, looked up briefly and, as if in agreement, put it down just as quick; giving out a slight huff.

Jim went over to his wife and grabbed her shoulders. 'You've blagged your way out of many situations and I'm sure this will be no exception. Remember the one with the white stripe on her nose was one of Brochan's. That will be a good place to start.'

Helen calmed down a little.

Does nobody have a brain in this family? Why don't they use their common sense and match the pup with the mother's nipple the puppy is sucking on. It's all about them titties guys... maybe old Woolworth's is more of an ass man? Let's just see how long it takes them.

Chapter 8

It was early afternoon and the tea shop was quiet. Helen was watching Frank through the kitchen window. He was playing in the mud patch outside and was filthy from head to toe. The weather was warm and the sun was shining. She'd sent May down the street with Jamie in his pram and, for once, didn't really have any work to do. Jim was in Glasgow and was having his vasectomy done. It had taken a few weeks for a free appointment and as it was a weekday, he thought it would be a good opportunity to skive off school.

Helen could see quite a bit of smoke passing by the window. She peered against the glass and tried to see where it was coming from, then thought it was best to go and inspect outside in case Frank had found a box of matches. He might have accidentally set something on fire! Helen quickly filled up the metal mop bucket with water from the sink and rushed outside through the back door into the garden area. The dogs were all lying lethargic on the ground, feeding from perhaps their own mothers (but nobody was really sure anymore). Frank had built quite an impressive mud castle on the muddy patch, with different structures from four plastic buckets he owned. He was holding up a long slithery worm and placed it on top of one of the castles.

Helen looked at her son, who was content in his own world, and thought perhaps she'd imagined the smoke, again, due to lack of sleep. She stared ahead and realised that her mind wasn't playing tricks – there was indeed smoke. She marched over to the back garden, through the gate, where the washing was kept. Without hesitation, she threw the bucket in the air, which released the water and completely soaked Grant and his punky friend, Gail, who he was snogging in between puffs of a cigarette. Helen had seen them, but thought she'd teach them a lesson as there were rules and two of them were being broken simultaneously.

'What the hell do you two think you are doing?' asked Helen as Grant looked closely at his soaking cigarette, annoyed that it had been distinguished.

'Come on, sis. We're just having a bit of fun. We're young—'

Helen butted in, 'Exactly. You're far too young to be smoking and eating the face off…' She pointed at Gail, who looked terrified with her previously spiky hair all flat. She began to shiver and was soaking wet, trying to hide her drenched limp cigarette under her leather jacket (one she'd bought at a jumble sale in the Millport Town Hall). Her family were well-to-do Christians, but she'd been going through a rebellious stage for a while and liked to sneak out to her friend Yvonne's house. They'd change into one of her punk outfits, then hang around Millport. Her family owned a tea room at the other side of the island, which made it unlikely she'd be spotted.

Helen continued to point at Gail. 'Who are you? Who's your parents?'

Gail looked terrified and seemed like she was going to pee her pants. The wet feeling on her clothes certainly didn't help.

'She's not from around here. Just came over on the ferry from Largs for the day,' Grant said, trying to dig himself out of a hole.

'Grant, your nephew is around the corner. Don't you think you're setting a bad example by sneaking a wee floozy into my garden, snogging her and…' She looked at the wet cigarette at the same time. 'Smoking. It's disgusting,' she continued. Gail was now on the verge of tears.

'Look, sis, she's not a floozy. She's my girlfriend.' Gail giggled (like the schoolgirl that she was) when she heard his words.

Helen looked at them both suspiciously. 'Thought you said she came over on the boat?'

'Please don't tell her parents. They are very conservative and she'd get into a lot of trouble. I promise we'll adhere to all of your rules,' said Grant.

Helen sighed and her face changed, remembering it was not so long ago that she had to sneak around with her boyfriends. 'Fine.' She held her hand out to Grant. 'Give me the cigarettes.' Grant placed the soggy cigarette on her palm and she threw it to the ground. 'Not that one. The packet.' He huffed a bit and pulled the packet of cigarettes from his flairs and handed them over. 'And the lighter.'

He looked pissed off handing over his gold Dunhill lighter, which he'd bought in an antique shop in Glasgow with well-earned cash. He knew he had to comply with his sister to keep her quiet and not dob Gail in to her strict parents.

'What's your name?' Helen asked Gail, who stayed silent for a second.

'Her name's Gail,' said Grant, quickly.

'Can she not speak? What's the matter, Gail? Cat got your tongue?' Helen asked.

Gail shook her head fearfully. She wanted the ground to swallow her up.

Grant took her hand and led her past Helen, who grabbed his shoulder.

'Where are you going?' asked Helen.

'You've got your contraband. What else do you want?' Grant said aggressively.

'Gail needs to know the rules. No sex!'

Gail went red as a beetroot. 'I promise I wasn't going to...'

Grant pulled her away by the hand. 'Enough, sis. I'm taking her back onto the street and I'll see you in the flat later. Have a go at me, but leave her alone.'

The pair went past Frank, who was now dive-bombing into his mud castles. He was covered in muck and looked like he was a little earth monster as he was so dirty. There was also a business of flies hovering around him, not phasing him at all.

Helen waited for five minutes until she knew they were gone and hid behind the clean washing on the line. She pulled a cigarette from the Player's No.6 packet, placed the end in her mouth and lit it with Grant's fancy golden Dunhill lighter. She took a long, satisfying drag and inhaled the smoke before puffing out onto the clean washing. This was the first one she'd had since finding out about her pregnancy. The plan was to stop for good, but recently life had been pretty stressful and the temptation was impossible to resist.

***

In Glasgow, Jim was having his vasectomy procedure done at a private hospital. He'd been given a lift from his co-worker and friend, Bill, who had jumped at the opportunity to also play truant from school and help out a mate. Jim had been given a local anaesthetic and seemed at ease as his tubes were being tied up. He missed his sex life and was glad the day had come. Helen was adamant that they weren't going to have any more children as two was enough along with the dogs, their pups, the tea shop and his teaching job. He sat and thought about it all for a few seconds, realising that the hospital was actually a very relaxing place compared to his home life – which was chaotic even on a good day. He wasn't precious about his body and didn't care who saw his private parts. This was actually turning out to be a really nice day out.

The doctor appeared next to him. 'Right, Mr Coyle, that's you all tied up.'

'I better not get myself a mistress who wants kids then,' said Jim, chuckling to himself.

The doctor didn't know whether to take him seriously or not and smirked slightly. 'Drink lots of water today, no sex for at least seven days and still use some contraception for the next twelve weeks. Just to be on the safe side, to allow the sperm to clear in your tubes,' he said.

Jim looked a bit shocked. 'Twelve weeks? I thought it would be instant.' he said slightly peeved.

'Afraid not,' said the doctor, who left immediately.

Jim lay in bed for a few minutes, but felt alright and decided he would get dressed and look for Bill. He'd been living a moderately quiet social life for a while now and thought that today would be the ideal opportunity to change this.

***

In Millport, the town was fairly quiet. May was over the road from the tea shop at the jetty with Jamie, who was in his Silver Cross pram. She was gabbing to one of her acquaintances. Grant, who was across the road with Gail, spotted her and decided to sneak Gail around the corner to Ritchie Street. He wanted to have a good old snog before she went to her friend's house to get changed out of her (now wet) punk gear.

***

Helen was enjoying herself in the back garden. The sun was out and she had nothing to do. She'd taken a deckchair out and was sitting round the corner from Frank, who was still quite contently playing in the mud. After smoking her first cigarette, she couldn't stop lighting up. It was as if she was trying to play catch-up for all the smoking she'd missed during her pregnancy. It crossed her mind that she was being contradictory towards Grant and his new girlfriend in regard to smoking, but nothing was going to spoil this delightful, sunny afternoon. She'd even been tempted to go inside to grab a Gordon's gin and tonic – it had to be Gordon's, as other brands turned her gaga. She liked to use the term "Mickey Finn" and had passed out on more than one occasion due to someone else slipping her a different brand. However, she'd decided against the gin as she was working that night – even though the tea shop would be quiet.

***

In Glasgow, Jim was in the car with Bill, knowing full well that Helen wasn't expecting him back that night because he'd have to recover from the vasectomy procedure, which would most definitely require an afternoon and evening in bed at his parents' house. He'd try to give her a quick call (to the phone box across the road from the tea shop) to let her know that everything had gone okay. He would tell her he was feeling too tender to drive back to Millport, even though he was actually fine. It was only a wee white lie and he would swear Bill to secrecy. He'd already informed him that he wanted to grab the opportunity to go out on the piss. Bill (who currently was a bachelor) was well up for an afternoon drinking session and Jim could stay at his flat on the couch. They just needed to park the car and find the nearest pub, before starting their night on the tiles.

***

In Millport, May was speaking to a lady called Grace, who was wearing a mink fur coat and a matching fur hat. She had visited Moscow and chose to wear it at all times to show off – even though she must have been roasting, as it was about twenty degrees outside. Grace was leaning on the pram with her hand, which had a cigarette in between her fingers. Jamie was wide awake and could smell the smoke that was blowing under his tiny nose and into his mouth every time he breathed in.

Oh, how I've missed you, sweet, sweet tobacco smoke. Pretty little cigarette, how I'd love to kiss you once again. Stupid baby body. Jamie was able to move a bit more than before and attempted to lift himself closer to the cigarette, but was strapped down in the pram. Some ash from the cigarette fell onto his blanket. *Old Dear! Are you not seeing this? The yellow-fingered Russian mafia lady nearly set me on fucking fire.* Grace had very wrinkled hands and a yellow tobacco stain all the way up her smoking finger – it smelt rotten. *She's no even smoking it. She's just letting that sexy white tobacco stick burn into my pram – what a waste. People like her shouldn't be allowed to smoke. She's too busy talking a load of pish.*

The blue-rinse brigade – Isa and Betty – came rushing over from the pier. They were really excited about something and stopped off next to May and Grace.

'You'll never believe it,' said Isa.

'The Waverley steam boat is coming in for the day,' continued Isa as Betty jumped in the air while clapping her hands, unable to contain her excitement.

'I wonder if our Helen knows. 'Cause she owns Ye Olde Tea Shoppe, you know,' said May in her put-on posh accent.

There she goes again - fake Queen Elizabeth. I'd have said she's lost her marbles but they're all very clearly in her fuckin' mouth!

Isa shook her head. 'Oh no. She won't, as it's had to do a detour and was meant to be going to Rothesay today. There's been a fire on the pier. Can you believe it?'

May and Grace gasped at Isa's words.

'Can you believe it?' asked Betty, repeating Isa's words.

'The boat is meant to be here in an hour, full to the brim and stopping for four hours,' said Isa.

Jamie stared up at the four women. Grace's cigarette was burned all the way to the butt. *Well, that's Blondie fucked. She thought it was gonna be a quiet day and Woolworths is away in Glasgow.*

May grabbed the handle of the pram, noticed the cigarette ash on the blanket and looked a little guilty, as she hadn't noticed her friend had nearly set her grandson's pram on fire – with him inside. She shook the blanket to shake the ash away, trying not to cause a scene, but then she spotted a burn mark and felt really guilty as she hadn't seen it happening.

Once again, one of Old Dear's friends nearly kills her gorgeous wee (favourite) grandson. Shame on you, Old Dear. Shame on you.

'Girls, I'll need to rush off and tell our Helen about the Waverley. She's not even got Jim today to help her as he's in Glasgow having a castration done,' said May.

The three women looked towards one another and gasped – completely shocked.

There she goes again, mixing up her words. I hope for Woolworths' sake, he's not been castrated. Mind you, it might do Blondie a favour.

May hurriedly pushed the pram across the road towards the tea shop entrance and met with Helen, who was on a mission. May attempted to speak to her.

'Mum, I need to check to see if Jim's okay. I've been telling him to sort out a phone line in the tea shop for months.' She was well past May by this point and appeared to be talking to herself.

Helen rushed into the red phone box on the jetty and quickly dialled a Glasgow number, then placed the receiver on her ear.

'Hello, Sadie,' said Helen.

On the other line, Sadie replied coldly, not acknowledging that she recognised the voice as her daughter-in-law's, the mother to her grandchildren.

'Has Jim arrived back from his procedure?' asked Helen.

'Who's asking?' Sadie said, deliberately cutting.

Helen sighed loudly in frustration before speaking, 'It's Helen. Your daughter-in-law.'

'Why would Jim be here?' Sadie said bluntly.

Helen was tensing up and was ready to knock the phone against the glass in the phone box, but she put on a forced smile and replied, 'Because he's having a vasectomy in Glasgow today and he's meant to be staying the night at your flat.'

'First I've heard of it,' said Sadie, before hanging up the phone without saying goodbye.

Helen aggressively put the phone back. 'That bloody woman!' she said.

May had done a U-turn and was now standing outside the phone box with Jamie in his pram, waiting for Helen to finish her call. Helen opened the door and spoke to her own mother. She was clearly agitated. 'Jim's mother is so awkward and cold.'

Jamie looked up from the pram. *Sounds like my kind of woman.*

'All she does is go to Catholic mass, smoke cigarettes and play cards,' said Helen, still wound up.

I like fags and cards, but you can keep your church unless they give me a large tanker of red wine.

'Any word on Jim's castration?' said May, seriously.

Helen looked at her like she couldn't cope any longer. 'It's a vasectomy, Mum. A castration is when they chop the balls completely off.'

May nodded her head and giggled. 'Think I might have told a few people that he was being castrated today.'

'Wonderful. The whole of Millport now thinks my husband has had his testicles chopped off. Thanks, Mum,' said Helen, aggravated.

Wonder if Woolworths is going to come back with a squeaky voice, like he's permanently sucking helium?

May began to look puzzled again. 'There was something I needed to tell you.' She put her hand on her chin as she tried to think. Helen was already stressed and no news would be good news. 'That's it. I've remembered.' May was pleased with herself.

'Well, spit it out,' said Helen gruffly.

May quickly glanced at her tiny gold watch, which was loosely strapped on her wrist. 'The Waverley boat is full today and will be coming in about thirty minutes,' she said.

Helen looked like a brick had fallen off a building and landed on her head. 'Mum! Why didn't you tell me sooner?'

'I tried, but you were all flabbergasted about Jim's castration,' said May and then quickly put her hand over her mouth, realising her blunder once again.

'Right, listen to me carefully. Where's Dad? I'm going to have to send him to the shops,' said Helen, in her old teaching voice.

'He's round the back of The Wee House, up a ladder,' said May.

'I'll get him. Frank's in the back garden covered in mud. Throw him in a bath, then meet me in the kitchen. I need you to help me make sandwiches,' said Helen.

'What about Jamie?' asked May, as she tickled his chest in the pram.

'Take him with you. Just place him where you need to,' said Helen.

I wish I could clap my hands for Blondie. Mother of the year award coming right your way. She's treating her wee gorgeous baby like a reject pass-the-parcel gift. Right, Old Dear, come on. Shove me somewhere where the sun don't shine.

Helen was already rushing across the road as May stood static - discombobulated.

Helen turned and shouted at her, 'Quickly, Mum! We don't have time to stall.'

***

In Glasgow, Jim was in a busy pub with Bill, who was encouraging him to down a full pint of Tennent's lager.

Two random guys beside them had overheard their conversation and began to chant, 'Down it! Down it.'

Jim, who was in a great mood, stood up from his bar stool, placed the glass on his lips, tilted it back, opened his mouth as wide as possible and gulped down the entire pint in a matter of seconds. He gasped loudly, burped and smiled, before placing the up-turned, empty beer glass on his shaggy head.

Bill stood up and shouted to the bar, 'This man's just had a vasectomy!'

The crowd in the bar cheered.

Jim laughed before shouting out, 'No more kids for me.'

The men in the bar then responded with a wild roar like they were at a football match - or at least that's the way that Jim was now perceiving it.

***

In Millport, Helen went down Ritchie Street to find Jimmy, so she could have him run a few errands for her. There was a small gate that led to a very tiny courtyard and one of the two windows for May and Jimmy's minuscule flat, which they called "The Wee House". They still mainly lived in their home in Busby and had bought The Wee House in the 1950s as a holiday home. Millport was very popular with the people from Glasgow and its outskirts for holidays. People weren't holidaying in Spain yet – There was no "sun, sea, sex and sangria" - instead it was beaches, bikes and blowing a gale.

Helen pushed through the gate with great difficulty and ended up squashing Grant and Gail, who were hiding behind it, snogging. Helen pulled them apart, saying, 'Can you two not keep your hands off each other?' Helen glared fiercely at her brother, then pointed up at Jimmy, who was high up a ladder, painting The Wee House windowsills. 'And with Dad up there. Do you want him to know your dirty little secret?'

Grant rolled his eyes and Gail looked to the ground. She hadn't really thought she'd have to deal with *all* of Grant's relatives; in a single day. She was worried about her own mum and dad finding out, but hadn't bargained on Grant having a judgemental sister, who would catch them snogging twice in the same afternoon.

Helen stepped back into her teaching voice, 'Right, Grant, you need to move your ass to the tea shop and set up as quick as you can.'

Grant shot her a dirty look. 'Sis, I'm not meant to be working today.'

'You are now, as the Waverley's coming in. You can get wee Gina to help you,' said Helen.

'It's Gail,' snapped Grant.

'Gina, Gail… to-*may*-to, to-*mah*-to,' Helen snarked at them as she marched off to find her father.

Grant was pissed off and Gail was a timid wee wreck, terrified of Helen. He apologised to her, before leading her away. He was beginning to have feelings for her, which was something he'd never felt for any girl back in Glasgow. Perhaps it was the sea air that was making him frisky.

***

Helen stood underneath Jimmy, who was standing ten metres up, painting a small windowsill. He'd noticed a few paint cracks that morning and had had a fairly quiet day, so decided to paint. Radio 2 was blaring from the wireless radio that was sitting on the ground underneath the ladder. This radio was actually plugged inside The Wee House, but would still be referred to as a wireless – like the ones pre-WW2 with the giant rechargeable batteries.

Helen shouted up at her father, 'Dad, Dad, *Dad!*'

He couldn't hear her at all and was in his own wee painting world. She bent down and switched off the noise of the radio. It took him a second to realise, then he shouted out, 'Who the fuck's messing wi' my wireless?'

'Dad, can you come down a minute? It's urgent,' shouted Helen.

He stepped down from the ladder gingerly, as he knew he wasn't getting any younger and had to be careful or it would be lights out for him.

'What is it?' he brusquely shouted at her.

Her glare became intense. 'I need you to go to the shops for me,' demanded Helen.

'Don't be so fucking lazy, 'elen. I'm fucking busy,' growled Jimmy.

'Please, Dad. I would, but the Waverley is coming in and I think the tea shop is gonna be mobbed,' Helen pleaded, desperately.

Jimmy half-grinned at his daughter. 'Fine. What do you want?'

***

Helen was in the tea shop kitchen, panicking, as the Waverley paddle steamer (which was a grand boat with two unique red-white-and-black funnels) had just docked on the Millport pier and was full, carrying about eight hundred passengers. The boat had been built in the 1940s and was famous in Scotland as she was one of the the last seagoing passenger-carrying paddle steamers in the world. It had been owned by the Paddle Steamer Preservation Society since the 1970s. One of its main routes was the Firth of Clyde and the boat stopped off on the Western Isles to allow the passengers some time on the islands.

Helen knew that the Waverley visiting meant busy days and she was determined they were going to make money. She'd roped in the entire family to come and help her – even Grant's new girlfriend, Gail, who was standing in the tea shop full of nerves, folding napkins as quickly as she could. She wasn't scared of the work as her parents also had a tea shop and she had to help them sometimes. However, she was petrified of Helen, who she thought was the most demanding and forthright woman she had ever met. May came down with Frank, who was all clean after his bath and annoyed 'cause he was about to be shoved into the sink to do dishes again. May had baby Jamie in her arms and stood next to a terrified Gail.

Who's this wee punk? Hey, Blondie, make her tie that hair up, otherwise she'll scare away the fucking customers.

Grant was setting tables away from her and this made her even more scared. May smiled at Gail and spoke, 'Hello, dear. Have you just started working here? It's my daughter who owns "Ye Olde Tea Shoppe", you know.' Gail smiled and nodded towards May, then did the maths in her head that this lady was Grant's mother. She'd only been kissing him for a few days and she was already working for the family and meeting the parents. She looked like she was about to hyperventilate.

'For fuck's sake! Would somebody come and fucking help?' Jimmy came through the door like a hurricane. He was carrying a load of groceries, shouting at the top of his voice. Gail was scared to look.

May turned and shouted, 'Grant! Grant! Help your dad.'

Grant sighed noisily and went over to retrieve the bags from Jimmy. Gail gulped really loudly and darted her eyes around, looking for an exit, unable to cope any longer. If it wasn't for the fact that Grant's sister was aggressively chopping a cucumber with a very sharp knife right in front of her, or that his dad looked as though he was about to explode like a grenade while blocking the door, she would have sprinted out of the tea shop to escape the nightmare.

***

In Glasgow, it wasn't even three in the afternoon and Jim and Bill were in a circle in the manner of a rugby huddle with five other drunk men, who had joined them in downing their drinks every ten minutes. They were like excitable wee boys singing their favourite song: "Loch Lomond". They were circling the table, singing, 'You'll take the high road and I'll take the low road, and I'll be in Scotland afore you.' The middle table wobbled and the few pints that had any drink left spilt onto the table.

All of the men were sporting similar looks – with their shaggy mops, moustaches, T-shirts and causal light-coloured short shorts. One of the guy's hairy testicles had popped out and was bouncing about due to the quick movement. They kept repeating the chorus over and over – out of tune – while dancing faster around the pub table each time. They were raucous and unsteady. The smallest guy in the group looked dizzy and was about to pass out. The landlord just stood and watched – waiting to intervene if things got out of hand. As it happens, this wasn't such a surprising occurrence. The little guy fell and grabbed onto the shorts of the guy with the loose testicle. His shorts came down and he was completely exposed – dick, balls and bush (it was the 1970s after all). Jim, Bill and the rest of the group seemed to pause for the briefest of seconds then cheered loudly and began to topple down like they were dominos. The grown men lay on the floor, laughing, as the barman (who'd had enough) marched over and shouted, 'Right! Enough! You lot, *out!*'

Jim looked at Bill. 'It's like being called into the headmaster's office,' he said as he stood with difficulty, wobbling like a Weeble. He grabbed Bill's hand and helped to pull him up. They left the bar, walked a few doors down and entered the next pub.

***

In Millport, Helen had had to organise the food for the afternoon in under an hour and had to improvise. She'd found some Scotch broth in the freezer – a big frozen block that had been kept in a container. There was also some lentil soup left over from the weekend, so she decided to mix them both together and call it "Scottish soup". She was a master at taking leftovers and transforming them into something completely different. She had all six of the gas rings on and was desperately trying to heat the soup in a giant pot before the customers arrived. Jimmy had bought cream buns, strawberry tarts and all that was left from the bakers. Helen would normally do a hot lunch for tourists visiting for the day, but had decided to do traditional tea-room style afternoon tea. May had even been roped in to make sandwiches. Under the hot lights were some scones that Helen had found in the freezer and put away for a rainy day. Today was *that* day (even though the sun was baking down).

Helen had to feed Jamie before the rush and had his mouth stuck to her nipple, sucking hard. He slowly came up for breath with breast milk dripping from his face.

Better suck up as much as I can from Laverne before I'm thrown in the pantry to shut me up.

Helen stared down at her four-month-old baby. 'Think it's about time we got you on the bottle – before those teeth come in, you little piranha.'

Jamie leered at his mother. *What the actual fuck. Laverne, Shirley – no! It can't be true. Please tell me it's a lie. You told me we would be together for life.* Jamie sucked on the nipple as hard as he could.

'Awl,' Helen said, as she pulled Jamie off her boob.

Come back. Girls, come back.

Helen handed the baby to May, whose hands were covered in butter.

'Mum, think I'll use formula from now on. It'll make my life a lot easier,' said Helen.

Your fucking life. What about my life? I put up with so much. It's the only pleasure I get. I have to hang around with people I despise. I can't drink alcohol, smoke or take drugs. I shit in a fucking nappy. My body's useless and all that I love is being taken away.

Jamie started to cry, but Helen had turned away and was now cutting sandwiches at a furious rate. Gail, who had been standing at the counter, looked on, terrified, still trying to plot some kind of escape route. Grant, meanwhile, was on top of his tasks and was quickly writing a sign to entice customers to come in. He went outside and turned the reversible sign to "Open" on the front door. He stuck the afternoon tea sign on the outside billboard. By chance, Norma was walking past and he tried to stop her in her tracks.

'Norma!' shouted Grant as she tried to walk by, ignoring him. '*Norma!*'

She stopped and looked over the road at all the people who were disembarking the Waverley and were quickly filling up the pier, soon to be in the tea shop having their afternoon tea. There was an agenda in her eyes and she turned to face Grant, speaking to him in her friendliest voice – which still sounded dour. 'Do you need me to help this afternoon?'

Grant was taken aback as he thought that he'd have to battle with her to get her to work. He nodded and was, for once, dumbfounded. 'Yes,' he said.

Norma turned and went inside the tea shop. Grant tried to figure out why she was being so obliging, but he didn't have time. The Waverley customers were now on the jetty across the road, eyeing up places to have refreshments.

The tea shop was filling up fast and Helen was in her usual panic. Her Scottish soup still hadn't heated properly and half of it had started off frozen. She had the large pan on one hob and was furiously ladling soup into two smaller pans on another two hobs. May was making slow progress with the sandwiches, trying to make as many as possible, she wasn't used to working so hard as she'd spent most of her life being a lady of leisure. Gail was standing with her head down and didn't know where to look.

'Gina,' Helen said to the poor girl, mid-ladle, as some of the soup splashed onto the hob. '*Gina!*'

Gail looked up, her eyes as big as soup bowl saucers. 'Yes,' she said meekly.

'Can you go and help your mother-in-law make some sandwiches, please?'

Gail's face turned redder than a tomato, but May was too busy concentrating on slowly making sandwiches (with her arthritic hands) to acknowledge Helen's dig at her son and new girlfriend.

Helen felt a little guilty and decided to be a bit nicer – she'd punished Gail enough. 'Come round here, Gail. You'll be paid for your work today and I do appreciate your help.'

Gail relaxed a little and was soon standing next to May. 'If you could just put the filling in the sandwiches – egg and cress, ham and tomato, and cheese and pickle. Cut them into triangles. One of each on a plate with either a scone or a cake,' said Helen.

"Gail started filling the sandwiches and was actually quite quick - much to Helen's silent relief.

Grant came over to the counter. 'Right, that's everyone seated. The place is heaving. You need to start lifting, now!' he barked at Helen.

'Yes, Grant. I'm totally aware, but I'm also not going to serve the customers frozen soup,' Helen replied edgily.

Grant then turned his attention to his mother. 'Can you not hurry up, Mum?' He looked over at his girlfriend, showing off. 'May, a monkey would be quicker at making sandwiches than you,' Grant said in a very cutting way.

May looked really upset. She had been trying her best, but her arthritis was really playing up and it had been a struggle. Gail wasn't impressed with her new boyfriend and looked at him disappointedly.

Helen began lifting bowls of soup and snapped back at Grant, 'Why don't you concentrate on the customers and leave Mum alone?'

Grant realised his blunder in front of Gail and grabbed the soups from Helen. May turned to face Gail. 'I've got really bad artificial-itis,' said May.

'She means arthritis,' Helen said. 'I'm sorry, Mum. I shouldn't have got you to help.'

Gail looked sad for May as she slowly moved her fingers to relieve the pain. Gail had already plated up six portions of sandwiches and a cake.

Helen looked across and was impressed. 'You can have a job here any time, Gail.'

Gail smiled. 'I help my mum in her tea room most days,' she said.

Frank was in his usual spot at the kitchen sink. The hot water was pouring out the tap and the soapsuds were forming and looked mountainous in the sink. Baby

Jamie had been put in his pram and placed a few metres from Frank. He had been fed and was currently asleep. Frank gathered up as large a handful of the soapsuds as possible in his two hands and jumped down from the sink.

Oh... mm... ah... it really tickles my nose... but... what's that rank taste in my mouth?

Frank was rubbing the suds all over Jamie's face and giggling at the same time. He was fair pleased with himself.

Jamie opened his eyes, sneezed and some of the bubbles floated above his head. *That wee dick-weed. I might of known the Wee Shrimp would be involved.*

Frank had his face right next to Jamie's, trying to taunt him, knowing full well that there was nothing Jamie could do. All of a sudden, baby Jamie projectile vomited Helen's breast milk all over Frank's face, covering his eyes, nose and mouth. He looked like a milk bottle (that had curdled) had exploded on his face. A shocked Frank burst into tears and Jamie stared at his big brother.

You soap me, Wee Shrimp. I baby sick and fuck you up!

***

In Glasgow, Jim and Bill were soaking up their twenty pints of lager with a typical Glasgow curry. The table was filled with enough food to feed four hungry men. They had already wolfed down a plate of vegetable pakora and a plate of onion bhajis each. There were a further four curries in front of them, with naan bread and rice. Jim was covered in red, yellow and an array of different coloured sauces – all over his face. The two men were so drunkenly engrossed in their food that they were unable to make conversation.

Jim glanced at his watch with his glazed eyes and drunkenly stuttered out his words, 'It… It's… ffffivvvee o'clock some… somewhere.'

Bill picked up a piece of naan bread and hit Jim on the forehead. Jim laughed out loud, before laying his face on his plate of curry, squeezing his cheek onto a piece of lamb. Bill stood up unsteadily and laughed, before he fell over his chair and landed on his back on the floor - rolling about like a pissed-up baby.

The three Indian waiters stood back, looking concerned. They were used to drunken buffoons on Friday and Saturday nights, but this was five o'clock on a Tuesday – it was still technically the afternoon. Luckily, the restaurant was empty and there was no one to complain about the two drunk men making an arse of themselves.

Jim, who'd completely lost sight of Bill, lifted his lamb Bhunna besmeared face off his plate, pulled up the tablecloth and threw himself under the table, onto the floor; looking for Bill, now only moving his legs and arms; like an upturned turtle. Bill was well over six feet and was wiggling his legs like they were an out-of-control crocodile tail. He hit a chair with a fast swoop from his feet; the chair fell into the table, which knocked over a full pint of lager and a plate of vindaloo curry onto the floor.

Jim had been crawling under the table when he heard the clatter of the glass smash on the floor and attempted to stand up – forgetting where he was. His back got stuck into the table and he stood up really quickly, which lifted the table in its entirety, spilling the entire contents on the floor, smashing his plate and glass of Tennent's as well. The floor was laminate and could be cleaned easily, but all the different curries were spread everywhere. The waiters scrambled around Jim and Bill, trying to clean up their mess as the two adult men acted like a couple of toddlers on the floor.

***

In Millport, the last of the Waverley customers left the tea shop and were ready to embark the boat to take them home. It had been a gruelling day for Helen and the family. They'd turned over the tables at least five times and had used every morsel of food that they had. Helen was counting the day's takings next to her mother, who was knackered and eating one of her own sandwiches, which she only now realised was made with two heel-ends of bread.

Helen handed Gail two pound notes from the pile of money. 'Thank you, Gail. I really appreciate your help today.'

Gail smiled and felt a bit more at ease. Grant stood behind her and subtly put his hand on her waist. She flinched, moving away from him as quickly as possible and raised her hand to May and Helen to say goodbye. Before leaving, she glanced at Grant with unhappy eyes and walked out. He sensed an issue and followed her out of the door.

Helen kept counting the notes and change that were on the table. 'Mum, I'm sure something's not right here.'

May looked at her and smiled with dazed eyes, which then shut for a second.

Outside the tea shop, Gail marched away from Grant, who was following her like a puppy.

'Gail, Gail, wait up.'

She stopped, huffed, then turned towards him. 'I don't think I want to see you anymore,' Gail said to Grant, who looked at her, shocked.

This morning, they had been like love's young dream and now she was rejecting him.

'I'm really sorry about my family... I know they're a lot, but you get used to them,' said Grant.

Gail shook her head at him. 'It's not your family; it's you,' she said and he looked at her incoherently.

'Me?' asked Grant.

Gail became quite animated. She'd spent the day in her shell, overwhelmed, but now she had to release all that pent-up frustration. 'Yes, Grant. The way you spoke to your mother, comparing her to a monkey, was disgusting and disrespectful. You're not the boy I thought you were.' She held her head up high (making her seem taller than she actually was - the spiky hair helping) and walked away from him.

Grant was speechless. He really liked Gail and was worried he'd messed up. He couldn't believe that it wasn't his family's fault, but his own. He went back into the tea shop and Helen and May were still sitting at the table next to the money. He approached his mum and threw his arms around her. She looked at Helen, confused as her son hadn't shown her affection since he was a wee boy.

Helen looked up at her brother. 'You okay, Grant?' she asked.

Grant whispered in May's ear, 'Mum, I'm sorry if I'm mean sometimes.'

May processed the information and initially seemed hurt, then she smiled at him. Helen took the opportunity and spoke out to her brother like she was reciting a line from a poem, 'Love is in the air...'. Grant rolled his eyes at Helen, while still hugging May, who was clueless about what was going on.

Grant stared at the money on the table and tried to change the subject. 'How much did we make?'

'There's only one hundred and ten pounds here. Weren't there about two hundred people today? There should be about a hundred and sixty pounds,' said Helen.

Grant thought deeply for a second. 'I have an idea of how to snare the thief,' he said.

Jamie had just woken up from a sleep in his pram. *The Artful Dodger might not be such a bad boy, after all.*

Frank crawled from under the table, where he had been playing with his toys. He screwed his face at everyone. 'Can we go for ice cream now?' he asked.

Helen suddenly remembered about her husband, who she hadn't heard a peep from all day. She stood up from the table and shouted to the rest of them, ' 'Jim. Where the bloody hell is Jim?!'

***

In Glasgow, it was seven o'clock at night and Jim was lying on Bill's couch, fast asleep and snoring loudly - cheeks still covered in curry.

Chapter 9

Jim woke up at three o'clock in the morning. He'd fallen asleep the night before on Bill's couch. They'd stumbled into a taxi after the Indian restaurant and had arrived home in the early evening. He was fully clothed and wide awake, and then he remembered that he'd forgotten to call Helen to tell her the vasectomy procedure had gone well. He knew she would be absolutely livid, as communication was one of the main stipulations she'd written in her vows… that, and no secrets. She liked everything to be laid on the table. He'd had a jolly the night before and he knew there would be a moment in the doghouse, but he'd enjoyed himself socially for the first time in ages.

He gathered himself together and made an instant Nescafé coffee – he took his coffee black. He slurped rather loudly and dribbled down his chin, mildly burning himself. Luckily, the Volvo was parked outside the flat as Bill had driven him to the hospital the day before. He could wait to drive Bill to his car (in the centre of Glasgow), but he was still asleep – Jim could hear the loud snoring through his bedroom door. He decided it was a better decision to drive back to Millport to face the wrath of Helen sooner rather than later. Bill was bound to understand his woman woes and the skelp across the arse he was about to receive from his very angry wife. He picked up his holdall and car keys, which he jangled in his loose fingers, and quietly left - his hangover followed.

***

Helen lay in her bed, worried senseless about Jim. It was 6am and she hadn't had a wink of sleep all night and had tossed, turned, gasped and sighed. She had gone through a mix of emotions, including (but not limited to) anger. She nearly went across the road to call the hospital and ask them if something bad had happened to him. It was meant to be a simple procedure – but perhaps he'd had an allergic reaction to the local anaesthetic and had to have his testicles chopped off. Damn her mother for putting that thought in her mind! There was also a chance they might have found something more sinister, like a cancerous lump. Why wouldn't Jim phone her and where the hell was he? The tiredness was really making her paranoid. Maybe he'd run away with a hot nurse that liked the look of him with his clothes off. Or another patient had gone on a rampage with a syringe, stabbed him with a needle and he'd had an overdose and died.

Helen wiped some uncomfortable sweat off her brow and adjusted the soaked bed sheets – worry made her sweat profusely. She was making too much noise and it woke Jamie up.

Come on, Blondie. What's all the racket about? Your baby needs sleep. Where's Woolworths? I knew that guy was a snake. He's got himself a new piece... a woman who's not been torn to smithereens by her little dick of a son – the Wee Shrimp. I wouldn't be surprised if that wee psycho came out her fanny with razor blades in his hands.

Suddenly, there was the sound of footsteps creaking down the corridor of the flat. Helen opened her eyes and heard the living room door make a swooshing sound. Then, the bedroom door slowly opened and there was a sudden smell of stale alcohol, BO and cigar smoke – he'd puffed a fat one in the car on the way back from Glasgow. Jim put his shaggy mop (which was in complete disarray) around the door. His hands were in the air like Lord Summerisle from *The Wicker Man*.

Good Gawd. Woolworths looks like he's possessed. Have I missed something? Yesterday he seemed normal; now, he looks like some kind of cult leader.

Jim was desperately hoping that Helen was asleep, to buy him a little more time before his severe scolding. He tiptoed across the room, trying to make as little noise as possible and almost stubbed his toe on Jamie's cot. Helen pretended to be asleep with her eyes tightly shut. Jim unbuttoned his shirt, slipped off his shoes at the same time, then unzipped his party flairs and let them fall to his ankles, before quietly slipping them off.

Jamie stared at him, as his cot was right next to where he was getting undressed. *Tut-tut, Woolworths. You're about to get your ass kicked and I've got front-row seats. Biggest fight since Muhammad Ali pummelled George Foreman.*

Jim carefully pulled the duvet back in the bed and slipped under as quietly as possible. Helen suddenly opened her eyes. She could feel him pressed against her. Anger took over as Jim settled and closed his eyes. Helen waited for a minute until she knew he was relaxed, before dramatically turning around, grabbing his shoulders tightly and whisper-shouting in a husky voice, 'Where the hell have you been?'

Jim shuddered as it had only taken him a minute to fall asleep. He thought he'd managed to buy himself a few extra hours. He smiled, hoping it would become infectious. 'Glasgow.'

Helen's eyes widened as her face became even more contorted with anger. 'I thought you were dead or you'd run off with someone else. Did you even get a vasectomy?'

Jim scoffed at her. 'I'm not dead, dear. I didn't run away with another woman and, yes, I did have a vasectomy,' he said.

'But where have you been? You weren't at your mother's.'

Jim wasn't one to keep secrets and decided to tell the truth. 'I went out on the piss with Bill,' he said, casually.

This made Helen even more livid and her voice raised another few octaves. 'After a medical procedure? You stupid idiot. You could have died and left me a widow with all this shitty mess.'

You tell him, Blondie. If I do say so myself, Woolworths has been a bit selfish.

Jim gave her a condescending look. 'Erm… perhaps you're exaggerating, dear.'

Helen looked like she was about to headbutt him. 'You were out on a bender while I was run off my feet – sorting the kids, the dogs and the tea shop, which was mobbed yesterday – and you have the cheek to say I'm exaggerating! What grown man in his right mind goes and gets pissed after a medical procedure and doesn't even call his wife,' she barked.

Jim shrugged his shoulders and sighed at her.

If I were you, Woolworths, I'd apologise to Blondie 'cause she's no happy.

'This is a marriage, Jim, which involves communication,' said Helen.

Jim laughed. 'Maybe one day you'll see the funny side, Helen,' replied Jim casually. In some ways it seemed like the drink was still talking.

'Are you brave or stupid?', challenged Helen.

He knew he had made some mistakes and should be sorry; yet he didn't seem able to say the right things. Helen shook her head at him. 'Just go. Get out my sight.'

Jim slipped out the bed as he didn't have anything else to say and actually felt that he might dig an even bigger hole for himself if he stayed. Once he was standing, he scratched himself on the arm, reassessing his silence. 'If it makes you feel any better, we were home by half five in the afternoon,' he said.

'Oh yeah, I feel wonderful hearing that,' Helen said sarcastically. 'Well, at five-thirty yesterday, I was knee-high in dishes and dirty nappies,' said Helen.

Was that a dig at me, Blondie? 'Cause I've been on your side up until now.

Jim started to look a little guilty.

'Oh, and something else, Jim. We could do with you working in the tea shop 'cause we're being robbed in broad daylight. That's something else I've had to deal with.' Helen rolled back over.

Jim waited a second before he left to go to sleep on the couch.

***

A few hours later, Jim's head was feeling a little less hazy. He'd tried to sleep on the couch for an extra hour but couldn't, so had gone down to the tea shop and set up the dining area and hoovered the floor. He knew the extra graft he was putting in was mostly due to guilt and trying to work his way back into Helen's good books after his misdemeanours. In hindsight, it probably was stupid drinking himself into oblivion just after having a knot tied in his dick.

Grant came through the side door. He was wearing a pair of navy, white-rimmed shorts and a black "Doors" T-shirt. He'd swapped a carton of cigarettes down at the Barra's in Glasgow for a pile of rock and punk T-shirts. He liked to think he was one of the cool kids, but felt a bit low in confidence after his altercation with Gail the day before. He really liked her and was desperate to make amends. He smelt the coffee that Jim had made in the filtered coffee machine, so went over and poured two large cups, then sat down next to Jim. They both acknowledged each other and sat and sipped.

After a long silence, Grant asked Jim, 'How do you… em…' Grant sighed and was lost for words. This love business was turning him gaga.

Jim turned and looked at his younger brother-in-law.

'Eh… I've… Em…' mumbled Grant.

'Women trouble, by any chance?' guessed Jim. He was used to Grant being a smart-ass and had never seen him stumble over his words.

'Yes. How'd you know?' Grant said, nodding desperately.

Jim chuckled quietly. 'Guess we're both in the same

boat… as I'm in the doghouse with your sister, hence the early morning start.' Jim gave off an unsure look. 'Not sure that I'm the best person to ask about women right now.' Grant looked disappointed. 'One thing I will say: women seem to love being given flowers. And I'll be going along to the shop later to pick up a bunch. Would you like me to buy an extra one for you as well?'

Grant smiled at him. 'Do you think that would work?'

'Probably your best chance. Oh, and an apology, of course. No matter what it is, just apologise. Women have periods and they act… different sometimes.' It was now Jim's turn to smile at Grant. 'Have you got yourself a lumber, young man?' he teased.

Grant instantly changed the subject. 'Did Helen tell you about the takings being way down again?'

'Yes, she mentioned it this morning. We really need to do something about that,' said Jim.

'I have an idea. I just need some pound notes from the takings to make the plan work,' said Grant, enthusiastically.

Jim pulled out a wad of notes from his pocket and counted out ten pound notes and gave them to Grant without hesitation.

Grant waved the money in the air. 'Today's the day this place will start making real money. I'm on it.' He went to leave.

Jim looked at his watch. 'The flower shop is about to open soon. I'll help you make things right with your little lady,' he said and both guys went off in different directions.

***

Later on in the morning, Grant was in the kitchen of The Wee House – his parents' Millport holiday home. The house literally was tiny: there was no toilet in the actual premises but there was a shared "cludgie" in the stairwell that contained a toilet and a small sink - luxurious for its day.

The few kitchen units were avocado coloured and the walls were covered with orange-and-yellow flowered wallpaper. There was a cooker, a small fridge and a sink, but it was very basic. The master stroke was that the kitchen also doubled up as a bedroom with a set of bunk beds. There was a wee window, which was the only extraction – and this meant that Helen and Mary could take turns and smoke out of it when they were growing up; as it used to be their bedroom. The living room had a small couch, a few lamps, tables and a recess bed, where May and Jimmy slept. The decor was fairly tasteful and looked fresh as Jimmy had kept up with the latest fashions on May's request. They had brown 1970s patterned wallpaper with yellow, orange and red swirls and a brown shag carpet (which was a nightmare to clean, especially with a 1970s hoover). Sometimes, there were up to twenty people squashed into The Wee House for one of their famous get-togethers and Jimmy was always the life and soul of the party. He'd sing and dance and be merry... singing "Doon in the Wee Hoose" (his very own version of "Doon in the Wee Room"). He changed the words to fit and he showed songwriters' pride every time he sang it. He'd also include all his friends in the song as a tribute to them – as they were always at the parties. The kids also had to do a party piece in front of all the guests. This was compulsory. May would make Mary and Helen dress up in pretty 1950s dresses with bows in their blonde hair – they'd link arms and sing the Doris

Day song, "Que Sera, Sera". Danny, the third eldest child, was made to stand on a chair wearing one of May's fur hats and sing "The Ballad of Davy Crockett". Every party was the same: lots of drinks, songs and plenty of fun, until the next morning when Jimmy was hungover and a bit grumpy.

Grant was sitting around the square table in the middle of the floor, which had a gingham tablecloth over it. He had handed over a few pound notes to his mum and some others to his dad.

'Aye, no bother, son,' said May. 'I'll talk to some of my pals when I'm down the street, so will your dad.'

Jimmy looked at May like she'd lost the plot. 'Are you fucking sure this has been happening?' asked Jimmy.

'Yes!' Grant said firmly.

'Jimmy. Our Helen says it's been going on for months,' said May.

'Alright. I'll see if Jock and Davie from the bowling club will help. It makes me sick in my stomach knowing someone would do that,' said Jimmy.

Jim had bought two bunches of roses from Jean Macleod's flower shop. He then popped into Barbara's shop, which sold confectionary, and bought Helen some Turkish Delight, which was one of her favourite treats. Back at home, he placed the roses in water. Grant was still away on his mission and hadn't picked his up yet. Next, he organised the tea shop for the busy afternoon ahead and had extra time to make scrambled eggs and toast, some coffee and orange juice for Helen to eat in the upstairs flat.

Grant came rushing through the door and approached Jim as he awkwardly carried the tray and flowers, which were held under his sweaty right oxter.

'Your flowers are in the vase over there,' said Jim.

'Great. And the plan is about to be put into action this afternoon,' Grant replied.

Jim gave him a nod of approval.

Upstairs in the flat, Helen was still in bed, so was Jamie, as they had both had a terrible night's sleep. Frank was pretty independent and had gone into the kitchen and made himself a bowl of Coco Pops, and was now sitting close to the TV watching *Swap Shop*. His parents didn't make him work on Saturday mornings, which was a relief as he could just be a regular kid, rather than the workhorse and number one dishwasher.

Jim awkwardly came into the room, holding his breakfast tray and the flowers under his arm, which had almost fallen onto the floor as he reached for the door handle.

'Frank!' Jim said.

Frank blanked him in hope that he would go away. This was his time to enjoy himself – it was far too early to be on the clock.

'Frank!' Jim said, louder.

Frank rolled his eyes and pursed his tiny lips in a scowl, which made creased lines on his forehead. He contemplated ignoring him further, but he didn't want to get in real trouble and jumped to his feet, toppling over the nearly empty bowl of Coco Pops onto the carpet. He approached his father.

'Grab the flowers and open the bedroom door.'

Frank took the flowers reluctantly, still scowling. Keith Chegwin had just come on the telly and they were about to do the "swaporama", where kids would swap their belongings with others. He desperately wanted to be on the show, but knew deep-down they would never come to Millport.

Frank opened the door with his shoulder and let Jim through with the tray in his hands. The scrambled egg was practically cold by this point. Helen was awake, holding Jamie in her arms and trying to feed him with a bottle, but he was having none of it and kept trying to dive-bomb into her clothed boob.

No way, José. I want the girls. You can shove your powdered crap up Woolworths' arse!

Helen was still really angry at Jim and pretended to ignore him when he came over with the tray. Frank got to the edge of the bed and stood back, still trying to see some of the TV. He threw the roses on the bed at his mum's feet and made his way back to the door.

'Frank! Don't throw them!' said Jim.

Yeah, Wee Shrimp. Have some fucking respect.

Helen glared at Jim. 'Don't shout at poor Frank. You're the one in the bad books, not him,' she said angrily.

'Mum, can I finish watching my programme?' said Frank.

Oh Mummy, can I watch my wee cartoons 'cause I'm such a wee fanny.

'Yes, of course, Frank. Your dad shouldn't be involving you in the first place,' said Helen.

Frank made a run for it before he was asked to do anything else. He tripped on the way out of the door, falling on his face. You could see his feet in the bedroom while his body and head lay in the living room.

They need to get the Wee Shrimp some proper medical treatment. He's got straw for brains.

Jim sat down on the bed next to Helen and placed the tray on her lap. He grabbed Jamie off her and held him in front of his face for a second, then lifted the bottle of formula milk.

Woolworths. See if you try and feed me that shite, I'll grab hold of your porn-star moustache and pull it right off your top lip.

Helen looked at her breakfast. 'It'll take a lot more than cold, soggy toast and runny scrambled eggs to make amends for your behaviour, but I'll take that.' She grabbed the Turkish Delight off the tray and placed it on the side, then took a sip of the coffee. 'Mmm. Lukewarm coffee. What an absolute treat. I feel just like a princess.'

Jim put the baby bottle between his knees while leaning across the bed to pick up the bunch of roses and held them in front of Helen.

She just rolled her eyes. 'Do you know nothing about me? I'm allergic to roses.' She sneezed into her scrambled eggs.

Jim had almost run out of ideas when he remembered that he hadn't apologised. 'I'm sorry, Helen. I was really stupid.'

Fucking right you were, Woolworths. You could have left us a family of three and then the Wee Shrimp would have to step up as the man of the house. We'd all be dead within a month.

Helen nodded her head. 'I'm listening,' she said.

'I should have called you and I shouldn't have got drunk yesterday.' Jim urged himself to stop talking and not to go into a speech about how much fun he had had and that he actually deserved a bit of a break because he was working two jobs.

Helen took a deep breath in, almost as if she was absorbing the apology. 'Okay, I forgive you. But don't do it again and don't run away with a hot nurse… 'cause I'll chop your balls off.'

If you're gonna do that, you may as well take off his plonker and all.

Jim gave a confused look, but held his tongue. He was ready to get on with the day. 'I'll take Jamie out for a bit and you can relax for an hour,' he said.

Helen moved the tray away from her lap and sprightly got out of bed. 'Don't be stupid, Jim. It's Saturday. The busiest day of the week.' She marched out of the room.

***

Gail was standing on the jetty with her friend, Yvonne, sharing a cigarette. Each time they took a puff, they would cough profusely afterwards. They were both from good families, but were typical teenage girls trying to be cool by wearing alternative clothes and smoking. They were pretending to take an interest in the boats coming in towards the harbour, but the real reason they were there was so that Grant would see Gail and realise how much he wanted to be with her and that he couldn't possibly live without her. Although Gail was still upset with him, she still really liked him and didn't know how long she would be able to resist the temptations of this boy. In some ways, she liked him because he was a bad boy. She loved the way he dressed and thought he was so cool, with plenty of swagger and a tonne of attitude. There was one thing that grated on her – she believed it was important to have respect for one's elders and she'd witnessed Grant crossing that line. His mother seemed like a sweet lady and certainly didn't deserve a comparison to a primate.

Gail had surprised herself when she had stood up to Grant, as she was normally quite timid around boys. She likened herself to Sandy from *Grease* and saw Grant as a bit of a Danny. Her and Yvonne had recently seen the film at Millport Town Hall. That's when she bought her leather jacket at the jumble sale. The film had sparked her rebellious stage. She fantasised about being Sandy and was trying hard to be like her at the end of the film - cigarette and all. She'd even got Yvonne to cut her hair to make her look like rock-Sandy, but Yvonne went a bit gung-ho with the scissors and had mutilated Gail's hair, so it had turned out to be a bit more Siouxsie Sioux. The first time she saw Grant – this bad boy, who was smoking and wearing hip clothes – she'd imagined a narrative in her head where Grant would rock up on a motorbike and whisk her off the island so they could live an exciting life somewhere exotic.

Yvonne turned towards the tea shop while stubbing out the cigarette (just like Sandy) and nudged Gail, who was dreamily watching the water.

'Gail,' whispered into Yvonne's ear. 'Look.'

Gail turned around and there was Grant over the road, waiting to cross and holding up a bunch of flowers. She feigned fainted onto Yvonne as she couldn't contain her excitement and was overwhelmed by the butterflies deep within her stomach. Yvonne held her friend up, which wasn't a difficult task as Gail was so small and light. Grant began to cross the road and Gail's eyes grew wider, like the proverbial dear caught in Grant's headlights.

'He's so dreamy,' she said to Yvonne and felt like she'd been transported into the *Grease* film then and there. She'd actually forgotten that she was meant to be mad at Grant.

He came closer to the two girls and had a really intense look on his face. He hadn't felt right for a few days. He was normally so sure of himself and his abilities, but meeting Gail had totally stumbled him. He smiled at Yvonne, who took that as her cue to give them a little space.Gail almost fell to the ground as her knees buckled - she'd lost her prop; Yvonne.

Grant caught her before she fell and slipped his arm around her waist. He looked into her eyes passionately. 'I'm sorry. I was an idiot yesterday and acted like a dick.'

He handed over the flowers and Gail could only smile at him. She literally smelt the roses and felt giddy. If you were to look at them from a distance, they looked like two drunk people stumbling on the jetty.

'Are we cool, Gail?' asked Grant.

'I do... I mean, yes,' Gail replied and then felt embarrassed as she'd been caught up in the wrong moment. Grant hadn't really noticed – he was just happy she hadn't dumped him. 'You're the one that I want,' Gail said, all lovestruck - the perfect line being lost on Grant.

Yvonne sniggered behind them.

Grant took out two pound notes from his pocket and handed them to Gail. 'My sister wanted you to come for lunch in the tea shop today as a thank you for helping out yesterday.'

Gail seemed pleased. 'She didn't need to do that,' she said.

Grant nodded at Yvonne. 'You can bring Yvonne. I'm working all day, but it would be great to be able to see you in one way or another.'

Gail giggled to herself uncontrollably, as if some of those butterflies had escaped from her belly.

Grant had only half told her the truth. He did want to see her – that part wasn't a lie – but he had an ulterior motive, which was part of the big plan to make the tea shop a financial success. He kissed Gail on the lips. 'See you later,' he said, before crossing the road.

Yvonne sneaked up behind Gail once Grant was gone.

'Golly gosh. Tell me more!', she smirked.

***

The afternoon shift in the tea shop was well and truly underway. The place was heaving and Helen had managed to rope in every member of staff. Grant and Jim were both working; Frank was on dishes; Helen was working solo in the kitchen; Norma the Grump was on the orders and was her usual cranky self; a couple of schoolgirls, Audrey and Morven, who helped out on Saturday afternoons, were there to clear the tables and to take out food; May and Jimmy were sitting down at a table in the corner and looking after Jamie, who was beginning to be a lot more physical and difficult to look after in public places. Today's menu was soup and sandwiches, as well as the option of a hot meal – fish and chips or gammon steak with a slice of tinned pineapple, plus chips and peas.

Plenty of tourists were enjoying a day out in Millport, some of which would come for lunch before or after a cycle around the island. The Isle of Cumbrae was a little more than ten miles the whole way around and would only take an hour or two to cycle its entirety. There were lots of cycle hire shops – the most famous being Mapes, which also doubled up as an amazing magical toy shop.

As well as the tourists, there were more locals than usual having their lunch. May's friends, Isa, Betty and Grace (once again wearing her fur hat), were sitting at a table in the corner eating scones, sandwiches and a pot of tea. The girls would normally visit the tea shop on a Tuesday afternoon with May and they would catch up with all the week's gossip. Norma the Grump was lurking around their table, desperate to talk to them. She knew them because she went to school with Isa and Betty, who were locals to the island, but they weren't friends. Norma had a large jug of piping hot water and approached the table, lifted the lid on their teapot and began pouring water into it.

Isa looked up at her and quipped, 'Are we not getting another teabag? It'll be all wishy-washy.'

Betty nodded in agreement.

Norma leaned in with very serious eyes. 'It's the owners. They're really tight. Much happier serving weak tea to their customers than forking out for an extra teabag,' she said, cattily. The girls looked at one another, knowingly. 'They're also slave drivers. They work me like I'm one of those donkeys on the beach… for practically no pay.'

Grace had lit a cigarette while Norma was bitching and making up lies. 'Aye, Norma, you seem rushed off your feet,' said Grace sardonically.

Norma eased back. 'I've got a bad back and a dodgy hip, you know.'

Isa raised her eyebrows, as did Betty. They knew something was about to go down today and they were glad to be a part of the circus.

'Oh, poor you, Norma. You're being treated just like one of those poor *donkeys* down on the beach and you move just like them as well,' said Grace.

Isa almost spat out the tea she was drinking and Betty burst into a fit of giggles. Norma was angry and affronted, and began backing away slowly.

May and Jimmy were three tables down and couldn't help but watch the girls' interaction with Norma. Jamie (who was in his gran's arms) watched as well. *The battle of the old birds. In the blue corner: Norma the Grump with a pot of boiling water. In the red corner: two clucking hens and a Russian Mafia lady, ready to stab the old grump in the eye with her giant cigarette.*

May turned to Jimmy. 'What do you think they're saying?'

Jimmy shook his head and poured some whisky into his cup of coffee from a hip flask from his pocket. 'I don't know, May, with all the fucking racket that's going on in here.'

May eyed the whisky. 'Is it not a little bit early?' she said.

Jimmy became defensive. 'It's fucking Saturday – and I was working this morning,' he said.

Jamie was staring at his papa. *Oh, let Grumpy Old Painter be. He's much better craic when he has a drink.*

Grant had been everywhere in the restaurant, but took a moment to stop off at his parents' table.

Jamie looked at him and Grant pulled a goofy face. *Please, sir, can I have some more of your brilliant comedy? Who's the funny one now, Artful Dodger? Not you… you're about as funny as Grumpy Old Painter's haemorrhoids.*

Jimmy spotted his three pals from the bowling club coming through the door – Jock, Davie and Drew. They were all dressed similarly with casual long grey trousers, shirts and the Millport bowling club official tie. They had just been to a competition and Davie was looking fair pleased with himself as he held up a small trophy. Jock was puffing away on a pipe, which created a cloud of smoke in the tea shop. From his table, Jimmy went to wave them over.

Before he had the chance, Grant grabbed his shirt and whispered in his ear, 'Dad, remember why they're here.'

Jim went to the door to greet the three elderly chaps and took them to an empty table – one that he'd reserved earlier, as he knew they were coming for lunch. Jim shook Davie's hand. 'Looks like congratulations are in order,' he said as he eyeballed the cup.

Drew held his hand up, which had a bandage wrapped around it. 'He just got lucky today. The club champion is out with an injury.'

Jim laughed lightly and escorted them to the table.

A few seconds later, Gail and Yvonne came through the door. Grant was still at the table with his parents and suddenly stood to attention when he saw Gail.

The two girls caught Jimmy's eye as well. 'The state of young people today is a fucking disgrace. Look at those two lassies' hair,' he said. 'Reminds me of a pair of paint brushes I've got in the shed.'

Grant glowered at his dad and went to greet the two girls at the door. May nudged her husband, as he was being loud enough for the entire restaurant to hear.

Grumpy Old Painter makes a good point. They look like they've been mowed over by a lawnmower.

'Those lassies look like they've had their haircut with a pair of fucking shears,' said Jimmy.

'Jimmy, the wee one works here, you know, and she's very nice,' said May.

'She'll scare away all the fucking customers with that haircut,' said Jimmy, now on a roll.

Jamie turned to his Papa and laughed. Jimmy caught his grandson's eyes. 'See, Jamie agrees.'

Yes, I fucking do! That's what I said about Wee Punk the other day. If we weren't both sitting with each other, I would think that I was Grumpy Old Painter reincarnated.

Jimmy was staring at his son, who escorted Gail and Yvonne to the table. 'Is the small one our Grant's girlfriend? He's awfy touchy feely with her,' said Jimmy.

'No. He knows her 'cause she works here,' said May.

Jamie looked up at his gran. *Old Dear, you're so yesterday's news. She's gonna have his babies soon. And they're gonna call them Sid and Nancy.*

'I bloody hope she's not his girlfriend. Mind you, I know what we could buy her for Christmas. A fuckin' bonnet to cover that barnet o' hers!' said Jimmy in all seriousness.

Helen was working up an extreme sweat in the kitchen. She was struggling to keep up with all of the orders, as she was working on her own apart from Frank, who was on the dishes. She'd pull the two Saturday girls around to the kitchen to plate up sandwiches when necessary. She was also feeling anxious about the plan that Grant had organised. Helen came across as a very tough cookie, but she was also a worrier and wouldn't be able to relax until the matter was dealt with indefinitely. She plated two fish and chips, then two gammon steaks, carefully putting the tinned pineapple on the middle of the meat, before placing all the plates under the hot lights.

Jim instinctively came over and picked up the meals. 'You okay, dear?' he asked.

Helen almost bit his head off. 'Yes, Jim! Why wouldn't I be?'

At this point, Norma the Grump walked past carrying one solitary plate in her hand loosely. Food fell off it and landed on the floor. Helen looked at her really angrily. She was tired of this woman taking advantage of her and her family – and the fact that she thought she was hard done by when it was the complete opposite. Helen just hoped that Grant's plan would work.

Frank was fervently washing dishes in the sink. He knew the faster he went, the quicker he could get out of there. Norma came up behind him and threw her plate into the sink, splashing him. His face looked like an angry rat with its teeth bared. When she turned around to leave, he splashed her on the back, then quickly turned around, picked up a plate and washed it in the sink. He pretended that he hadn't done anything. She turned towards him and was absolutely livid. She leant over him and gawked in his direction. He had to stop himself bursting into giggles.

'Did you just soak me, boy?' she asked menacingly.

Frank came off all innocent, like butter wouldn't melt. 'Meee?'

Helen turned around and saw what was going on. 'Is there an issue, Norma?' she asked.

Norma scowled back at Helen as she walked back onto the tea shop floor. The atmosphere was intense. Frank shook his fist towards Norma when he knew his mother wasn't watching anymore.

***

By mid-afternoon, most of the customers had finished their meals and had left the tea shop. However, Isa, Betty and Grace had sat at their table all afternoon – they seemed to be waiting around for something exciting to happen. Jock, Tam and Drew had finished as well and were paying Norma for their meal. She picked up the cash and bent down for a second, pretending to tie her shoelaces. She then took the money over to the till, where Jim was counting the cash. She threw the money on the table next to him and he looked at her with contempt – a facial expression that you would rarely see from Jim. Yvonne and Gail were the only other table left, except for May, Jimmy and Jamie.

Grant locked the front door. Helen was cleaning the kitchen and the two girls, Morven and Audrey, were wrapping cutlery. Jim knew that all the takings were in and he'd taken the written cheques and counted the amount that should be in the till. As usual, the money was down by thirty pounds. The afternoon had been very busy and the takings should have been a hundred and fifty pounds, but there was only one hundred and twenty in the till. Jim stood up with the money in his hands and addressed all the staff.

'I need all the staff to come into the kitchen for a meeting.'

Grant came forwards and helped guide Morven and Audrey into the kitchen.

Norma looked at her watch. 'I'm due to be off the clock, so I'm going home,' she said, a little worried, perhaps sensing something wasn't right.

Jim approached her, his steely eyes pinning her to the spot. 'Kitchen *now!*' said Jim.

She seemed genuinely worried, as she'd always looked at Jim and Helen as complete pushovers who were new to the business, but, suddenly, he had become really scary. She reluctantly stood in the kitchen lined up with the other staff, who all looked like they were in a police line-up. Grant also stood with them, but Frank was told to go and sit with his gran and papa.

Helen stood behind Jim, who was pacing up and down the line of staff members - hands behind his back, like a police sergeant. 'It has come to my attention that someone has been stealing from the takings,' said Jim.

Morven and Audrey looked absolutely terrified, but Norma rolled her eyes. She was much cleverer than the Coyle family... or so she thought.

'This has been happening for several months—' continued Jim.

'We need you to empty your pockets to prove your innocence,' Helen butted in, unable to control her outburst.

Jim wasn't happy as he had the situation under control. He placed his hand up at her. 'Helen. Let me deal with this,' he said and Helen backed off.

'This is a violation of our working rights,' said Norma.

'Oh really,' said Jim. 'If you are innocent, you'll empty your pockets and we'll say no more on the matter.'

The two girls emptied their pockets, as did Grant, who'd included himself in the search. None of them pulled out anything of any significance; a few hairbands, pens, notepads.

Norma emptied her apron pocket and became all defensive. 'I brought money with me today 'cause I'm going for my messages later,' she said, pulling out a wad of pound notes.

'You won't mind if I take a look at the money?' asked Jim as he grabbed the notes off an exasperated Norma.

'I've got a good mind to phone the union rep and the *Largs & Millport News*. This business will be finished and your horrible family will be run out of town,' said Norma, flapping like a hen that's been startled by a fox - a cunning fox.

Jim flicked through the pound notes and kept eight of them aside, holding them up in front of her. 'You see, Norma. This morning, Grant took ten pound notes from the takings and put a very distinctive red dot on these notes,' said Jim.

Grant smiled at Norma smartly.

'He then distributed these notes to some of our family friends and acquaintances.' Jim pointed at the three sets of tables. 'They were asked to come and spend the notes they were given in the tea shop today, which they have, and somehow these notes have ended up in your pocket.'

Norma looked incredibly worried, like she wouldn't be able to worm her way out of the mess she'd got herself into.

'This is, in fact, a police matter,' said Jim. Norma pretended to come over all light-headed.

Isa, Betty and Grace moved closer. 'Don't fall for her antics. She used to do this in gym class when she wanted to go home,' said Isa, excitedly instilling herself into the drama.

'Yes, she did,' said Betty.

Norma knew she'd been well and truly rumbled.

'We have all these witnesses that have seen your true colours now,' said Jim. 'If I hear one negative comment from anyone in Millport about this tea shop and my family that is linked to you, I will go to the police and you'll never work in this town again.'

Norma put her head down and slowly made her way past all the locals who were there. Isa shouted at her, 'Shame on you, Norma.' Betty nodded in agreement. Grace was a little more uncouth with her comment, 'You common dirty thief.' Norma then went past May, Jimmy, Frank and Jamie. Frank was the happiest of everyone as she'd made his life miserable. He stood up on the chair and shouted behind her back, 'Hope I never see you again, Norma the Grump!' He shook his fists at her. Jimmy laughed at his grandson as May pulled him back down.

Jamie watched her walk away. *I could have saved you a load of cash. I knew months ago.*

Norma walked out of the tea shop and the atmosphere changed instantly.

Helen felt the weight lift from her shoulders. The matter had bothered her for a long time and it had finally been resolved.

Jim stood forward and shook Grant's hand. 'Well done, Grant. You did good. We might even give you a pay rise,' said Jim, rather chuffed with his own performance too.

Helen butted in, 'Yes, he's done well, but a pay rise? Think we might need to discuss that.'

Jim rolled his eyes at Grant and nodded at Helen, using his favourite catch phrase, 'Yes dear', then they both chuckled

Chapter 10

Friday afternoon had been busy all day in the tea shop and Helen was rushed off her feet with only Grant helping her - as usual. May and Jimmy were in Busby at their own house, which meant Helen had no daytime care for her children – particularly Jamie, who was now crawling and standing, and had become very curious - a total nuisance to be honest. She didn't have enough eyes to watch him all the time as she was understaffed, busy and stressed. Jim hadn't arrived back from his last day at school before the summer holidays and wasn't available to help. There was only a small window between the lunch shift and the early evening dinners. She was doing a Chicken Maryland night, with banana and pineapple fritters. She'd done it once previously and the feedback had been excellent. The dinner service was fully booked and Helen was frantically trying to batter her fruit fritters, while pan-frying chicken and looking after Jamie, who was crawling around the kitchen floor. He picked up a piece of pineapple and stuck it inside his mouth. Helen saw him do this and quickly grabbed it, to prevent him from choking. Doing the Heimlich manoeuvre to her baby wasn't on her list of daily tasks.

Come on, Blondie. I don't get given any good food. Just that shit powdered milk crap, now that you've let Laverne and Shirley run dry – just like Old Dear's Sahara Desert saggers.

Helen was fully aware that there was oil spitting from the frying pans and picked Jamie up from the floor. She needed to figure a way for him to settle in his pram for a few hours while she dealt with the nightly rush. She went into the fridge and picked up a pre-made bottle of powdered milk.

No, I'm going to go on a hunger strike if you keep feeding me that crap.

You could tell Helen was thinking deeply with a worried expression on her face. She walked over to the shelf where she kept the alcohol for cooking her sauces and grabbed a bottle of Grouse whisky.

I've been pissed off with you for a while, Blondie, but now we're talking.

Helen looked around the tea shop to check no one was looking and unscrewed the bottle of Grouse, then poured a teaspoon's worth into the bottle of baby milk. Jamie had a massive grin on his face, showing his two front baby teeth, which had half come in. Helen looked at her baby son. 'The whisky is just for the pain from your poor wee baby teeth. They must be sore,' she said.

Aye, right. You want to put me to sleep to shut me up for a while. I tell you, Blondie, it's the best plan you've had in ages.

Helen was contemplating putting the bottle of whisky away, but decided to pour another teaspoon's worth into the milk.

Ye wee beauty! I'm gonna have a rare old night the night.

Helen put the cap back on the bottle and hadn't noticed that Frank had sneaked up on her and was standing behind her like Damien from *The Omen*.

'Mum, are you putting whisky in the bottle?' asked Frank.

Helen screamed and jumped with fright, knocking the whisky bottle on its side and spilling some of its contents.

Trust the Wee Shrimp to waste good alcohol.

'Frank! You scared me,' said Helen.

'If he's having whisky, can I have some?' asked Frank, knowing full well she'd put some in the baby bottle. 'Don't be ridiculous, Frank. Jamie isn't having whisky. It's for Mum's sauces,' said Helen, trying to cover up her antics.

Jamie laughed out loud with his baby gurgle. *Ha ha! You tell the Wee Shrimp. Only adults and babies get whisky... ha ha!*

'Mum. Are you sure? I think I saw...'

Before Frank had a chance to finish his sentence, Helen pretended to look at her wrist like she had a watch on it, even though she didn't. 'Frank, go and wash your hands and face. You'll need to have your tea before we get busy,' said Helen.

He frowned at his mum, knowing she was telling him white lies. He wanted whisky like his brother and not to have to do dishes. He crinkled up his little face and stamped his feet as he walked towards the sink. Helen sighed, thinking she'd got away with it, and tilted the baby bottle into the mouth of an eager Jamie, who – for once – was desperate to feed from it. He gulped down the liquid like an alcoholic would drink a bottle of booze wrapped in a brown paper bag. Helen was too busy thinking about that night's dinners and the prep she still had to do to notice her baby gulping down his medicine.

Frank made eye contact with Jamie, who was still feeding. He was sick of his baby brother having the life of Riley. He didn't need to work and was mollycoddled by whoever went near him. He also got to sleep when he wanted and now he was being fed whisky in a bottle.

Jamie stared back at Frank as he guzzled his milk. *Ha ha! The Wee Shrimp is jealous.*

He took his mouth away from the bottle and cackled out loud, spraying Helen's shoulder with milk.

Frank noticed and knew Jamie was trying to torment him. He began shaking his fists at Jamie, who smiled sneakily and went for the bottle once again. Frank came over like he was a mini hardman coming out of a pub, drunk and ready to fight the nearest passer-by. His face was squelched up as he danced behind his mother's back, pretending to air punch – missing hitting Helen by mere centimetres. She sensed something was going on and turned around suddenly. She banged into Frank, who lost his footing and fell onto the tiled floor on his bum. Jamie laughed out loud and spat out of his mouth - this time spraying Helen on the face.

Helen was flustered as she turned to face him. 'Oh, for goodness' sake, Frank. What were you doing behind my back?' asked Helen.

Frank pouted his lips and his eyes welled up, as he stared towards the chequered tiles. 'Nothing,' he mumbled.

Jamie just smiled and went to finish off his bottle. Helen grabbed some blue roll paper and wiped the milk from her face, then her kitchen clothes.

'Frank, get yourself ready. It's gonna be a busy night again,' she said to her son. She lifted Jamie around to face herself. 'And you are going outside to fall asleep in your pram, as it's such a lovely night.'

I… I am… fee… ling slee… ee… py.

Frank was really angry now and was shaking on the ground with his fists clenched tightly. He watched his mother take his privileged little brother to have a lovely little sleep while he worked again. 'Rubbish life,' he grumpily said to himself.

Helen walked down the tea shop floor, tightly gripping an unconscious (and perhaps drunk) Jamie. She passed Grant, who was setting up the dining area. He really wasn't his efficient self as he was unusually clumsy – he was dropping cutlery onto the floor and banging into tables and chairs. He looked like he may have an untreated brain injury, but had actually been struck down by a completely different kind of illness – the love bug.

Gail and Grant had been spending as much time together as possible and were finding it more difficult to keep their hands off one another – they were like a couple of love doves. This posed a problem on a small island, as Gail was always trying to hide him from her parents who definitely wouldn't approve. He was a working-class boy who smoked, drank alcohol and had been expelled from school without any qualifications. She was only fourteen and they didn't think she should have boyfriends, especially one who didn't attend their church. Grant and

Gail hadn't yet delved into the topic of religion, although Gail knew in her heart she was a Christian. She didn't have the guts to ask him about his beliefs, as she was scared that if they didn't match up, then she'd have to finish with him. They were having too much fun together and – for both of them – ignorance was bliss. They spent their time talking about bands, films and other general topics, which was fine for now. They liked to hang out on the pier and the fairground in the Garrison – where they would snog on the swing boat ride. It was the perfect place for Gail and Grant to be together. There was little chance that her parents or any of their friends would catch them snogging there, as they didn't frequent the area – unless there was a big event on, like the yearly gala that saw the crowning of the Cumbrae Queen.

It was a long-standing tradition, which had occurred for quite some time. Each year, there would be a new queen crowned and she would be paraded through the town with her two young pageboys on a carriage. They would be followed by the glorious sounds of the Millport pipe band. Gail had been telling Grant that morning about her own humiliation when she'd been voted as the Cumbrae Queen by her classmates. She'd felt she didn't have a choice and became painfully shy when dressed up in her regalia as she sat in front of the Garrison – feeling unbelievably exposed with all eyes staring at her for what felt like an eternity. It had only been recently that her confidence had grown and she had started to wear outlandish clothes – ones that she thought were fashionable, but the jury was out on that one. The older residents of the town certainly thought her and Yvonne dressed in a shocking manner.

Grant's legs were beginning to feel like jelly – these new emotions were making him inherently uncomfortable. He had this nervous feeling inside his gut and he didn't really like it. He had been too sensible recently with having a serious girlfriend and a career. It all seemed a lot for a fourteen-year-old. He sat down at one of the tables in the tea shop and placed his hand on his forehead. Earlier, he'd managed to score a bottle of vodka from a guy called Robert, who was happy to buy underage teenagers some drink for a couple of spare fags. Grant had already swigged a good quarter of the bottle already and had hidden it in the dogs' kennel. If Helen saw him there, he would just say he was checking the dogs, which was something that he did anyway. He convinced himself that the alcohol was medicinal – to help calm his out-of-control nerves.

He stood up and walked across the tea shop floor, towards the back door, and went outside. The weather was decent and the dogs were all lying down outside the kennel. The puppies were growing fast and were almost ready to be sold to their new owners. Grant went inside the kennel area. A few overstimulated red setter puppies tried to escape, but he pushed them gently back inside and shut the door. Several of the puppies jumped on Grant, licking his hairy bare legs. Normally, he would have been delighted with their excitability and cuteness, but today he felt really flat and had no energy to give them any attention. He was there for one purpose only and that was to find his vodka. He placed his arm inside the kennel where Tana was hiding from her own puppies.

Grant acknowledged her. 'You seem like you're in the same mood as me,' he said to the tired-looking, overweight dog. He grabbed his vodka, which he'd placed up against the inside of the kennel. Brochan grazed past him as he stood up and he patted her for a second before he left the dogs' area.

Grant sauntered to the back of the garden, feeling sluggish, and eventually stood under the birch tree. He sat on a tree stump where another tree had previously lived before being cut down. He stared up at the branches and lit a cigarette, then took a giant gulp of the straight vodka, barely gagging as the harsh clear liquid went down his gullet. Nothing bad had happened with Gail, but he just had this unsettled feeling. He was beginning to think he was too young for a serious relationship. They'd been seeing each other for a couple of weeks and it had been brilliant, but also intense. He was worried he was losing part of himself and that he had become entangled with Gail – that they were becoming one. It was all a bit too much and he was now questioning whether this was where he should be at such a young age. He wanted to go to wild parties and have sex, drugs and rock 'n' roll in his life. He didn't want to be married with children and settling down by the age of sixteen. He was worried that he had given her a false impression. There were two voices in his head – one that was telling him that he was madly in love and the other that was telling him to sew his wild oats.

He emphatically swigged the vodka and had now drunk another quarter of a bottle. He'd also been so deep in thought that he hadn't noticed that his cigarette had burnt all the way down to the stub. He stood up and left the vodka by the tree – there was no way Helen was going to be looking there today and there was not a chance that he wasn't going to polish off the whole bottle by the end of the night. He stood up and swayed and had to hold himself up with the tree trunk, as he was feeling light-headed and a little drunk. He put his hand inside his pocket and pulled out a packet of Wrigley's P.K chewing gum and placed a piece inside his mouth. His eyes were beginning to glaze over, so he put his prescription glasses on in order to see better - the ones he only needed for reading. He wanted to hide his eyes from Helen, who would definitely give him a bollocking if she knew he was drunk. He walked back towards the tea shop rather unsteadily.

Helen was at the front of the tea shop and was placing Jamie inside his Silver Cross pram, being extremely careful not to wake him up. She stared down at her sleeping baby, who seemed gloriously happy and content. This made her mind go into overdrive, worrying that she'd perhaps put a bit too much whisky into his bottle – had she completely knocked her baby out? Women in Scotland had been doing this for years just to get a bit of respite. Her own mother did it to all her children – who now all really liked to drink alcohol. In fact, everyone she knew in Scotland drank excessively – was this because they'd made their children dependent on it from when they were babies? She stuck her head into the pram to check him. He was breathing rather heavily, but that was probably because he was in a deep sleep. 'You're fine,' whispered Helen.

She rocked the pram and enjoyed the fresh sea air for a little while. She'd spent so much time in that hot, stuffy kitchen lately and hadn't had the opportunity to enjoy what she loved. Helen adored the sea, which was one of the main reasons they had moved to Millport. She'd loved her time on the island as a youngster with her siblings – life was just so much more laid-back than in the hustle and bustle of Glasgow. The city didn't have the holiday vibe that Millport had to offer. Everything felt much heavier and Helen thought that a move to Millport would lighten the family's load. They had both been quite naive thinking that owning a small hospitality business would be a walk in the park. It had been the opposite: irregular hours, weekends and nights. Solid work for the entire summer. When everyone was out enjoying themselves, they were at work, stressed and usually rushed off their feet. When she wasn't in the kitchen, she would tend to her children and dogs.

Helen looked across to the busy pier and then over to Wee Cumbrae (a smaller island a few miles away, which was currently uninhabited). Helen sometimes wished she had a boat so she could go over to the wee island and escape for a day or so. She sighed deeply, then shook herself out of her daydream and suddenly remembered she'd left a batch of battered pineapple fritters in the hot oil of the pan. 'Shit!' she said in a panic as she ran back inside the tea shop, leaving Jamie sleeping heavily in his pram. Not even the overbearing squawks of the seagulls could wake him up.

***

Frank was sitting in the middle of the dining area floor on the old tartan carpet, which was covered in stains and spillages. He was staging some kind of protest in the hope he'd be listened to by his mother. He didn't want to work anymore, but the main reason for his annoyance was that his baby brother was being treated far better than him and he didn't like it. He wanted things to go back to the way they were – life BJC (Before Jamie Coyle). He would love to rub his brother away with his fancy dolphin rubber that he'd bought in Mapes toy shop. He was sick of his voice not being heard. Therefore, sitting on the floor was his only option until somebody listened to him and maybe agreed to throw the baby in the bin or, even better, the sea. He didn't want him to die, but if he could just be swept away by the tide in a rubber ring – never to be seen again. Frank was so involved in his own head that he failed to notice that the kitchen had filled up with smoke due to Helen's pan of cremated fritters. The smell was a harsh burnt smell and it engulfed the entire tea shop. Health and safety wasn't in place in the 1970s – you just had to improvise.

Grant staggered into the tea shop feeling worse for wear. He'd been a good boy lately and hadn't been hitting the bottle since he'd started work here. He took a few paces and tripped over his nephew, who was on the floor. Frank screamed out as Grant went flying onto his front, knocking off his glasses as he skimmed across the floor on his stomach, enduring some painful carpet burns. He then banged his head on a metal table leg.

Helen came bounding up the tea shop floor, totally aware that the kitchen could be on fire. Her eyes peered ahead and she failed to spot Grant, who was now sprawled across the middle of the floor. She tripped over his torso, screamed like a banshee and landed on her boobs – which helped to cushion the blow and prevented her from hitting her entire face on the kitchen floor. Frank was crying loudly – more from shock, as Grant had barely grazed him. Grant was semi-unconscious – not because he'd badly hurt himself, but because he was drunk.

Helen gathered herself up from the floor and spotted the other two. She stared towards the open-plan kitchen, which was now hidden due to the smoke. 'The kitchen's on fire!' she screamed as she ran towards it. 'Grant! Come and help!'

Grant slowly came to and was really confused about what was actually happening. Helen frantically felt around the cooker to turn off all the gases. The oil pan was on fire and she could barely see. Fortunately, she knew the kitchen like the back of her hand and was able to navigate around it. She bent down and grabbed a load of dishcloths, then ran over to the sink and soaked them with cold water. Grant stumbled into the kitchen and his eyes were drawn to the burning flame. Helen ran back with the wet dishcloths and pushed him out of the way.

'Open all the windows and doors, Grant!' shouted Helen. He kept staring towards the small flame in the pan. '*Now*!' she screamed at him, as she threw a wet cloth over the burning flame in the pan, then another two. She managed to extinguish the flame, but had to get rid of the smoke and stupidly picked up the roasting hot metal handle with a wet cloth, lifting it over to the sink. She burnt her hands and this made her throw the pan into the water. There was a cacophony of crackles, hisses and spits and then some prolonged sizzling as a cloud of smoke came from the water into the air.

Grant was making slow progress trying to open the back door, so Helen took it upon herself to open all the windows in the kitchen. When she'd completed the task, she shouted to herself, 'Shit!'

'You swore, Mum,' said Frank through the cloud of smoke.

'Not now, Frank! Can't you see there's a catastrophe in the kitchen?' Helen picked up a metal pot lid and tried to waft some of the smoke out of the window. 'What's the time, Grant?' Helen shouted out to her brother.

Grant had gone to the front door and opened it as wide as possible, but hadn't banked on the fact he was unsteady on his feet and fell forwards, similar to a tree after being cut down by a chainsaw. He landed on his chin and was lying flat down on the street, and didn't have the energy to pull himself back up again. Gail happened to be across the road with Yvonne because she couldn't bear to be away from her love – she was on the verge of obsession. She saw her boyfriend falling to the ground and rushed over to help him, with Yvonne closely behind. Grant was very groggy. In her rush to get to him, Gail brushed against Jamie's Silver Cross pram, where he was still fast asleep outside the tea shop.

Gail kneeled beside Grant. 'Grant! Grant!' She shook him to try and rouse him. He flinched and raised his hand, gently pushing her away. 'Grant, it's Gail. Are you okay?' she asked, worried.

He slowly lifted his head to face her and scowled at her. 'Why are you always here?' he asked, staring at her as though he hated her.

A tear dripped down her cheek. Yvonne, who'd finally

made it across the road, grabbed Gail's shoulder. 'Come on. He's not himself,' she said.

Gail went closer to him again. 'Grant, it's Gail,' she said desperately.

'Why don't you just fuck off?' said Grant, completely out of character.

This time, Gail burst into tears. She couldn't believe this was the same Grant. They'd been in the Garrison earlier and everything had been wonderful. What had changed in an afternoon? Yvonne, who was much taller than Gail, pulled her up and made her walk away. She was crying loudly.

Grant soon stood up, having completely forgotten what had just occurred, and staggered back inside the tea shop.

The tea shop was almost free from smoke, but had a burnt fat odour that was impossible to shift. Helen was on a mission to still make her Chicken Maryland night a success. She'd only burnt one batch of fritters, but the biggest issue was her sore hands. She'd filled a plastic container with cold water, so she could dip them inside to relieve the pain when she had the opportunity, but this wasn't often as she had so much to do. Self-employed people don't get the opportunity to call in sick – if there's something wrong, they just have to grin and bear it. She'd had worse burns before and knew that they'd eventually clear.

Frank was still sitting in protest, pretending to sniffle on the tartan carpet. He was becoming quite annoyed as his mother hadn't noticed him. His plan hadn't worked at all. He was out of sight from Helen, who hadn't seen him as he was hidden across from the servery. Helen turned her oven down and looked across to the pile of pots in the washing sink.

'Frank! Frank!' she shouted.

He thought about ignoring her completely, but he wanted to be noticed and pushed a chair over, which made a loud banging noise on impact with the ground. Helen jumped back, then rushed out of the kitchen to see what was going on. Frank was lying on the ground next to the toppled-over chair.

She knelt down beside him. 'Oh Frank, did you fall over?'

He burst into pretend tears and nodded at his mother. This wasn't his original plan, but he liked the attention and hoped that maybe she'd sympathise and let him watch cartoons for the rest of the night. She picked him up off the ground, which was something she hadn't done for a while. She embraced him tightly and he reciprocated. It was a cuddle that they both seemed to need and this made Helen quite emotional – she began to worry that she was neglecting her children due to her heavy workload. She carried Frank into the kitchen as Grant stumbled up towards them.

'Grant, pick up that chair, please,' Helen said, without making eye contact.

***

Jamie was lying in his Silver Cross pram. His eyes opened wide unexpectedly and his head began to move slowly away from his lifeless body. His neck stretched itself and thinned out. All the skin began to look like a slithery snake, which was now high above the pram. He was smiling as he rose up towards the sky, higher than the tea shop – relieved that his useless body was being left behind as it had only been a burden to him. His neck broke away from his floppy mess of a body completely and now looked like a very long umbilical cord, which flopped around in the air below his baby head. He was now close to reaching the clouds and at last had the freedom he desired. He suddenly burst through the clouds and opened his mouth with the desire to eat the fluffy candyfloss. Unexpectedly, his neck broke off from his head and was swept up by a flock of flying geese in the sky. They hungrily feasted on the string of skin until it had been entirely eaten. He didn't care that he'd lost another body part, though, as he was ecstatic about being a lonesome head – a gorgeous wee head.

Paradise existed through the clouds. There were big, beautiful, succulent mountains of all different shapes and sizes. They had glorious white rivers of lovely milk, which splashed down them and came from their wonderful tips: red ones, white ones, black ones, brown ones – all spurting out like a volcano. The milk was splashing onto Jamie's head and he opened his mouth wide, allowing gallons of milk to enter inside. The milk didn't fall out of the hole where his neck had previously been, but each gulp increased the size of his head – bigger and bulgier. His head was beginning to look like one of those giant balloons that you could win at the fairground. He was increasing in size and getting closer to those beautiful mountain breasts. He was lapping up the situation – this was what he'd always dreamed of since he was born. *Those that say dreams can't come true are blatant liars*, he thought. He was rising higher and higher – he was now the size of a hot-air balloon – and closer to his first giant nipple. A lovely large brown one, which was gushing out milk. Jamie opened his giant hole of a mouth, placing it over the entire nipple, and the increase in his head size was instantaneous. His head was now humongous and was nearly as big as the mountains themselves, but he was still thirsty and wanted more. Greed was taking over as he sucked up the entire brown nippled boob mountain inside his head. *Ha ha! I'm the king of all boob mankind and will have all the milk in the universe – ha ha!*

The giant baby head guzzled up the pink nippled mountain in one large suck – milk spluttered from his mouth all over his face. A voice could be heard in the sky, 'Hello, gorgeous!'

He stopped sucking for a moment. *I am pretty gorgeous. Who goes?*

'Isn't he such a cutie?'

There was suddenly a horrendous pong in the air, which Jamie breathed in through his nose. He then vomited out an ocean's worth of milk from his mouth, his head decreasing at a rapid rate.

'Yes, he's a very cute little baby,' said a creepy voice in the sky.

Jamie continued to vomit out milk and he was desperately trying to reach the last existing mountain – still wanting to be the king of milk and boobs. He composed himself, trying not to breath in through his nose, as the awful stench was still in the air. He was determined to reach the top of the boob mountain. This one was different, though, and didn't look as appetising as the other ones. It had a much crustier surface;

however, it was all that was left and he had no choice but to explore. There was only a slight drivel of milk coming from the tip. He fought his way upwards, supping up each and every dribble of milk that slowly poured down, and eventually reached the top, then looked over the horizon. The nipple tip was releasing smoke and was covered in harsh brown marks that had large clumps of thick black grass sticking out from them. He licked up the remainder of the milk, which was more of a yellow colour. It tasted rank in his mouth, but was the only way his head would increase and take him to the tip. He finally arrived near the tip and was horrified to find giant hairy moles surrounding a giant nipple, which was oozing yellow puss.

Jamie suddenly opened his eyes and woke up from his baby nightmare. He had a very bad feeling that something terrible was going to happen. Staring at him were two people who looked very fuzzy, as he was still feeling the effects of the whisky. The awful odour from his dream could still be smelt through his tiny nostrils – it was absolutely ghastly, grotesque even, and was beginning to make him feel ill.

'Hello, you gorgeous wee cutie pie,' said the lady's voice, one he was sure he'd heard before. He could feel a harsh rubbing of his chest.

'Why don't we take him for a walk up to our flat for some sweeties?' said a man.

Oh, that smell. That's totally rank. I feel like I'm being pressed down. Where the hell am I?

Jamie tried hard to open his eyes to see who was there. He knew the voices, but they weren't overly familiar. This wasn't Blondie, Woolworths or any of the other regulars who surrounded him normally. It definitely wasn't Old Dear or Grumpy Old Painter either.

'Come on, Muriel. Let's take him before his mother sees us,' said the man.

Muriel... Muriel... who in the hell's Muriel again?

'Don't you think we should go and ask Helen first, Tam?' asked Muriel.

Muriel and Tam, Muriel, Tam. Who are they again? Eyes open, eyes open and stop being blurry. Jamie's vision became clearer. *Nooo!*

Muriel and Tam were both staring down at him, right up close, and Jamie looked at them like a dear in headlights.

The Hills Have Eyes! *Somebody help me! Help me!*

Muriel smiled at him with her toothless grin and Tam breathed heavily through both his mouth and nostrils. Jamie's head flew forwards a little and he projectile vomited some milk onto them.

Phew. Thank Gawd for baby sick. Hopefully they'll fuck off now.

Muriel leaned in more and Tam grabbed his baby blanket and rubbed his grotty face with it. 'He's such a little cutie. Aren't you a little cutie?' said Muriel, as she tickled him over the covers. As she did this, his own baby sick dripped from her chin back onto his own face. He started to bawl loudly in the hope that someone would come and rescue him, but that was wishful thinking as they were the only ones there.

Help me! Help me! The Hills Have Eyes *have captured me and I think they're going to eat me.*

His cries continued, but this didn't deter Muriel.

'You're going to come to Aunty Muriel's and Uncle Tam's for a chocolate biscuit, aren't you, cutie?' said Muriel, still tickling him.

No, no. I don't want to. I'm not even on solids yet. I just drink milk and whisky, that's all. Please fuck off!

Muriel stood up properly with the help of both of her walking sticks. 'Come on, Tam. You push him,' she said.

Tam leaned into the pram, opened his diseased mouth and bared his rotten teeth. 'We're going to have fun with you,' he said, before laughing like a cartoon villain.

Yuck! What a minging pong! And what the hell does he mean? Please, please, if there is a God, I beg you, now's the time to help me. The Hills Have Eyes couple have got me and they're going to cook and eat me. Somebody do something. Strike them down with a lightning bolt or open the ground and let them fall inside to their deaths. Please, please rescue me. I promise this time I'll be a good little boy.

***

Inside the tea shop, the Chicken Maryland night was at full capacity. Helen had managed to vanquish most of the smoke, but there was still a harsh fatty odour. Grant was still swaying about and Helen had been so busy that she'd failed to notice he was a wee bit drunk – even though he was covered in cuts and bruises. Frank had calmed down after his cuddle and his mum had given him a large bowl of ice cream before he started his shift on dishes – this had placated him.

Grant picked up two plates of chicken, which Helen

finished off by putting a pineapple and a banana fritter on top. He managed a few steps before he tripped over his own shoelace, lost his balance and fell to the ground. He managed to hold onto the plates, but a couple of fritters flew into the air and landed on the table of an older couple. One of the fritters even positioned itself onto the lady's plate next to the rest of her meal. Fortunately for Grant, neither of them noticed. He lay on his front for a few seconds. Helen was giving him the evil eye and was embarrassed, but was unable to shout as there were customers in earshot. Grant stumbled around on the ground, placing the plates down and happened to find his glasses that fell off earlier during the fire.

Helen shouted, 'Grant! Grant!'

He turned to her as he placed the glasses over his eyes. 'Just needed my glasses, sis.'

Helen was aware that some of the customers were now watching the debacle and she stared ahead with a forced grin. Grant stood up while holding the two plates and was about to walk towards the table.

'Grant!' Helen shouted.

Grant stopped in his tracks and went to the servery, placing the plates back under the light.

'What the hell is wrong with you?' whisper-shouted Helen.

Grant pointed to the two plates. 'Think these ones need more fritters.'

Frank's ears perked up and he looked at his uncle like he was chewing a wasp, which was one of his famous facial expressions. Helen placed more fritters on the plates and Grant took them out to the table.

***

Muriel gasped for breath as she slowly walked up Cardiff Street, which was on a large slope. She used both her sticks, which enabled her to walk, but the task was almost impossible as she was so unfit. Tam was pushing Jamie (who was terrified and crying loudly in his pram). Tam would stop every few seconds and smile at the baby with his rotten teeth and tickle his chest harshly with his dirty fingernails. He did this every time he waited for Muriel to catch up with them, and every time she did, she would lean inside his pram and sing "Rock-a-Bye, Baby". It made her hopeful that he would stop his crying and warm to herself and Tam.

They lived at the very top of Cardiff Street in a ground-floor flat. It was a really bad location for a severely disabled woman. Tam had gone out and bought the property without Muriel's knowledge. He liked the idea of her having to walk up the hill to punish her for being overweight, even though she had two dodgy knees and an out-of-place hip. Muriel was actually a really pleasant woman, who had happened to marry an awful predator of a man. Unfortunately for her, babies couldn't see beyond her physical appearance and she somehow managed to frighten the life out of them. As a couple, they were terrifying.

Jamie's cries were desperate in the hope that somebody would come and rescue him. *Please! When I grow up, I promise I'll do only good. I'll go to church. I'll volunteer to help the elderly and the sick. I'll even stop swearing if you just fucking help me!*

They had nearly reached the top of the hill and were very close to the entrance of their flat. Tam jiggled about in his pocket and looked for his key. He used his other hand to lightly grip onto the handle of the pram. Muriel was a good five metres behind, and was making slow progress.

Gail and Yvonne were at the top of the hill. They had been moping around on the swings at the West Bay swing park – well, Gail had been moping as she was still devastated about her altercation with drunk Grant and had been crying solidly for a few hours. Yvonne had had enough and was desperate for her to talk about something, anything, else.

Tam spotted the two fourteen-year-old girls and looked straight at their chests. He made a sinister phwoar noise, before he looked at their eyes. 'Hello, girlies. Fancy meeting you here,' he said creepily.

Yvonne stared at Tam with utter disgust – thinking he was a dirty old pervert. She did a double-take at the pram, thinking it odd. Gail kept her eyes to the ground, caught up in teenage heartbreak.

Jamie was bawling his eyes out, trying to alert the girls' attention. *Come on, Wee Punk and Punky Big Pal! These people are going to cook and eat me. I'm just a wee innocent baby.*

Yvonne pulled Gail away from Tam. She was ill at ease and feeling queasy. She rushed past as quickly as possible - all the time being ogled by the creep.

He stared at their backsides and made another (almost involuntary) perverted noise. 'Oh, lovely,' he said as he licked around his lips. At this point, he forgot he was holding onto the pram and let go with his hand. Muriel was only a few metres from Tam and the pram – she was completely out of breath and was seeing stars in her eyes.

Inside the pram, Jamie noticed that there didn't seem to be anyone there, so he moved as much as he could. *Come on… roll… fucking roll.*

The pram's wheels began to slowly move as the brake hadn't been placed on by Tam, who had been too busy predatorily watching the two underage girls, who were now rushing down the hill. Jamie rocked as much as he could, so that the wheels began to turn and the pram slowly rolled down the hill.

Tam was oblivious to the fact that the baby he'd taken was about to embark on his very first joyride. He was turning the key into the front door of his flat. Muriel – on the other hand – had seen the baby's pram move towards her. It was on course to bang right into her, which prompted her to throw her walking sticks to the ground in the hope that she'd be able to catch the pram. Her breathless shouts towards her husband went unnoticed, as she could barely speak.

The pram picked up a bit more speed. Baby Jamie was delighted. *Fuck you, you fucking pervert!* The pram was well and truly away from Tam now and only a metre from Muriel, who was wobbly on her feet without her crutches. *Crash! Crash into her! Knock her down the hill!* Muriel panicked as the pram approached her and she tried to jump out of the way, but only managed a wobble. The pram hit Muriel on the stomach with the handle and spun around like a fairground waltzer. Muriel fell onto the pavement, landed on her fatty rolls and began to roll down the pavement. *Smash, bang, die! Hills Got Eyes, die!*

Tam finally turned around and was shocked to see his wife rolling down the hill. He ran towards Muriel to rescue her and completely ignored the runaway pram with the baby inside. The pram had spun around and was now travelling down the hill - hood first. Tam managed to stop his traumatised wife, who was trying to tell him to catch the baby, but was having a full-blown asthma attack and couldn't release any words from her mouth. He cuddled into her and placed his hand inside one of her fatty rolls, like a viper setting fangs into its prey.

The pram continued rolling downhill so Jamie could only see uphill. He was giggling away to himself – delighted that Muriel and Tam were lying on the pavement. *That'll teach you to kidnap a baby – the baby flattens you and turns you into a roly-poly.* The pram's speed was steadily increasing and was moving towards Gail and Yvonne, who were still walking down the hill, arm in arm. They hadn't noticed and when it finally reached them, the pram knocked hard into Yvonne's back and she fell onto Gail, causing both girls to tumble over. The pram spun around once more on impact with Yvonne and veered onto the main road, almost toppling over when it hit the curb. The two girls weren't hurt, but it took them a while to gain their composure and realise what had happened.

Gail looked onto the road. 'Yvonne, that's Grant's nephew's pram! He's rolling down the hill – towards the pier!'

Yvonne, who was laying on the ground, turned to face the road. 'Somebody stop that baby before it's too late!' she shouted.

Gail quickly stood up and bolted down the hill like she was the Road Runner.

***

Jim was driving into the town after disembarking the last ferry. He had three boys in his car – they were from his school and were called Paddy, Seamus and Pierce, aged fifteen, fourteen and twelve. Three brothers of Irish descent. He'd brought them over for the summer to have a holiday, which he'd promised them a while ago, but also because they could really do with help in the tea shop. Their parents were more than happy to get rid of them for a well earned break. Jim's usual parking space was outside the tea shop, but there was somebody in his spot. He decided to go and park by the chip shop next to the pier. The boys were really excited as they'd never visited a seaside town before. Jim was about to turn left when he came to the Cardiff Street junction, but had to do a sudden emergency stop when a pram came flying past them, rolling towards the pier at a rapid rate. The pram was swiftly followed by Gail, who was running extraordinarily fast for such a tiny girl.

Seamus leaned over towards Jim, who was in shock. 'Was that a baby in the pram?'

Jim stared, transfixed. 'That's not *any* baby.' He quickly opened the door. 'That's *my* baby! Jamie!' he shouted as he exited the car.

The boys got out of the car and all left their doors wide open. Paddy (the oldest brother) was staring goggle-eyed towards Gail, who had just run past him. 'She's gorgeous,' he said in his thick Irish accent.

The pram rolled onto Millport Pier, changing the tempo of the ride from a gallop to a slightly slower (but more unconformable) bumpy trot. Jamie was now terrified, as he realised his predicament was not looking good. *Holy moly. If I fall into the water, I'll drown... these arms and legs are fucking useless.* The pram veered to the side of the pier after several attempts by people to grab onto it and stop it, but the speed and momentum from travelling downhill was too much. There were two bollards that could stop the pram in its tracks, but there was also a large gap and a drop right into the water – which was at least ten metres deep. There wasn't much time either as the pram was only ten metres away from falling off the pier. *Fucking hell, it's like I'm on the* Titanic. *I'm trapped! I cannae get these straps off me... even if I could, I'd still not be able to jump out.* The pram was only five metres away now and was on course to go right through the middle of the two bollards.

Jim was running for his baby's life and was followed by Gail, Seamus and Pierce. The pram was only a few metres from falling into the water and Jim was still a few metres away.

***

Helen was oblivious to what was happening with her baby as she finished off her first round of Maryland meals for the night. Grant had been absolutely useless for the first time and she was wondering what was wrong with him. He had been clumsy all night and had even stuttered a few times. She hadn't had time to give him the third degree, but his cards were marked and she'd jar him later. There was a short lull in the tea shop, so she took the opportunity to check on Jamie and bring him in for a feed. She went out the side exit to avoid the customers, popped her head around the door and her stomach dropped to her feet. Her baby was gone. Hopefully, somebody would have just taken him for a short walk.

There seemed to be a kerfuffle over at the pier – lots of screaming and shouting. She could see something fall into the water. Then, the penny dropped. She ran, her worst fears suddenly a reality.

***

The pram fell into the water. *For the love of Barbara fucking Streisand... "What's up, Doc?!" I'm only a wee baby and cannae swim.* Seconds later, Jim didn't hesitate and jumped in after his baby. He was swiftly followed by Gail, who did an impressive dive. The two Irish boys couldn't swim without armbands yet and had to stop dead at the edge of the pier. Paddy, the oldest brother, came from nowhere and also jumped into the pier – Jim had given him swimming lessons in the school pool and he'd become rather good. There were huge splashes in the sea. The pram bobbed up and down and hadn't started to sink quite yet.

My! Hasn't this been an adventure?! Oh look... there's reliable Woolworths coming to save the day... oh, and Wee Punk with flat hair.

Jim and Gail managed to grab either side of the pram to keep it afloat, while they frantically kicked their legs like egg beaters under the water. Paddy swam up to them and grabbed the front. Gail made eye contact with Paddy and he smiled at her with a big cheesy grin as they all swam together, trying to keep the baby from sinking in the pram.

Jamie looked at Gail and Paddy. *Uh oh, the Artful Dodger ain't going to be pleased. Someone's about to steal his bird.*

Jim began to panic as the pram was becoming too heavy and was starting to sink.

Helen, meanwhile, spotted a man on a small motor boat, which was sitting in the water at the jetty. She jumped inside like she was Wonder Woman.

'What do you think you're doing?' asked the man.

'Drive! Over there – my baby's in the water,' Helen said in a panic, pointing towards Jamie in the pram.

Without hesitation, the man fired up the engine and steered his way from the jetty towards the sinking pram.

Jim was trying his hardest to save his baby and managed to unfasten the straps and flip the hood down. Paddy and Gail worked together to keep the pram from sinking.

Save me, Woolworths! I cannae swim! 'Cause somebody made me a useless lump of lard.

A small boat came speeding over as fast as it could, with a very scared screaming mother leaning over – frightened her baby was about to drown. Crowds had now gathered on the pier and the jetty – all anxious about the outcome. Jim managed to grab Jamie from the pram and was using one arm to tread water and the other to hold Jamie in the air. Gail and Paddy let go of the pram, allowing it to sink into the sea.

I'm glad that piece of shit has gone and now those creepy Hills Got Eyes folk won't be able to kidnap me again. Fair kudos to Woolworths for rescuing his beautiful wee baby. Oh, and here comes Blondie – where has she been?

The man in the boat stopped near where they were all swimming and Helen leaned over and grabbed her baby from Jim, lifting him inside the boat. She made eye contact with her husband, who shot her an extremely fierce look. Jamie stared at his mother, who was now crying.

That's another fine mess you got us into, Blondie!

Chapter 11

The day had been extremely traumatic for everyone. Jim sent Grant to cancel all the rest of the night's bookings as the family needed to recover from the terrifying incident on the pier. Jim was livid at Helen, who was cradling Jamie tighter than she'd ever done before.

Gawd! First I nearly drown, now she's trying to suffocate me.

Helen was unbelievably upset and felt a tremendous amount of guilt for leaving Jamie outside. This was something that she'd done with Frank. This was what every mother did with their bairns. Who took him? And why had he fallen off the pier? She was relieved that he'd come to no real harm, but it was a really close call. She worried that everyone would think she was a terrible mother. At that moment, she felt like an abysmal mother.

Gail and Paddy were sitting, shivering, still wet with towels around their shoulders. They were next to the calor gas heater, which had three orange bars burning. Jim was pacing about trying to work out why his son had ended up in the sea, but he didn't want to make a scene in front of everyone else. The two other boys, Pierce and Seamus, were spotted by Frank as they came in the door. He had met them a few times when Jim had taken him to swim in the Maryhill School swimming pool. They were all on the same level and still had to use armbands. They would watch Paddy dive in after a rubber brick from the bottom of the pool and retrieve it. Frank was delighted to see the boys. He went up to the flat to find his Fisher-Price aeroplane and brought it down to show them. He'd made them sit on the stained tartan carpet and then explained to them the names of all his Fisher-Price play people. He particularly liked the wobbly Weeble and held him up.

'I sometimes take him down to the kitchen sink and place him on the side. Then, I hit him hard and he goes flying into the soapy water, bouncing up and down covered in soap,' said Frank, laughing so loud that spit flew from his mouth. The other two boys laughed, too – humouring him. Frank became really animated with his little chunky Weeble, who had brown hair and a wee smile. 'One time, I hit him so hard and a plate smashed in the sink,' said Frank, all excitable, before quickly changing his expression to worried in a split second. 'But don't tell my mum.' Frank's eyes darted between the two boys. 'She doesn't know.'

Seamus patted him on the back and said, 'Don't worry, wee man. Your secret's safe with us.' Pierce burst into laughter, knowing his mum probably wouldn't care at this precise moment.

Grant had sneaked back into the garden after he'd managed to explain to the unhappy customers that the tea shop wouldn't be able to continue the Chicken Maryland night. He'd said the kitchen cooker was broken and there was no way of fixing it. In the garden, he'd downed another quarter of the bottle of vodka he'd left there. When he came back into the tea shop, he was horrified to see Gail sitting cosily with Paddy – he didn't have a clue who he was. Paddy couldn't keep his eyes off Gail, who would occasionally glance at the cheeky Irish chappie. Grant couldn't believe that she'd moved on so quickly. He had no memory of the altercation they'd had outside earlier and now felt that Gail was just a wee player – the type of girl who'd move on from one guy to the next in a blink of an eye. He stared towards Gail and Paddy and felt incredibly jealous. There was a strange pain inside his stomach and it wasn't the vodka. Gail glanced at Grant for a split second and then turned to Paddy, who was already looking in her direction. She smiled at him. Grant couldn't bear it any longer and marched back to the garden to polish off the entire bottle of vodka.

Jim approached Helen, trying to contain his anger at what had just happened with their baby. He could tell Helen was really upset with herself and when he sat down next to her, she burst into tears. 'He could have died, Jim, and it would have been my fault,' Helen spoke through her tears.

Jim now felt sad for her, as she was breaking her heart. He could tell she'd been punished enough for her mistake and instead of interrogating her, he gently placed his hand on her freckly bare arm. Jamie was asleep on her shoulder and seemed to be breathing normally. 'It's okay, Helen… he's absolutely fine,' said Jim softly.

Jamie opened his tiny eyes and his fingers wriggled; finally resting in what resembled a "middle finger" position. *Am I fuck! Those Hills Got Eyes people were going to kill me and eat me.*

Helen was shaking her head. 'No, Jim. It's not okay. How did it even happen? Who took him away and why did his pram roll down Cardiff Street and onto the pi…' She couldn't finish her sentence before bursting into tears. *It was that creepy bastard and his scary, hairy wife.*

Jim tried to be rational. 'Why don't we take this as a warning to be more careful in the future? We obviously can't leave him outside,' said Jim.

No shit, Woolworths!

'and let's be thankful we've not had a knock on the door from the polis!' continued Jim

'I'm just not coping at the moment, with having to work all day and night and trying to look after the children. I don't think I can do this anymore, Jim.' She shook her head. 'I really don't.'

Jim rubbed her arm. 'I've brought the three boys from school to help in the tea shop for the summer,' he said.

Helen looked around. She hadn't noticed the three Irish lads and this put Helen into an even bigger panic. 'Jim, no! Where are they going to sleep? This is an even bigger disaster,' she said.

Jim shrugged his shoulders. 'Don't worry, dear, I have a plan in place,' he said. 'We brought camping gear from the school and they're going to live in the back garden.' Helen placed her sweaty palm over her face and couldn't believe what she was hearing. 'They were delighted to come and help, and we're calling it a working holiday. All we need to do is feed them, give them some pocket money and allow them some free time to go to the beach and the shows.'

'Where will they even wash?' said Helen, still not convinced.

'They can use the tea shop toilet for basic washing and can occasionally come upstairs for a bath,' Jim said, relaxed. 'They're really looking forward to going in the sea – in fact, Paddy's already been in for a swim.' Jim laughed.

Helen looked like she was coming round to the idea. 'I suppose we do need the help,' she said.

Jim stood up from his chair. 'And it will give our Frank the chance to take some time off from doing the dishes and act like a normal child,' said Jim.

Frank's ears pricked up at the mention of his name and his eyes almost bulged out of their sockets with excitement, as he saw cartoons and ice cream in his eyeballs.

'I suppose. We have worked him really hard this year,' said Helen.

Just then, Yvonne came rushing through the door to see Gail flirting with Paddy, which made her look twice. She then approached Helen, who was still holding on tightly to her baby.

'Helen,' said Yvonne quietly, as she stood behind her back. Helen turned to face her from her chair and gave her a curious look. Jim had been listening as well. 'There's a phone call for you over the road.' Yvonne felt timid. She'd now gained the attention of the whole room. The whole room apart from Paddy, who was still gawping over Gail. That and Gail had told her how scary she'd found Helen and didn't know what to expect.

'For me?' asked Helen, pointing to herself.

'Yes. It's your mother. She says it's urgent.'

Helen sighed deeply as she felt heavy nerves in her stomach. She looked up at Jim. 'Jim, could you go? I don't think I could handle bad news right now.' Jim nodded at her and patted Yvonne on the shoulder. 'Thank you, I'll handle this.' He was very much playing the hero of the moment... again, and went off to answer the phone.

Yvonne stared over at Gail, who was now giggling like a silly little schoolgirl at every word that came from Paddy's mouth. Yvonne was a bit shocked at her friend, who only a few hours ago had been devastated about Grant. She shook her head and left.

Grant was standing at the side door, staring at them. He could barely stand up.

Helen started biting her nails – she'd had a horrible day and was stressed out to the max. All these horrible thoughts went through her head about her father having a nasty accident – maybe falling off his ladder. She always worried about him up there, especially at his age. What else could it be? Why would her mother be calling at this time? Something must be wrong and it must be something really bad.

Outside the tea shop, Jim was over the road on the phone and he didn't seem to be too concerned. He listened and shook his head. Grant came stumbling out the family entrance door, which allowed access to the upstairs flat. Yvonne was walking past just as he did this and he almost fell into her, knocking her off her feet. Luckily, her reflexes were decent and she managed to grab him and hold him up.

'Grant. What is wrong with you today?' Yvonne said firmly. 'You've been acting like a dick all day.'

Grant's eyes were darting around their sockets. 'She's in there with another boy, little whore,' said Grant.

Yvonne pushed him against the wall and pointed in his face, 'Don't you ever dare disrespect my friend again,' she said firmly. 'She really liked you, but you blew it.'

Grant moved his face closer to Yvonne's and went in for a kiss. Yvonne grabbed his forehead and pushed it against the wall. 'Sort yourself out, Grant. Maybe stop drinking alcohol. You're normally a decent guy, but this version of you is pathetic,' she said. She let go of Grant's forehead and he slumped down to the ground. Yvonne shook her head and was about to walk away, but then she remembered about the dirty old man who'd made lewd gestures to her and Gail. At the time, she had been so disgusted by his actions that she'd failed to help Jamie and rushed off.

Yvonne came back inside the tea shop at the same time as Jim, who was precariously carrying an old-fashioned orange tent that he'd borrowed from the school for the summer. Yvonne held the door for Jim and as soon as he came through, he shouted out, 'Boys, come and grab the tent.'

Pierce and Seamus, who were playing with Frank's play people on the floor with him, jumped to attention and ran over to grab the wobbly wooden poles from Jim.

He looked over at Paddy. 'Come on, Paddy. We need to put this up before dark or you'll have nowhere to sleep,' said Jim.

Paddy was in a world of his own, gazing towards Gail. Yvonne was shaking her head at her friend, who was also staring back at her new love interest.

'Paddy!' shouted Jim.

Paddy almost fell off his seat when he heard his name and went over to help.

Yvonne approached Helen, who was still holding on tightly to Jamie. She was far from recovered from the incident that could have killed her baby. 'Helen,' said Yvonne. Helen turned to face her and was confused at why she had come back. 'I just wanted to let you know that I think I know who had your baby,' said Yvonne.

Helen stood up from her chair. Jim was now next to Yvonne. 'Who?' asked Helen, desperately.

'I don't know their names, but I've seen them about. He's a slimy man who ogles us when he sees us,' said Yvonne. Helen started to think who it could be and a person's name popped in her head, but she wanted further clarification. 'His wife is very disabled and I think they live somewhere at the top of Cardiff Street,' said Yvonne.

'Tam and Muriel!' said Helen, angrily. Jim looked very serious. 'I'm going to kill that horrible man. How dare he take my baby!' said Helen, as she rushed towards the door with baby Jamie in her arms.

Jim ran after her and grabbed her shoulder. 'We'll deal with this tomorrow. You're far too angry to go and talk to them tonight,' said Jim calmly.

'They kidnapped our baby, Jim, and nearly killed him,' said Helen.

'They were probably just taking him for a walk,' said Jim.

Jamie opened his eyes. *No, Woolworths! Those revolting cannibals were going to eat me. Blondie's right... let's go and smash them up. We could use her sticks to batter him on the head.*

Jim placed both his hands on Helen's shoulders. 'We'll both go up tomorrow, when we've all calmed down after a good night's sleep,' said Jim, being the voice of reason.

Helen was still angry, but her anxiety had calmed slightly. 'Well, tomorrow I'm marching up there to give them a piece of my mind. They're lucky we aren't calling the police on them,' she said. Jim hugged her and Jamie.

At this point, Yvonne grabbed Gail's arm and encouraged her to leave. She was sitting by the fire like a loved-up puppy, but Yvonne wasn't sure who she was loved up with. She barely recognised her sweet, innocent friend anymore. Yvonne lightly pulled Gail outside through the main tea shop entrance.

Helen was still in an embrace with Jim when she remembered to ask, 'What did my mum want? Is everything alright?' Jim pulled himself away from his wife. 'Nothing too serious. Your sister has broken her leg again. They're bringing her to Millport to convalesce,' said Jim.

Helen's face lit up when she heard his words. 'At last, some good news,' she said.

Jim looked at her disapprovingly and Helen realised what she'd just said. 'I mean… Mary can babysit Jamie. She can stay on the couch,' explained Helen, pleased with the new arrangement. 'I mean… of course it's not good she's broken her leg – again.' Helen scratched her itchy scalp. 'She still blames me for the last time she broke it, after falling off the ski tow up Cairngorm Mountain, and no doubt I'll be blamed for this one as well – but maybe this is the lifeline we needed. She'll probably have the plaster on for six weeks. Problem solved. This wee bundle of joy has a new babysitter.'

'I suppose,' said Jim, not convinced it was good that Helen's sister had broken her leg and his wife was pleased because it provided a babysitter.

Jamie was staring at his mother with his mouth wide open. *Are you fucking kidding me, Blondie? Who the hell is this Mary? I'm about to be palmed off with another stranger. I nearly died and I'm your responsibility. Blondie will never learn.* Jamie managed to shake his head and Helen smiled at him.

Jim went over to Frank, who was on the floor, still playing with his toys. 'Right, son. It's time you got ready for bed,' said Jim.

Frank scowled at his dad. 'But the big boys might come back. I haven't showed them all my toys yet,' he said, desperately wanting to stay up later.

'They're going to be here for the summer, so I think toys will wait until tomorrow,' said Jim before he addressed Helen. 'Are you going to take the kids to bed? I'm going to help the boys put up their tent. Where's Grant?'

Helen looked at her husband. 'He's been acting really weird today. Something's not right. I'm going to speak to him in the morning,' said Helen. 'He was useless in the tea shop tonight. It's really not like him.'

Jim raised his eyebrows. 'Perhaps girl trouble. I saw that wee Gail smiling at Paddy a lot tonight.'

Helen sighed heavily. 'That's all we need. Two teenage boys fighting over one girl. That little Christian's a dark horse. You'd think butter wouldn't melt in her mouth,' said Helen.

Jim went out to help the boys.

***

Grant was hiding in his usual corner with his bottle of vodka, which was almost finished. The world looked twinkly and blurry for Grant as he swayed on the wooden stump next to the birch tree. Across from him, he could hear the three Irish boys disastrously trying to erect the tent without much luck. The main poles were still lying on the ground and Pierce was inside the cloth part, standing up.

Jim came down the garden and was shaking his head. 'Did you three not learn anything when we all went camping with the school?'

'It appears not,' said Seamus in his Irish accent.

'We're all feckin' useless,' said Paddy.

'Pierce, get out from there! And Paddy, hand me those wooden poles,' said Jim, matter-of-factly.

Grant hid himself further behind the tree and took another giant swig of his vodka.

***

Later on in the evening, Helen was standing next to Jamie's cot and watching him sleep. Jim – who had been a boy scout in his youth – had perfectly put up the tangerine tent, leaving the three Irish boys happy in the garden with bottles of Coca-Cola and several bags of Smith's crisps. Jim had forgotten to check on Grant and presumed Helen had put Frank to bed, and he was now lying in bed feeling a bit hopeful that tonight could be the resurrection of their sex life and that maybe he'd receive a bit of loving from his darling wife. He'd previously stripped off and was laying comfortably under the covers.

'Helen, Jamie's fine. Come to bed,' said Jim, patting the top of the covers.

'I'm just worried there might be some repercussions from the incident today,' said Helen as she rubbed her baby's head, in his cot.

Stop fussing, Blondie. Get to your bed 'cause baby needs his sleep.

Helen waited another few minutes and climbed into the bed.

**

Grant stumbled through the front door of the flat and banged against the walls. He was really drunk and couldn't speak. He fell into his and Frank's bedroom and landed lightly on the ground. Frank sat up on the bed, but couldn't really see what was going on because the room was dark. Grant lay on the ground and fell asleep. Frank, too, was so tired that after looking around and satisfying himself that all was well, he lay back down and went to sleep instantly.

**

In Jim's and Helen's room, Jim was cuddling into Helen and acting very friskily. Helen was still feeling rather vulnerable as he kissed her neck, facing away from the cot. She'd had a terrible day and enjoyed the comfort of her husband spooning her. She'd been feeling a bit more normal in the downstairs area and was prepared to try – especially because Jim had had his vasectomy. They kissed and routinely began their lovemaking session.

Jamie was soon woken up by little grunt noises coming from his parents' bed and couldn't believe what he was hearing. *Seriously, Woolworths! That's no right! Please stop! I need to distract myself. What's not sexy? The Hills Have Eyes… no, I've had enough of them. Margaret Thatcher… that new prime minister. She's definitely not sexy with her orange hair and her stupid pearl necklace. Oh no, yuck!*

The groans in the bed next to Jamie became even louder and the bed was starting to creak.

This has been the worst day of my life. Nobody should ever have to suffer this. Maybe if I stand up, they'll realise I'm awake and they'll stop!

Jamie rolled over in the cot and, holding onto the wooden bars, pulled himself up and faced his parents, who were now in full flow with their lovemaking. Luckily, they were under the covers.

Now, that's disgusting, with kids watching, too. Maybe standing up wasn't such a good idea. They've not noticed me. Now, I just look like a wee pervert watching his parents do it. I'm a sick wee bastard!

***

Next door, Grant was lying in front of Frank's bed. He suddenly stood up and dry-retched a few times. He was unsteady on his feet so he placed his hands on Frank's bed, before he projectile vomited all over Frank, who was lying sleeping. Frank woke up, terrified, and Grant tried to move, but was so disillusioned that he only managed to move closer to Frank and, once again, was sick on his nephew. This time, there was even sick in his eyes. Frank screamed and Grant fell backwards onto the floor, this time. Frank jumped off the bed and was shaking – devastated that his uncle had been sick over him. He ran out of the room, gagging himself, then went into his mum and dad's room and (peering through his stinging eyes) got an even bigger shock – his dad practicing the pommel horse on top of his mum!

Helen spotted Jamie first.

Aye, I've got your cards marked Blondie. I can see what you're doing and it's disgusting.

'Dad! Why are you hurting Mum?' asked Frank, bawling his eyes out.

Jim, who was slow to realise, made a final groaning noise before being pushed off by Helen.

'Don't worry, Frank, your Dad was just helping Mum out with a medical issue,' she said.

Aye right, more like a groin sandwich. That gullible Wee Shrimp will believe anything she tells him. Woolworths, you dirty dog!

Helen jumped out of bed and sorted out her nightie. Jim lay on his back, exhausted. *What the hell's that rank smell?*

Jamie walked around his cot until he could see his brother. *Gawd, think I'm gonna puke.*

Helen turned on the bedroom light to see Frank covered in Grant's sick from head to toe.

Look at the state of the Wee Shrimp. Dirty wee bastard!

Jim was under the covers.

'Frank, dear. What's happened? Have you got an upset tummy?' said Helen

Frank shook his head, still crying. 'No, Uncle Grant was sick all over me,' he said as he rubbed his eyes. 'And it's even in my eyes.'

Helen looked at Jim. 'Jim, go and sort out Grant and I'll put this wee soldier in a bath.'

'Think I might have to wait a minute, dear,' said Jim, pulling the covers right up.

Helen looked at him knowingly.

Woolworths can't move from under those covers! It's not the first tent pole he's had to deal with tonight. Dirty dog!

***

A short while later, there was absolute chaos and an awful smell of sick in the bathroom. Jim held Grant's head above the avocado toilet as he continuously hurled and Helen bathed a traumatised Frank in the bath.

'You can sleep in Mum and Dad's room tonight, Frank. And Dad will make sure Uncle Grant's okay. He must have eaten a dodgy mussel or something, which made him sick,' said Helen, then she turned to Jim and, pointing at Grant, mouthed, 'he's for it in the morning.'

Jim looked at her in all seriousness and mouthed back, 'How come it's me that has to sleep in the poky room with your brother?'

''Cause you're the man of the house and Frank will want his mum,' said Helen, whispering very loudly.

Grant puked into the toilet once again.

'That's right, play the gender card, Helen,' said Jim, now in a normal volume, as more vomit met with toilet water.

'Okay, Jim. You deal with all the sick in the room. All the sheets and bedding,' said Helen.

'No, I wouldn't know how to clean them properly,' said Jim.

'Exactly, Jim. Now, make sure he doesn't choke on his own vomit tonight,' said Helen. She grabbed a large towel and lifted Frank out of the bath. 'Right, Frank. You can come in Mum's bed and it will be all cosy.'

She carried him out of the bathroom and into her bedroom, then placed him on the double bed.

Jamie lay in his own bed with a smile on his face. *What a fucking night. I tell you, this family should charge money. We've got freak shows, sex shows and the incredible Vomiting Trapps!*

Chapter 12

May and Jimmy drove down Millport high street in Jimmy's old white banger. Mary (Helen's sister with the broken leg) had been tied up in the large boot with all his paint and painting equipment. She'd had an extremely traumatic journey and had been rolling around. Jimmy had tied her down with some bungee straps, to protect her leg and stop her banging about so much, but it had taken them three hours to finally reach Millport - leaving her stressed and anxious. This was meant to be a convalescent period for her to recover from her broken leg. She was a hairdresser in Glasgow city centre and had been signed off work until her leg was better. May was desperate to go back to Millport, though, and had persuaded Mary that she would be better off coming as well. Little did she know Helen's plans for her. The only reason that Mary had agreed to come was because she'd recently been dating an old friend of hers from Millport – Paul. They'd been going on dates for quite a few months and she was thinking about moving in with him, but hadn't yet told her family. They'd been enjoying the excitement of meeting in secret. The other reason was that Helen and Paul used to constantly fight when they were all teenagers and Mary wasn't ready to discuss her relationship with her sister yet.

Jimmy parked his van right outside the tea shop, then got out and opened the door for May. Jim was standing at the front of the tea shop with Jamie in his arms and Frank beside him – who was eating an ice cream from the Ritz Cafe. After the fiasco with Grant the previous day, they thought it was best to spoil Frank to keep him happy and if that meant giving him ice cream at 10am, then so be it. Frank was delighted while he licked his ice-cream, as his parents had promised him a day off the dishes.

May kissed Frank on the forehead. 'Are you enjoying your ice cream, Francis?' she asked.

He looked up at her with one of his trademarked scowls and ice cream all over his face. 'Who's Francis?' he asked, before spotting his papa. 'Hi, Papa. Will I help you paint today?'

Jimmy ruffled his grandson's blonde hair with his hand. 'Not if the walls end up as messy as your face,' he said to Frank, who was trying to work out what his papa was saying.

May then kissed baby Jamie on the cheek.

Well, look who's back – Old Dear and Grumpy Old Painter. Suppose they're here to add more disorder to this already chaotic family.

There was a loud banging noise coming from the inside of the van, which everyone ignored.

May smiled at Jim. 'How's everything been since we left?' she asked.

Well, your pals kidnapped me; I rolled down the big hill while I was drunk on whisky, fell off the pier, nearly

*drowned and was rescued by Irish Lothario and Wee Punk;
the Artful Dodger puked all over Wee Shrimp; and both me
and Wee Shrimp witnessed a rather disturbing sex show
when Woolworths bonked Blondie.*

Jim kissed May on the cheek. 'Everything's fine,' he
replied.

The knocking on the side of the van became even
louder and there were faint screams.

Jim raised his eyebrows at Jimmy and asked, 'Is there
something you need to tell us? Need I ask what or who is
inside the van?'

Jimmy sighed and hit the side of the van. 'Calm down
and don't wet yourself,' he said, pissed off. This made Jim
even more curious and he looked at Jamie with intrigued
eyes.

*What the hell is going on in there? Has Old Dear and
Grumpy Old Painter kidnapped someone to be murdered?
Are we in a mafia family now?*

Frank continued to devour his ice cream – there was
more dripping from his hands than actually going inside
his mouth.

Jimmy opened the van door, which let the sunlight
flood in and illuminate the inside of the van. There was
Mary – blinded by the sun, covered in white paint, tied up
with bungee straps and very angry.

'For fuck's sake, Mary. You've wasted a whole tin of
Magnolia,' said Jimmy to his daughter.

'I've wasted your paint! Look at me, I'm covered – and
'cause you tied me up, I couldn't stop it happening, Dad!'
said Mary, all in a tizzy.

May came to see the cavalry as well. 'What are you

doing in there, dear?' she asked Mary, whose eyes were close to popping out of her head.

'You promised me a relaxing time in Millport, Mum. I almost died in here,' said Mary.

Jimmy raised his eyes at May. 'Always the drama queen, our Mary,' he said and tutted.

Mary was about to explode and looked even redder underneath splashes of white emulsion. 'My plaster is covered in paint. I'll never get it off.'

'We could stick you in the harbour, dear, then it'll wash the paint off the plaster and you'll be all clean before you know it,' said May.

Mary rolled her eyes at her mother. Jimmy climbed into the van and untied the bungee straps from the plaster and the other areas that were tying Mary down. Jim walked round to the back of the van with Frank and Jamie – they all stared inside, looking rather confused.

What's going on in here? Was Blondie kidnapped last night and dipped into a shrinking bath? She's half the size she used to be.

Jim waved inside the van. 'Frank, wave to your Aunty Mary,' he said.

Frank waved inside the van.

Gawd there's even more of them! Where do they keep coming from?

Jimmy helped Mary exit the van and placed her crutches under her armpits. Paint was dripping off her plaster and covered her bare leg and denim shorts. She had long blonde hair, which was identical to Helen's. Her face was similar as well, with freckles and pale skin, but she was a foot shorter and much thinner than Helen.

Mary was livid and couldn't hide it. She looked at her father and mother. 'You said it would be more than comfortable in the boot of your van when you shoved me in and tied me up,' she said.

'I didn't know you were in there. I thought you were taking the train to Largs,' said May.

'Mary, stop your whining!' said Jimmy.

Jamie looked towards his aunty, who was angry at her parents. *Mini Blondie's making a right fuss over a bit of spilt paint and a broken leg.*

***

Inside the tea shop, Grant was sitting opposite Helen. He was hungover and feeling sorry for himself. He'd been awake since five in the morning and knew he'd messed up. Helen wasn't happy.

'Where'd you get the drink, Grant?' asked Helen.

'I wasn't drinking. Just a bit of food poisoning,' said Grant, not doing a very good job of creating a cover-up story.

'Do you think I was brought up on a banana boat?' Helen looked at him suspiciously 'Did you steal it from the tea shop?'

Grant looked her in the eyes with a serious expression, not wanting her to think he was a thief. 'Okay, sis, I'm rumbled. I got some lowlife to buy me vodka from the shop.'

Helen shook her head at her brother and spoke, 'Right, that's it. You can go and live with Mum and Dad again. You keep breaking my rules! If you can't behave, you're being shipped out back to Busby.'

Grant looked downhearted and decided to play the sympathy card. 'It's girl trouble. My head's all mushed. Please let me stay. I promise I'll just put my head down and work for the rest of the summer,' he said desperately.

Helen was hard on the surface, but soft on the inside like a strawberry cream chocolate. She looked at her brother and said, 'You promise me you'll adhere to all my rules?'

Grant nodded his head and seemed relieved.

Jim – who was holding Jamie in his arms – opened the tea shop door. Frank came bounding in and was covered with ice cream. He shouted out, 'Can I go and see the big boys in the garden?'

Jim moved towards Helen and Grant, while shouting to Frank, 'I suppose so. Go and jump on them and cover them in ice cream.' Jim chuckled, pleased with his cheeky idea.

May was next to come through the door and said, 'Our Mary is here. She's hurt her knee and has a plaster on it.'

Helen looked up at her mother. 'Thought she broke her leg?'

'Oh yes. She was skiing and broke her leg,' said May.

Helen rolled her eyes.

Grant stared at May. 'It's July, Mum. Where was she skiing – Mount Everest?'

May grabbed Jamie from Jim. 'Oh, how I've missed you, my little sausage,' she said as she did a funny face to Jamie.

How many times do I have to tell you, Old Dear... I'm a real human boy!

Jimmy kicked the door open and Jim rushed over to hold it, but before he reached the handle, Jimmy shouted, 'Oh for fuck's sake, would somebody help?'

Jim opened both sides of the double doors. Mary came hobbling through on her crutches being dramatic and making little whimpering noises. The paint was beginning to dry on her plaster. Jimmy had taken a load of old sheets and wiped off as much as possible in the street, but a few drips now splashed onto the old tartan carpet.

Helen quickly rushed over to her sister, who was concentrating on each tiny step. She grabbed a few cloth napkins from the nearest table, bent down in front of Mary and began to dab some of the wet paint. 'Hold on, Mary! You're dripping paint on the carpet,' said Helen.

Mary stared down at Helen with a fierce scowl. 'This is all your fault! If you hadn't made me take that job up Cairngorm Mountain in that stupid Ptarmigan Cafe, then I wouldn't be in this mess.'

Helen stood up and shot Jim a look. 'Told you she'd blame me.'

Mary huffed at her sister. 'I had a perfectly healthy leg and you were… "Mary, you need to try new things", "Mary, you should expand your horizons", "Mary, you should fall off a ski tow and break your leg!"' said Mary, all wound up.

'Where did you actually break your leg this time?' asked Helen.

'I tripped over a loose plank at the hairdressers… but it's only because—'

Helen jumped in, 'So that's my fault? You've always blamed me for everything.'

May came over to the girls, while holding Jamie. 'Girls, no fighting,' she said as Jimmy walked away from them, shaking his head.

'For fuck's sake,' said Jimmy.

Jamie stared towards the two sisters. *Battle of the Blondies. Big Blondie in the blue corner, using her brute shot-putter strength. Mini Blondie in the red corner, matching the colour of her face. Think you're well and truly fucked, Mini Blondie, unless you manage to hit her on the head with one of your crutches.*

Helen put her arm round Mary's shoulder, remembering she needed her to look after Jamie pretty soon. 'I'm sorry I suggested you went skiing. It was all my fault,' she said as Mary gave her an untrusting look. 'Let's get you nice and comfortable in the upstairs flat. I'm sorry you've broken your leg again. I'll make you a nice piece of bacon and a cup of Nescafé coffee.'

Mary pouted her lips and didn't know whether to trust Helen or not. She did like the idea of being looked after, though. She was dying for some comfort – a bit of sleep, a bacon roll and a coffee did sound good. Helen and May led Mary out of the tea shop.

Grant was sitting with his head in his hands and Jim went over to him, patted his head and smirked. 'Hangover, boy-o?' he asked.

Grant looked up at Jim apologetically, not in the mood for any form of telling-off. Jim nodded his head. 'Been there, done that and bought the T-shirt. Don't worry, I'm not going to lecture you. Your punishment is the hangover while you work – all day. Best get those tables set up. It's going to be a very long and busy day.'

***

In the upstairs flat, Mary was being helped onto the couch by Helen. May held onto Jamie, who was asleep with his head on her shoulder. Once Mary was comfortable, Helen helped her to lift her broken leg onto a cushion, under some plastic bags in case paint went over the couch – not that it really mattered, as it was trash. Mary was tiny and only took up a small portion of the couch.

'There you are, Mary. Now's your chance to convalesce,' said Helen as she went over to Frank's toy box, which was near the window that looked out onto the pier. She grabbed a blanket from the top and placed it over Mary's legs. 'Right, let's get you that bacon roll and a coffee.' Helen signalled to her mother to give her Jamie. 'Mum, we are going up to see your friends now – after they nearly killed my little bundle of joy.'

Helen grabbed Jamie off her mother and placed him on top of the blanket between Mary's legs. Mary looked at Helen with a look of astonishment. She had wide eyes and an open mouth and was about to speak, but Helen spoke over her quiet chatter.

'Yes, Mum – Muriel and Tam! You're coming with me 'cause if you don't, I think I'll throttle them.'

May looked extremely puzzled as Helen marched out of the door, but she soon followed, even though she was feeling very worried. She despised any kind of confrontation.

Mary tried to shout after them, 'Don't leave me here with the baby! I've got a broken leg. How do you expect me to tend for your child when...' She gave up speaking when she heard the front door slam shut. She was fuming.

Jamie woke up while lying between his aunty's legs and made eye contact with her, as she stared down at him. *What's the matter, Mini Blondie? Do you want to reject this bundle of pure heaven?*

'Damn you, Helen. Always putting me in the shit,' said Mary out loud. 'Your mother is a total nightmare,' Mary said to the baby, both of them still staring at one another.

You think she's a nightmare? You haven't spent time with me yet. I tell you, Mini Blondie, you're in for a rare treat as I'm going to make your broken leg seem like a day out at Disneyland. You'll wish you never met me by the end of today. Jamie managed to manoeuvre himself onto his front and he began to stare at Mary.

First things first, let's see if this one's got water in her wells. They're quite big considering she's so wee. Jamie began to climb up Mary so he was level with her bosoms and cuddled into them.

She put her hands on his back. 'This isn't so bad. You're a good boy, aren't you?' asked Mary, petting Jamie like a dog.

Jamie looked up at her and grinned with the biggest, cheekiest smile – showing his two new baby teeth. *Aye, I'm a fucking angel!* He opened his mouth wide and stuck it onto her blue swirly- patterned jumper, then he bit with his two small teeth and sucked as hard as possible to try and extract milk through the cloth.

'Awl! Stop that. Oh. Stop it. It's weird!' said Mary as she lifted him away from her breast.

You playing hard to get, Mini Blondie – baby needs milk!

***

Helen walked furiously up the Cardiff Street hill with a mission on her mind. May was desperately trying to keep up with her and was in a blind panic, worried about Helen confronting Muriel. They'd been pals for over thirty years and she didn't want anything to jeopardise their friendship.

At the top of the hill, Helen was banging on Tam and Muriel's front door with her fist. A night's sleep hadn't managed to calm her down so she was about to confront them with all guns blazing.

Tam suddenly opened the door with a smarmy grin and Helen fell forwards, landing on his shoulder. 'Helen,' said Tam as he glared towards her breasts, absolutely shamelessly and guilt-free. Saliva formed around his mouth and he licked his lips.

Helen pulled herself up with the door edge and shoved him hard on the shoulder so that he fell to the ground. May had just arrived at the door and was looking embarrassed at her daughter's brashness.

From inside the flat, there was a noise. 'Tam, who's at the door?' shouted Muriel from her living room.

May called out to her from the front door, trying to diffuse the situation. 'Muriel, love. It's just May and Helen here. Nothing to worry about. Just coming in for a chat.'

Helen barged over Tam and made no attempt at being careful. He just lay on the floor like he was sunbathing with his hands behind his head, staring up towards May's private areas – all excited. Helen, who was now on the other side of him, faced directly towards the smug bastard. 'Mum. He's nothing but a dirty sex pest,' she said.

May sighed in disapproval, at the language she used, before saying, 'Helen. Behave yourself.'

'Me? I need to behave myself? He's glaring right at your crotch, Mum,' said Helen angrily.

May looked away as she was unable to cope with the situation. Muriel came through the living room door, completely out of breath and desperately holding herself up with her walking sticks. She looked up at Helen like she was a little lost girl. Her mouth was orange, it had Heinz tomato soup all over it and was also dribbling off the whiskers on her chin. There was a white cloth napkin hanging over her dirty woolly jumper – which hadn't been washed for weeks. The napkin was also completely covered in the orange liquid and little bits of soup soaked up bread.

'Helen… I am… so… so… sorry,' said Muriel between heavy breaths.

Helen began to focus solely on Muriel. 'What you sorry for, Muriel? The fact you abducted my baby? Or that you lost control of him and his pram rolled down a hill and he fell into the sea and nearly drowned?' Helen took a breath and May, who hadn't properly heard about the previous day's events, looked on in dismay with her mouth wide open and a tear forming in her eyes. Helen continued her rant, 'Or are you sorry that you married the most revolting, disgusting, grotesque sexual predator, who controls your every move – Muriel?'

Muriel looked a sorry sight; Tam, however, seemed unfazed as he lay on the ground and instead appeared to be getting off on Helen's anger.

'I've known you since I was little girl and trust me, Muriel, when I tell you this: you'd be better off by yourself than living with this…' Helen paused for a moment and thought clearly about her words. She stared down at Tam. 'Filthy animal! If he was my dog, I'd have him put down,' said Helen.

May didn't know where to look and was devastated. She'd spent years burying Tam's horrific actions under the carpet and pretending to Muriel that she thought he was a lovely man. Helen stepped back over Tam and kicked his crotch with her foot and he squealed out, but smiled straight afterwards through his rotting teeth.

Before Helen left the flat, she turned and addressed the couple, 'Stay away from Jim, me and my children. Both of you! Or I won't be responsible for my actions.' Helen barged out of the front door, feeling relieved.

Muriel was crying. 'I'm so sorry, May,' she said through heavy tears.

'It's okay, Muriel. She'll calm down soon. She just needed to suck off some air,' said May, mixing up her phrases and still not wanting to face the cold, hard facts.

***

In the upstairs flat, Mary was in a tizzy as Jamie kept trying to suck milk from her breasts. She'd had enough and was angry that she'd been left helpless with her broken leg on the couch, looking after Helen's youngest, who had become feral. Jamie dived head first into her breast for the tenth time.

Mini Blondie, we can do this the easy way or the hard way. I wish I had a better set of teeth, then I'd be able to extract milk from this bouncy duo much easier.

Mary weakly lifted him above her head, having had enough. She placed him on the floor, lay back on the couch and took a deep, angry breath. 'Convalescing, they said… I'd be better off in the nuthouse,' Mary said to herself.

Jamie climbed up the couch and eventually made himself stand up. He stared at his aunty's body. *So, you want to play games? Well, you're just in luck 'cause baby can stand up now. And maybe it's time baby learnt to walk and all. You don't feed me; I destroy your quiet afternoon, Mini Blondie.*

Mary closed her eyes for a minute and Jamie turned himself around. With the assistance of the couch, he began to walk until he was at the very end and a metre from the kitchen door. He let go of the tattered couch arm and stood on his own for the very first time, then took an unsteady first step and somehow managed to keep his balance. He then took a second and a third step.

I'm walking… I'm fucking walking and nobody is here to give me a congrat-u-fucking-lations! Mini Blondie is just lying there like a sad sack of potatoes! Where's Big Blondie and Woolworths and the rest of this useless family? Bet there was a parade with fireworks when the Wee Shrimp took his first steps.

Jamie managed to make it to the kitchen. He held onto the kitchen door and giggled when he saw inside. *So, this is the lair where they keep all the good shit!*

***

Downstairs in the tea shop, Grant was working hard to finish setting up for the busy lunchtime. Jim had just collected two of the Irish boys from the back garden. They were all due to start work, but Paddy was missing. When Grant saw Jim with just Pierce and Seamus, his heart sunk to the ground. He knew exactly where the missing Irish boy was and at this point realised the consequences of his actions the previous day. The fact that he felt sick with a pounding headache didn't help either. He was beginning to realise that he did really like Gail, but it was too late. In a teenage strop, he dropped the loose cutlery from his hand and smashed it onto the floor.

Jim lifted his head and shouted over, 'Everything okay, Grant?'

Grant bent down and picked up the cutlery. 'Butter fingers,' he replied. He felt heavy around his stomach area, feeling like he was going to be sick.

Jim showed the two Irish boys to the sink, where there was a small pile of dishes waiting. Frank was standing on his ladder, all high and mighty – he was rather excitable as he'd always had to do most of the dishes himself. He finally had the opportunity to boss other people around and he liked the idea of this a lot. He rubbed his hands together and said, 'Big boys, this isn't going to be easy for you as dishes is a hard job. But the best thing is to keep washing and drying the dishes until there are none left.' Jim stood back and watched his son impressively manage his new team of staff. 'When I first started, nobody really taught me and I had to work it out myself,' Frank said, smugly. 'And you two are lucky 'cause there are two of you. One can wash and one can dry.'

Pierce was eye-level with Frank on his stool. 'And what are you going to do, wee man?' he asked Pierce.

Frank nodded his head. 'Make sure you clean them properly. We can't be serving food on dirty plates.'

Jim laughed and then went on the hunt for Paddy, who was also meant to be in for training.

***

May chased after Helen all the way down the Cardiff Street hill. She was out of breath and in a confused state of mind. Although she agreed with Helen that Muriel was reckless for taking Jamie and losing control of her grandson's pram, she knew it wasn't deliberate. She was feeling so awkward about Helen's accusations towards Tam. Her generation didn't deal with these things, as it was far too shameful. You just tried to protect your own as much as you could. Helen was different; she clearly knew right from wrong and wasn't afraid to let those around her know when they were out of order and sometimes criminal.

Helen was about to cross the road at Ritchie Street when she spotted something that concerned her. Gail was snogging Paddy at the back of The Wee House – he was practically devouring her like she was a marshmallow ice cream from the Ritz Cafe. They were completely oblivious to their surroundings, acting like two typical teenagers who had just discovered one another's tonsils for the first time. There was even a seagull at their feet, eating up the remnants of a discarded bag of chips from the night before. Helen slowly sneaked up right next to where they were. '*Gail! Do you come here with all your boyfriends?*' shouted Helen in Gail's ear.

The two teenagers quickly unstuck their mouths and jumped back. Jim, who had been looking for Paddy, also arrived at the scene as well. Gail had to press her hands against her stomach as she felt like pee was about to burst right through her. Why did Helen keep catching her snogging? Gail was becoming more scared of Helen than she was of her own strict and conservative mother.

Jim grabbed Paddy's arm. 'Right, boy! You were meant to start your shift twenty minutes ago,' he said, as he escorted Paddy back to the tea shop.

Helen was left alone with a terrified Gail. 'What you playing at? It was only days ago that I caught you here with my brother and now you're eating up a boy that just came off the ferry last night,' said Helen, harshly. Gail couldn't help but burst into tears. 'Oh, come on, lassie. Waterworks won't work on me. I've got two boys that are infatuated with you working in my tea shop.'

Gail looked up at her innocently. 'Grant's infatuated with me?' Gail asked.

Helen sighed and rolled her eyes. 'Quit playing games. I've got a good mind to inform your parents 'cause, quite frankly, I'm sick to the back teeth of your little schoolgirl dramas.'

Gail put her hands in the prayer position in front of Helen. 'Please don't, Helen. It's Grant I like, but yesterday he told me to "f" off and it broke my heart.'

Helen turned her head to the side. 'He did what?' said Helen. Gail cried again, but this time the tears seemed genuine. 'Did you think snogging the first guy you saw would make things better?' asked Helen.

'I'm ashamed to say, but I just wanted to make him jealous,' Gail said through some very loud tears.

'I wish I could say I didn't understand, but it wasn't

that long ago I was a fourteen-year-old girl. Look, go away for a few days – away from both boys – and have a good think about who you really like,' said Helen.

'It's Grant. Definitely Grant, but I don't think he likes me anymore,' said Gail.

'I beg to differ,' said Helen, who gently grabbed Gail's arm. 'Go back home and let everybody cool off. We've got a busy weekend at the tea shop.' She bent down and made eye contact with the tiny girl. 'And when you come back… no more silly schoolgirl antics. Choose one boy and only one.' Gail nodded at Helen, who responded with, 'And don't sleep with any of them. Boys are obsessed with their willies and our… bits, as well.' Helen gave her a knowing look.

***

Jamie was running riot in the upstairs kitchen. He'd found a whole load of interesting items in a basket on the floor.

'Come back, Jamie! What are you doing in there? You're in a lot of trouble,' shouted Mary from the living-room couch.

Jamie had a punnet of six eggs in his hand, which he was pushing along the floor while crawling back into the living room. He appeared round the door and Mary was stressing on the couch.

'What's that you've got? That better not be what I think it is,' said Mary.

Jamie paused for a second and laughed. *That's exactly what you think it is.* He continued to push the punnet of eggs towards his aunty and stopped near her broken leg, sat on his bum, opened the paper punnet and lifted an egg

– holding it up. Mary looked possessed as she crunched her teeth while staring at her nephew. He made his way to the couch and managed to stand up with the egg intact in his hand. *Ye wee beauty. Did not think I'd manage to do that.* Mary was leaning forward as much as she could and was trying to grab the egg off him, but because of her broken leg, this was an impossible task. Jamie launched the egg towards her and she managed to make contact with her hand, but the egg cracked a little and flew towards her breast where it smashed all over her jumper. Jamie giggled. *Scrambled tits!*

'You little shit!' shouted Mary to her nephew. 'My new Jaeger jumper! I only bought that last month – with most of my wages.' Mary started to try and wipe off the egg.

Jamie had become rather agile and managed to find the box of eggs while Mary was distracted. He crawled along the floor and disappeared out of her sight, then pulled himself up on the arm of the couch where Mary's blonde hair was hanging down. He smashed the egg on her scalp and she screamed out.

Mini Blondie-omelette. Lunch, anyone?

'Damn you, Helen!' said Mary as she screamed the roof down in the hope that someone would save her from the nightmare she'd found herself in.

***

Downstairs in the tea shop, Helen had just arrived back in the kitchen to start her day's work. Frank was standing over the kitchen sink on his stool, inspecting all the dishes that had been washed by Pierce and dried by Seamus. He lifted a plate up that still had some food staining on it and threw it back into the soapy water-filled sink. 'No! It's still dirty. You'll need to do better, big boys.'

Seamus looked towards his brother, while rolling his eyes.

Pierce said, 'You're running a tight ship here, wee man.'

Helen laughed out loud behind Frank's back and he turned around. 'We have standards here, don't we, Mum?' said Frank. Helen almost couldn't contain her laughter, as she must have said the same thing to Frank a million times.

Out on the tea-shop floor, Jim was showing Paddy how to roll the cutlery into napkins. Grant was over at another table and was glaring towards the young Irish chap. He felt intense jealousy and was really struggling to control his emotions. He gripped onto a porcelain plate and really wanted to smash it over Paddy's head – or against the wall, at least. It took an immense amount of willpower to stop himself. He was in enough trouble and knew he'd be shipped back home if there was any funny business. He took a deep breath and went to go outside – a cigarette could help. He walked past Jim, who then turned around.

'Where you going, Grant?' asked Jim.

'A jobby,' he replied.

Paddy gagged at the thought of him on the toilet and this made Grant instantly regret his choice of alibi.

***

Outside, Grant stood inside the dog kennel area. He was hiding – while patting his favourite dog, Tana. The puppies were feeding off Brochan, who seemed much more comfortable as a mother. Tana was nonplussed about her puppies. She saw them as a chore and an inconvenience, while her sister seemed to thrive.

'Life can be one big hassle sometimes, girl,' Grant said to Tana, as he patted her beautiful silky red coat. He took a long drag of his cigarette. 'I mean, what's this Irish idiot got that I don't? He seems like he's thick as mince.' The overweight dog looked up at him pitifully. 'You get my drift, don't you? You're used to being the least popular one as well.'

He patted Tana and cuddled into her. The two were bonding and it was like she understood exactly what he was saying. Grant looked her in the eyes. 'You might not be a pedigree dog like your sister, but you are the smartest one. She's also thick as mince *and* Irish – just like that Irish wanker.'

Grant ruffled her ears, then stood up and took a last long draw of his burning cigarette, before throwing it to the ground and stubbing it out with his Converse trainer. 'Well, back to hell I go.' He looked at his watch. 'Only ten hours left.' He smiled at Tana and walked away.

***

In the upstairs flat, Mary was tearing her hair out and was looking like she was about to cry. She was covered in broken eggs from her head down to her toes.

'Where are you, you horrible little rascal? This is not funny. You're not too young for a skelp on the backside,' she said.

Jamie had temporarily gone into the kitchen and Mary was beside herself wondering what he was about to do next. Jamie crawled through, dragging a bag of flour that was scattering a trail of white dust behind him. His hands and face were covered. He looked like Casper the friendly ghost or, in Mary's eyes, Casper the little shit. Mary couldn't see him from where she was sitting, but she could hear.

'Where are you? I swear if you do anything else, you'll be put in jail. The big policemen will take you away for being a bad little boy,' said Mary.

Jamie stopped for a second and giggled. *Is she having a fucking laugh? I'm not even a year old. I'd fit right through the bars in the cell.* He continued to drag the flour along the floor, making sure he kept himself out of sight of Mary. He crawled all the way to his favourite spot, next to the arm of the couch, and stood up. The bag of flour was half empty and Jamie managed to lift it as high as possible. Mary sensed he was behind her this time and managed to grab the flour off him.

'Got it. You think you're so smart, baby…' she said, as she lifted the flour above her head and poured the entire contents over her own head.

Jamie laughed out loud and Mary screamed, and coughed, and screamed and coughed. Now it was her who looked like a version of Casper – the unfriendly ghost. She was absolutely livid. She ruffled her hair in an attempt to get some flour out, but inadvertently formed a batter between the eggs and the flour on her head. Jamie looked at her and laughed once again. *You could make pasta on Mini Blondie's head – spaghetti-alla-Blondie.* Her cross blue eyes flared behind the white flour. Puffs of white powder were floating in the air.

She shouted at Jamie, 'You're a ghastly little boy – absolutely awful. Frank's my favourite! He never behaved so badly, you terrible child!'

Jamie stared at his aunty through a cloud of flour, standing far enough away from her so she couldn't reach him and let out a little cute sneeze. *The Wee Shrimp's your favourite, is he? Big mistake, Mini Blondie… big mistake!*

***

Downstairs in the tea shop, there were plenty of staff for once, but there was an intense atmosphere. The Irish lads had shifted the dynamics of the place. Grant was angry and uncomfortable. His mood was slowly simmering into a darker place and he didn't know how long he could control himself. Paddy was swanning around – happy as Larry. In Grant's mind, Paddy and Gail were already loved up and he felt like Dr Bruce Banner waiting to turn into the Incredible Hulk. Maybe they'd been talking about him behind his back, taking the mickey out of him. He would have to stamp his authority in some way. If he hadn't won the battle of the girlfriend, he could at least boss the Irish boy in the tea shop – something that Grant excelled at.

Grant crept over towards Jim, who was training Paddy and showing him how to properly clear plates the professional way – by using three fingers to hold the bottom plate and placing the other plate on the raised thumb and pinky, then placing the fork on the bottom plate sideways and the knife underneath the fork, facing the other direction. Grant barged his way between them, but only made contact with Paddy, pushing him out the way. Jim had been too busy concentrating on his teaching to notice the unnecessary aggression. Paddy, however, did notice and was taken aback.

'Jim! Do you want me to finish training…' Before Grant finished his sentence, he turned to Paddy and looked him up and down. 'I don't know your name,' Grant said as he shrugged his shoulders and shot him a condescending look.

Paddy looked at Grant suspiciously, but cheerfully answered, 'It's Paddy. I met you earlier.'

Jim placed the plates onto the table. 'Good idea, Grant. I've got plenty to be getting on with,' said Jim and walked towards the kitchen.

Grant smirked at Paddy, who could also sense a load of tension and was unsure why.

In the kitchen, Helen was at her usual spot, stirring a large pot of minestrone soup for the afternoon lunches. There was a tray full of warm homemade scones, which smelt appetising, and some freshly whipped cream and homemade jam next to it. Helen was making the most of her extra time due to the increased manpower.

Jim came over and kissed her on the cheek. 'Feeling better today, dear?' he asked.

'What do you mean today?' replied Helen, defensively.

'Less drama, perhaps. Mary's looking after Jamie. We have loads of staff. Frank's not being worked like one of those 1800s chimney sweeps,' Jim replied.

Helen turned around to her son, who was in full flow bossing the Irish boys around. 'Yes, but we have to be careful with that one. He's becoming a proper little dictator.' Helen looked at Jim a little concerned and then with a much more serious expression. 'Do you think that's how Hitler started?' she asked.

Jim made an "eek" face back at her. 'I hope not 'cause we'll be the first to be taken down,' he replied.

Helen looked round at her son again – he was standing high and mighty on his ladder and had forcefully thrown a metal pot back into the sink of water, shouting, 'No, big boys. *Not good enough*! Again!' The two boys were beginning to look a little exasperated and already seemed like they were ready to throw in the towel.

Helen kissed her husband on the cheek. 'Think you need to take him outside before he starts World War Three. We may have created a monster,' she said as Jim casually laughed out loud, then went over to Frank, swept him up off his ladder and carried him outside.

Seamus turned to Pierce and whispered to him, 'That kid's a fecking psycho!'

Pierce, who looked a little shell-shocked, replied, 'For a minute there, I thought we'd ended up in a borstal prison.'

Helen heard the conversation and didn't know whether to laugh or cry.

***

There was chaos in the upstairs flat. Jamie was sitting in the middle of the living-room floor in an (almost) state of undress – he'd managed to take his shorts off and his cloth nappy, which hadn't been put on properly as Jim had dressed him in the morning. The nappy was half hanging off. He'd already wrecked the kitchen, and the living room was in disarray and covered in flour. Poor Mary was also a frustrated and flustered mess. She was angry at her whole family for putting her in this position. She was an invalid and should have been looked after, rather than having to watch her sister's rotten baby. Jamie was just sitting there, staring at his aunty in his state of undress – he wasn't a normal baby.

'That's right. You be a good wee boy for Aunty Mary,' she said.

He smiled slyly at her. *Don't you worry, Mini Blondie... everything will... Oh... Oh... Oh yes... that's it... That was a right fucking good one.*

Mary watched her nephew's face screw up and all of a sudden she smelt an awful smell and knew exactly what he was doing. 'No, no, don't you dare!' she shouted at Jamie, who smiled back at her. Mary panicked and reached towards him. Her outstretched arms meant she didn't have the right balance on the couch, so she rolled over and off it– landing on her back, with her broken leg still propped up on the couch backwards. She was uncomfortably contorted and stuck, which gave the baby the edge.

Jamie smiled with relief as his satisfying poo ended. His cloth nappy was being held together by one little safety pin. *Tut-tut, Mini Blondie. Should have given me that milk from that juicy titty when I asked so nicely... you've had a terrible afternoon, you poor wee soul. Look at the state of you. You'd make a great circus act, Mini Blondie – the very white ghostly contortionist with the mangled leg.*

Jamie quickly crawled towards her. Her eyes were tightly closed as she lay in the most awkward position between the couch and the floor. Jamie stood up next to her without her realising, then put his hand in his dirty nappy and grabbed as much poo as possible. And now, for the grand finale. He rubbed his clean hand on Mary's face and she actually thought he was being quite nice, so she turned to him, but then he put his poo-covered hand on her breast and she screamed.

***

Jim was outside, standing next to the dog's kennel. He'd just dumped Frank in the mud pit and told him to spend the day there and to relax and enjoy himself. Jim hadn't banked on him becoming an out-of-control dictator when showing the Irish boys how to do the dishes.

Jim puffed heavily on his Cuban cigar – a treat he'd allowed himself while the tea shop was quiet. He smiled watching his son acting like a normal child for once and wondered if they'd done the right thing by making him work at such a young age. Their lives had been hectic since they'd bought their small business and this meant that family time sometimes went out of the window… basically to work.

He watched the dogs and their puppies, who were all outside now – and looking rather lethargic, as it was the beginning of a sunny Millport summer's day. He puffed the cigar once again and the smoke exited his mouth and covered his black moustache. He breathed in and enjoyed the exotic flavours rising up his nose. He stared towards the puppies and this reminded him that the new owners, which also included the pedigree crufts people, would soon be coming to pick them up. He looked serious for a second, thinking that was a good thing, and then chuckled to himself that they didn't really know which pups were which. It was all going to be guesswork when it came to passing the right pups to their owners. This didn't faze Jim at all, as he had this wonderful ability to never really worry about anything – quite the opposite of Helen.

Jim stubbed out his cigar on the wall and gazed at Frank for a second to check he was alright – he was and was currently having a punch-up with a mud sandcastle. *Better that than a human*, thought Jim. He went back inside.

***

On the tea shop floor, Paddy was cleaning the salt and pepper shakers with a cloth and Grant was standing over him, militantly. He picked up one of the salts that Paddy had allegedly cleaned and held it up to his face.

'Does that look clean to you?' Grant said harshly and threw it down. It landed on the side and salt flew out of it onto some of the other clean ones. 'Come on, this isn't rocket science. A four-year-old could do this job.'

Paddy was beginning to fizz, but was desperately trying to hold in his anger. He could sense an underlying issue between him and Grant, but was clueless at what that was as he'd only just met the guy. Paddy turned to Grant and spoke calmly, 'Fella, maybe if you weren't standing over me like the Garda, then I'd be able to clean these little fecking salt and pepper shakers.'

Grant puffed out his nostrils. 'I'll be back in five minutes to check your work,' he said, thinking he'd got the upper hand, when he was actually just hindering the day's work.

***

Jim was walking upstairs towards the flat as he wanted to change his shirt for the afternoon shift. He heard a loud screaming – like some poor lassie was being tortured. He ran into the corridor of the flat, worried that something was wrong with his baby son. He barged through the door to find the scene of an absolute massacre and his poor sister-in-law stuck between the couch and the floor covered in flour, eggs… and shit. She was screaming blue murder with her eyes closed.

Jamie was sitting on the floor, half naked, with his nappy hanging off, but with a massive cheesy grin on his face. *Woolworths, pal. Welcome to the circus.*

Jim bent down and gently rubbed Mary on the shoulder to try and calm her down.

'I've had enough. Leave me alone, you horrible baby,' she said with her eyes closed.

'Mary. It's Jim,' he said calmly.

She stopped screaming and turned towards him. 'You tell your wife that I'm not speaking to her ever again. Look what that child has done to me,' said Mary.

Jim almost came over in a fit of giggles at the fact that his young baby had managed to cause so much chaos. He looked towards his son and laughed.

Jamie stared back at his dad. *Woolworths, you tell Big Blondie that this is her punishment for leaving me – again.*

Jim helped Mary off the couch into a better position on the floor, still trying to contain his laughter.

'Take me to the telephone box, Jim,' demanded Mary.

'Do you not want me to help clean you up first?' asked Jim.

'Now!' she screamed.

Alright, Mini Blondie... don't wet yourself – or do 'cause then you'll stink of piss and shit.

Mary started hobbling down the stairs on her crutches. She was still in a right state and was covered in paint, flour, eggs and baby poo. Jim was standing behind her, holding onto his son, who he'd quickly wrapped in a blanket. He desperately wanted to warn Helen, who would be unprepared for the wrath of her sister. Mary could be quite a fierce character; often Helen's only fitting adversary.

When they finally reached the bottom of the stairs, it took Mary a few seconds to sort her crutches out. Jim squeezed past her and Jamie waved at his aunty, who he'd spent the morning tormenting. *Bye bye, Mini Blondie. Hope you had as much fun as I did.*

Mary made her way down the corridor to use the other exit and Jim went back into the tea shop. He approached Helen, who was lifting bowls of minestrone soup for some of the customers. Lunch wasn't quite in full flow yet, but there were a few early diners.

'Helen. Helen,' Jim said to his wife.

She looked up at him. 'Not now, Jim, I'm busy.' Helen spotted Jamie – who was wrapped in a blanket, but was covered in flour and smelt disgusting. 'Jim, take him out of here. He stinks of...' Helen paused, then loudly whispered, 'He stinks of shit and we've got customers in.'

Charming, Blondie. What a way to greet that poor wee neglected baby of yours.

'Where the hell's Mary? And why is he covered in flour?' asked Helen.

Jim sighed and smiled. 'I don't think Mary will be coming back any time soon. If you think he's bad, you should go outside and see her.'

Helen's face sank to the ground. Everything had been going swimmingly for... five seconds. She untied her apron and threw it on the kitchen counter.

Grant was serving a table with four minestrone soups and Paddy was behind him with a plate filled with sandwiches and scones. Paddy put the plate between two of the customers. Grant laid down his final plate of soup, then readjusted Paddy's plate, centering it in the middle of the table.

'I do apologise. We just can't seem to get any good staff,' said Grant to the customers, who seemed rather perplexed.

Paddy stormed away from the table and was at breaking point with Grant. He marched towards the kitchen, as Grant swiftly followed him. They both stormed over to the kitchen servery and stood facing each other - fizzing.

'You really shouldn't show the customers that you have a bad attitude, son!' Grant said.

'Right, fella. Outside. I don't want to make a scene in front of the precious customers,' Paddy replied.

Grant looked a bit worried – he hadn't banked on a potential boxing match.

***

Mary was in the red phone box across the road from the tea shop. She angrily hung up the phone – which was now covered in egg and flour – after chatting to her boyfriend, Paul. Helen was crossing the road and Jim was standing watching with Jamie on the other side. He'd decided it was best to keep out of any sibling squabbles.

Helen opened the door to an agitated Mary. 'Oh Mary, let's get you all cleaned up,' Helen said as she grabbed Mary on the arm, but Mary pulled her arm away just as quickly.

'Get your hands off me. You only brought me here to use me as a babysitter,' said Mary.

'Mary. No, I brought you here because I knew Mum and Dad wouldn't be at home to look after you and I knew I could,' Helen replied.

'Look after me? You liar… you left me on my own with a broken leg and your ghastly child,' said Mary.

Helen looked hurt by Mary's comments. 'He's just a wee harmless baby,' she said in defence.

Mary was beetroot underneath the flour on her face as she fumed at her sister. 'A harmless baby? He's the devil incarnate!'

Helen looked really upset now. 'That's harsh and pretty cruel,' she said.

Mary pointed at the state she was in. 'Well, look what he done to me. You're right, it's not his fault.' Mary lifted up her crutch and stamped it down next to Helen's foot, which was holding the telephone box door open. 'It's your fault. My broken leg. The fact I'm covered in flour and shit.' She stamped the crutch next to her sister a second time and hit her on the foot.

'Awl, Mary. No need to get violent,' said Helen, who was exaggerating her pain.

A car pulled up outside the phone box and a small man with thick black hair, who was dressed in smart work clothes, a suit, shirt and tie, stepped out. He looked angry, puffing his chest out like a pigeon, as he assertively walked over to the phone box. He barged past Helen and helped Mary outside. Helen, who was taken aback, eyed him up and down.

'What the hell do you think you're doing? You wee shit,' said Helen to the man.

'I'm here to rescue my fiancé,' he said. 'Come on, love.' He grabbed Mary's hand.

Helen was agog in disbelief. 'What does he mean by fiancé, Mary?'

'Exactly what Paul said. We're engaged to be married,' Mary replied.

'Since when?' said Helen.

'Well, maybe if you paid more attention to other members of your family, you'd have noticed I'd got engaged,' said Mary.

'I didn't even know you were dating,' said Helen as she eyeballed Paul. 'And him. That wee troublemaker. Always starting fights.'

Paul stood next to Helen, pigeon-chested. 'Oh aye, Helen. Miss High and Mighty. I tell you, Mary, you can choose your friends but you can't choose your family.'

Mary hobbled towards the car, using her crutches. 'That's for sure, Paul,' said Mary slyly to her sister.

'I'll run a hot bath for you at my mum's house,' said Paul as he helped her into the car.

'If I'd known you were engaged, I'd have thrown you an engagement party,' shouted Helen as Paul slammed the car door shut.

He eyeballed his future sister-in-law before climbing inside himself.

'How dare she think that I don't care!' said Helen to herself. 'I'm always looking out for her.'

***

In the back garden of the tea shop, an irate Paddy – who had finally been pushed to his limits – was squaring up to Grant, who now didn't seem too cocky. The thing about Grant was that his mouth was his main weapon. He was articulate and had the gob of the century, but he was physically quite weak with a puny build. Paddy, on the other hand, had been boxing for years and came from a long line of amateur Irish boxers. Grant was beginning to realise that he may have pushed the wrong guy into a corner. Paddy was dancing on the spot with his fists in the air and was now intimidating Grant, who was slowly backing away – full well knowing he'd never actually been in a physical fight. They were standing opposite Frank's mud patch and they hadn't spotted him as Frank was camouflaged by the mud. The only bit of colour on the wee lad were his blue eyes. He was fascinated watching the two boys, who he thought were outside having a play fight.

'What's your fecking problem, fella?' Paddy said to Grant and then swiped his fist at him to scare him; not to actually hit him. Grant panicked and lost his balance, before he fell to the ground and landed on his bum. 'Knockout – and I haven't even touched you yet,' said Paddy. He faked more aggression and Grant put his hands up – scared he was about to be punched.

'I'm sorry. I've been a dick to you and I'm sorry,' Grant sniveled in a panic, worried he was about to get battered.

'Well, that's pretty clear, but why?' asked Paddy, wanting answers.

Grant stood up and dusted himself off. 'I've been jealous,' said Grant.

Paddy lowered his fists and seemed confused. 'Of me? I'm hardly David Cassidy, fella.'

Grant thought it was best to just tell him the truth. 'I'm not jealous of you,' said Grant and Paddy scratched his head, feeling confused. 'It's who you're with – Gail.'

The realisation of what the real problem was could be seen on Paddy's face.

Grant nervously scratched his arm. 'She was my girlfriend only yesterday,' he said and Paddy looked horrified hearing this news.

'Yesterday? But that's when she started flirting with me,' said Paddy, who now seemed upset.

'We've been dating for a few weeks and we had a bit of a bad day and, suddenly, she was with you,' said Grant.

'I had no idea. I'm sorry, fella. I never step on another man's toes, ever,' he said, upset that his own morals had been compromised.

'It's not your fault. It's mine… I think I was mean to her yesterday… I was drunk,' said Grant.

'Well, I've been there, fella. Drink and women don't mix too good,' said Paddy, who put his hand out for Grant to shake, which he did. 'Look. I came here with my brothers to work and to be by the seaside for a bit. I'm not interested in some love triangle.' They prolonged their shake to the discomfort of Grant. 'I will certainly step out your way, fella, and – as they say – there are plenty more fish in the sea,' added Paddy, full of grace.

Grant suddenly found he had a new-found respect for him. 'I really am sorry… that I've been hostile towards you since you arrived. You're a great guy. I can see that now,' said Grant as they continued to shake one another's hands.

'Water under the bridge. Friends,' said Paddy.

'Friends,' said Grant.

They finally released their hands from one another and Grant had to shake his off for a bit as Paddy's handshake was pretty deadly.

'Stink bomb!' shouted Frank from his mud patch.

Suddenly, a lump of dirt came flying towards Paddy and Grant. Paddy had excellent instincts and ducked down, allowing the mud ball to pelt Grant across the face.

Frank laughed loudly.

Chapter 13

Jim and Helen were fast asleep, but Jim was snoring very loudly and seemed like he was about to choke every time he breathed through his mouth - like a blocked drain. Jamie was wide awake and was lying in his cot beside a stiff orange teddy bear – the kind of bear with moving leg and arm joints. He had been Frank's first bear and it had been bought for him when he was born by Uncle Grant. He'd since upgraded to a softer, larger one, which was floppy and green and aptly named Big Ted. The little orange one was Little Ted. Both names came from the TV show *Play School*. Frank had always wanted a Humpty Dumpty – one of the other toys from the show – but had never been bought one. He also hadn't seen the egg-shaped toy with the thin arms and legs in Mapes toy shop or he would have purchased one with his money from doing the dishes. Now, though, he'd got to the point that *Play School* was too babyish for him and instead chose to watch the more grown-up cartoons like *Scooby-Doo*.

Jamie was becoming more and more agitated in the cot and pushed Little Ted out of his way. *I hate this little orange twat! It scratches my skin.* He looked towards his parents lying in the bed. *What about these two useless baboons? I'd be as well taking care of myself. I've pissed and shat in my nappy. My stomach is rumbling. I'm starving. My mouth is dry and I'm dehydrated. I'm bored out my mind 'cause there is nothing in here except for this stupid, pointless reject toy from the Wee Shrimp – what a fucking baby with his little teddies. And to think that they think I'd want this.* Jamie pushed the teddy out his way. *Give me booze and fags any day of the week. Fuck this!*

Jamie climbed up from his lying position using the bars and stared at his parents. He attempted to try and pull himself up and over, but soon realised his body wasn't there yet and became frustrated. *The sooner I become independent, the better. I'm sick of having to rely on this family. Look at them just lying there. Blondie's gonna be in for a huge surprise when she wakes up and it's not Woolworths' chopper behind her back. Woolworths has withheld some very important information from her and she is going to be livid!*

Jamie started to cry very loudly. *Fuck this for a game of soldiers.* He raised the decibels of his crying even louder and this woke Helen.

She started to nudge Jim harshly. 'Jim, Jim, *Jim!*' shouted Helen.

Jim woke up and sat up, startled, like a folding deckchair. 'What's going on?' he asked, dazed and confused.

'Did you not hear your son crying?' asked Helen. 'It's your turn to go and feed him and change his nappy… which I can smell from here.'

Alright, Blondie… maybe if you sat me on the toilet, I

could piss and shit in there. I'm not a simpleton like the Wee Shrimp. I'm perfectly capable.

Jim got out of bed and scratched his balls. *Woolworths, you better go and wash your hands. I don't want all your ball sweat over me.* Jim swept Jamie up from his cot using his two hands. *Think I'm gonna puke.* Jim lifted Jamie above his head, then made a face at him.

'You do smell bad,' said Jim to his son.

I'm a fucking baby! What's your excuse, Woolworths? And now I've got your saggy ball sweat under my armpits – disgusting!

'It's probably best that you woke us up at 7am, as Mum and me have got a huge wedding to do today. Who gets married on a Wednesday?' Jim muttered to himself.

And there it is. Helen suddenly sprung up like her back had just bounced off a trampoline. 'Jim. What did you say?' she asked, thinking she'd misheard him.

Jim turned to her with Jamie in his arms. 'The wedding, Helen. The one I told you about a month ago – when the two couples came in. The double wedding,' said Jim, as he watched Helen slowly begin to steam up. 'You were at the dentist and when you came back, I told you about it. Forty people at half past two.'

Helen was now standing by the side of the bed, having quickly jumped out. She had two clenched fists and a serious scowl on her face. 'You did not tell me, Jim!' said Helen, who was ready to burst.

Jim looked at Jamie puzzled. *You didn't, Woolworths, you clown.*

'I swear, Jim, if you weren't holding our child right

now, I would slap you across the face,' Helen said as she marched out of the room.

Kick him in the balls, Blondie. It's what he deserves.

After Helen stormed out the room, he looked at Jamie. 'Oops-a-daisy,' he said.

More like, how am I going to squirm my way out of this fucking mess, Woolworths!

Shouting could be heard through the wall. '*Frank! Grant! Get up! Jim's messed up again!*' blared Helen.

Jim looked at his son. 'Bit harsh, don't you think?'

Jamie managed to shake his head. *No!*

***

Soon after, Helen gathered the troops in the tea room to prepare for the surprise wedding that had suddenly cropped up and ruined her day. All the boys – the three Irish lads, Grant and Frank – were lined up and ready, after having been woken by the foghorn of Helen's voice.

'Right, boys. We have an impossible task to deal with today as *someone* forgot to mention that the tea shop will be hosting its first ever wedding,' said Helen and then looked at her watch.

Jim, who was holding onto Jamie, was flicking through the bookings book, desperately trying to find the wedding booking to prove to Helen that she should have known. The book was there for everyone to view – particularly Helen, who used it to check how much food she needed to order from her suppliers and to see exactly how many people were dining each day.

'We have six hours to pull this out of the bag,' continued Helen to the boys. 'One big issue is that we don't know what these brides and grooms have ordered to eat, as "Manuel" over there has lost all the paperwork!'

Grant went over to the desk where they kept all the paperwork, slipped himself next to Jim and pulled open a drawer. 'I found this on the floor a while back. Couldn't make out a word of it as Jim's writing is incomprehensible, but I knew it might be important,' said Grant as he handed it to Jim.

'There it is!' said Jim, relieved.

Jamie stared at his dad. *Come on, Woolworths. Maybe you should do something else with your life. Don't know if you're cut out for this restaurant malarkey.*

Jim walked over to Helen and handed her the sheet of paper. She glanced at it for a few seconds and hit him on the chest with it.

'Are you serious? What the hell does that say?' said Helen, annoyed with him. The boys in the line-up were trying to hold in their giggles.

Woolworths, you'd be as well digging the hole now. 'Cause I think Blondie's gonna bury you.

Jim took the paper back. 'Rona, John, Margo and Dennis,' read Jim in monotone.

'Not their names. The time, the food. All the key details. Don't you think you've messed this up enough already?' said Helen, frustratedly.

Paddy bent down and whispered to his two brothers, 'You can see who wears the trousers in this relationship. Glad it was Mr Coyle who's our teacher and not Mrs Coyle. She's a right ball-buster.'

Pierce and Seamus giggled. Helen glared towards them and their faces straightened.

Jim started to read out the menu. 'Starter – prawn cocktail.'

Helen let the words resonate and seemed okay with the starter. 'Go on,' she said.

'Main course – steak Diane,' continued Jim.

'Jim, are you kidding me? I need to pre-order with the butcher to order steaks. You'll need to go to the mainland if he doesn't have enough,' said Helen in a panic.

Jim gestured his hands to try and calm her and dared to speak. 'Calm down, dear.'

Jamie snorted. *Big mistake, Woolworths. Big mistake!*

'Calm down? Are you having a laugh?' said Helen, clearly pissed off. 'It's your fault we're in this predicament and you've got the cheek to tell *me* to calm down!' Helen was almost bursting out of her skin.

'And they're not having a wedding cake—'

'Great,' Helen interrupted, sarcastically.

'They want Black Forest gateau,' said Jim, matter-of-factly.

'What if we don't have enough in the freezer?' said Helen.

'Then you'll need... to... make them,' said Jim.

All the boys ducked down, expecting Helen to go berserk.

Woolworths has turned himself into a steak and is about to be ravaged by the big blonde lion.

Jim began to realise what he had just said. Helen turned her back on him and gave him the cold shoulder. Grant returned to the line-up and Helen addressed them all.

'Paddy. I'm going to write a list of items I need you to pick up. First off, the butchers…'

***

Paddy was soon walking fast down the main street, having been given his orders by Helen to go to several different shops. She'd only allowed him an hour to complete all the tasks. He was staring down at the lists and was trying to work out what some of the items were. Helen had been in a bit of a panic herself and hadn't really taken the time to explain properly. He well and truly felt the pressure and then, all of a sudden, bumped into someone, who fell on the ground.

'I'm really sorry,' he said and placed his hand out to help them up. At first, he thought he'd knocked down a small child, then realised it was Gail who was laying on the ground, helpless.

Gail had already seen that it was Paddy and wanted the ground to swallow her up. She'd realised that Grant was the one for her and felt embarrassed that she'd even kissed Paddy, who was definitely a rebound fling.

Paddy was a gentleman and helped her up. Gail had gone her usual embarrassed crimson colour as they stood awkwardly together in the street.

'If I'd known you were with someone else, I wouldn't have kissed you,' said Paddy, seeming a little hurt.

'I'm sorry,' mumbled Gail, realising that someone must have told him about Grant.

'You shouldn't lead guys on like that. You know we have feelings, too,' he continued and this made her feel really guilty. 'I'm a one-woman man and was brought up with morals and you obviously weren't.'

Gail's heart started to jump loops. She had been brought up with morals. Morals were so important to her. She desperately wanted to tell Paddy this, but it was her act the day before that had compromised her own principles.

'In some ways, I think I've had a lucky escape. That fella, Grant – he deserves to be treated well. He's breaking his heart, you know,' said Paddy.

Gail desperately wanted to tell Paddy that Grant had behaved disrespectfully towards her and that's what had ignited the breakdown of their relationship. What exactly had Grant been telling Paddy?

'Maybe think twice before you play two guys off one another next time,' said Paddy, before he hurried off – remembering that he was in a rush.

Gail stood there, astounded. The whole one-sided conversation had made her out to be a villain. She was desperate to make up with Grant, but she didn't like the fact he must have played the victim to Paddy.

***

Helen pulled out two boxes of frozen Black Forest gateau from the chest freezer and four bags of frozen prawns. She wasn't sure if she had enough of the gateau. Most of their supplies came from the cash and carry in Glasgow and she wouldn't have time to collect more. There were many items that you couldn't find in Millport's shops.

May and Jimmy had just come through the front door and were smartly dressed. Helen raised her head when she heard her father shout, 'Oh for fuck's sake, can someone not fix that door?' as he tripped and stumbled into the tea shop. He'd held the door open for May and she was already halfway up the dining area. She'd learnt to block out Jimmy's irate swearing.

May waved to Jim, who was carrying Jamie under his arm and seemed perplexed. He was still in Helen's bad books and she'd decided to completely ignore him and take full control of the day. All the teenage boys had been delegated their jobs and were all on the dining-room floor, setting up for the wedding.

May approached Helen and stood at the servery. It was the first time that she'd been in the tea shop for a few days. She had felt embarrassed about the whole Tam and Muriel incident. She just needed a bit of space to incinerate all the details in her head and not think about it anymore. May struggled to cope with this modern way of thinking, which was a speciality of her daughter's. She had decided to approach Helen with a clean slate and with the "incident" well and truly buried under the carpet, never to be dredged up again.

Jimmy wasn't far behind his wife and shouted out to Helen, 'Helen, I'm going for a starry night.'

May looked up at her daughter. 'But it's still the morning,' said May, who'd heard the phrase a million times but still found it confusing.

'He's going for a number two, Mum,' said Helen.

May still looked befuddled.

'What rhymes with night?' continued Helen, but May shook her head. 'Never mind, Mum. While you're here… I really need you to look after Jamie for me today.'

'I would, Helen, but it's the bowling Summer Champions day,' said May.

Helen was pouring bags of frozen prawns into a colander. 'Mum, I'm desperate. Can't you take him with you?' asked Helen.

'I would, but I'm bowling as well today. Sorry, Helen, but we'll see you later at the prize-giving,' said May. She looked down at the prawns, excited. 'Are we getting prawn sandwiches?'

Helen looked up at May like she'd completely lost her mind.

'See you at five, dear, for the prize-giving buffet,' said May as she toddled off, leaving Helen scratching her head. May stopped off where Jim was folding napkins (the fancy maroon ones for special occasions) with one hand and holding a restless Jamie under his other arm. She patted Jamie on the head. *Hope I'm not being sent to the bowling green with Old Dear. That place stinks of death.* 'Looking forward to our buffet today, Jim. Thank you very much for doing it for free,' said May. Jim looked up at May, unable to hide the shock on his face and then over his shoulder at Helen, who was glaring at him while holding a very sharp knife.

'Jim! Over here now!' shouted Helen.

Take me to the living cemetery, I beg you, Old Dear, before Blondie stabs us all! I'll even put up with the smell of talcum powder and Old Spice.

Jim sheepishly walked over to Helen, who was still pointing the knife in his direction. He didn't really have any excuses other than bad management.

'What the hell have you done this time?' barked Helen at Jim.

Woolworths, that's another fine mess you got us into.
Jamie was smiling at his dad's incompetence.

Jim put his only free hand up in the air. 'Helen, I have royally messed up,' he said with his tail between his legs.

'That's an understatement. You've booked a wedding and organised a bowling club buffet on the same day and you've not even told the bloody cook!' said Helen.

'Look, dear. We will manage… we always do,' said Jim, nonchalantly.

'What are we going to do… stick the bowlers on top of the wedding guests? We only have one room and forty fu…' Helen was desperate to swear, but withheld herself at the last minute. 'Forty seats. And food. I don't even know if I've got enough for the wedding party… never mind the free bowlers' buffet. I mean, free, Jim?' said Helen.

Jim shrugged his shoulders. 'I thought it would be good PR. Old people love tea and scones.'

'Yeah, while sitting at a table,' retorted Helen.

Jim thought long and hard for a minute. He looked out of the window and realised the weather was sunny. 'I'm a genius, Helen,' said Jim, pleased with himself.

Helen shook her head as she poured mayonnaise into a container. 'No, Jim. You're an idiot,' said Helen.

'You wait and see, Helen. I have a plan. We can do both the wedding and the bowlers,' said Jim.

'Abracadabra – wedding food for forty. Alakazam – a buffet of food for fifty bowlers,' said Helen, still really annoyed at Jim for getting her into this stressful predicament.

Just then, Paddy came rushing through the door, holding bags of shopping. Sweat poured from his forehead as he panted out of breath. He'd taken Helen's one-hour challenge seriously and had managed to collect the goods within the time limit. He dumped all the bags in the kitchen, next to Helen's feet.

'I hope there's gold in those bags, Paddy,' said Helen.

'Not quite gold, but certainly a bag full of silver,' said Paddy, jokingly.

'How many steaks?' asked Helen.

'Twenty-five sirloin,' said Paddy.

Helen tried to calculate the maths in her head. The sirloin steaks were usually pretty big, so she could definitely flatten them down by banging them with a rolling pin and try to make forty. She picked up the shopping bags with the steaks and placed them all out on the worktop.

'The butcher only had twenty-five steaks,' she shouted over to Jim, who was finishing setting up for the wedding, still holding onto Jamie.

Jim came rushing over. 'Do I need to go over to the mainland?' he asked.

Aye and just stay over there. You're as useful as drinking a bottle of Babycham to try and get you pissed.

'Luckily for you, your wife is a master and the butcher has given us huge steaks today, which I can batter,' said Helen as she glared at her husband. She walloped one of the steaks really hard with her rolling pin and the blood splattered on her apron. 'You're lucky that it's not you being battered, Jim Coyle.'

Just one hit, Blondie. That'll knock him out.

Jim gave her a cheeky smile, then went over and kissed her on the lips. 'Sorry, dear. Next time I'll do better,' he said.

You two make me want to be sick in my mouth.

'What you doing about the bowlers?' asked Helen.

Jim was pleased with himself. 'Outside. It's a sunny day. We could put the buffet on the jetty across the road and get the Irish boys to serve them.'

Maybe a few of the old bowlers will fall into the sea to put them out of their misery? Woolworths, perhaps you're not as daft as I thought.

Helen mulled the idea in her head and made a so-so face. 'Where are they all going to sit? We need all the tables, chairs, crockery, cups for the wedding and—'

Jim interrupted Helen, 'I've just looked in that room across the hall. The one we could never be bothered to clean out and there is a load of stuff in there. Tables, chairs – all we need. I'll get the boys to shift it across the road.'

Helen seemed unsure and sharply said, 'You just deal with it. I've got enough on my plate with a spontaneous wedding breakfast and a buffet to sort out.' Helen looked at her watch. 'Oh – in two hours. Damn you, Jim.' She whacked another steak with her rolling pin. He took this as his cue to leave.

Jim pulled open the door of the room they'd completely ignored since buying the place. There were piles of old tables, chairs, lamps, containers filled with cutlery and other useless tit-tat that needed to go to the dump. Grant was standing beside Jim, while Seamus and Pierce were behind him. Jim was still holding onto Jamie.

Fuck me, Woolworths! The dust in here is unbearable. How to make your baby asthmatic in five minutes. Jamie started to cough. *I feel like I've just smoked forty fags, for fuck's sake!*

Jim passed Jamie to Grant. 'Better take him out of here,' said Jim.

Now you care, Woolworths?

'Jim, the wedding guests are going to be here in an hour and I need to sort out the glasses of Blue Nun,' said Grant.

I'd love a glass of that to numb the pain.

Jim took a breath inwards before delegating. 'Okay – Grant, you sort out the wedding guests.' Grant handed Jamie to Seamus and then went back in the main room. 'Seamus, you get Paddy and he can help move the furniture,' Jim continued. Seamus passed Jamie to Pierce. *Not the old pass-the-fucking-parcel routine again.* 'I'll work out what we need from here…' said Jim and stepped into the large junk room, leaving twelve-year-old Pierce holding a disgruntled baby. Pierce held Jamie awkwardly under his arms, up in front of his face, and stared at him.

What you staring at? It's slim pickings for babysitters these days.

Jim hadn't realised that Pierce had been left with the baby and shouted from the room, 'It's a bigger job than I thought. Think I'll need all three brothers in here.'

Pierce walked down the corridor, looking for somewhere to leave Jamie. He went into the main room and saw that everyone was really busy. Helen was cooking, Frank was doing dishes, Grant was filling glasses with Blue Nun. He went back out into the corridor and opened the door to the inside dog kennel. The two dogs and all the puppies seemed pretty subdued and were snuggled together. He thought maybe he could just place him down beside the dogs until someone who wasn't busy could look after him. He gently put Jamie on the floor, laying him in between two of the red setter puppies.

Jamie was astounded. *Am I being brought up by the fucking dogs now? To be fair, they'll probably do a better job than this family. It's actually really quite cosy in here.*

Pierce left the room and shut the door.

***

Jim was knee-high in boxes and covered in dust. He'd managed to find a load of tables and chairs for the bowlers' buffet and the three Irish lads had taken them outside. In the process of all this, he'd had the realisation that this room would be a brilliant extra room and would increase the tea shop's capacity by about twenty people - but he resolved to tell that to Helen another day. He picked up a box of cups, saucers and plates and carried them out of the room. They needed to be washed before being used for the dinner guests.

Jim took them into the kitchen where Helen was red raw from the steam of all the cooking she'd had to do. She was bashing away at her final few steaks, trying to draw them out. There were trays of sandwiches and freshly made scones for the bowlers. The place was cluttered. Frank had done a great job of keeping up with the dishes, but seemed exhausted and fed up as he'd had no help at all.

Helen quickly glanced at Jim, who barged past her with the large box of crockery. He was almost about to drop it and had banged into her. 'Jim! What the hell you doing?'

Jim placed the box awkwardly onto the floor and there was a loud rattling noise.

'How much more are you going to mess up today?' said Helen, looking him up and down. 'Look at the state of you.' Jim was covered head to toe in dust, his hair was in disarray and sweat was pouring from every pore. Helen glanced at the time on her watch. 'The wedding guests will be here any time now and you need to be ready. You look like Worzel Gummidge.' She wasn't trying to be humorous.

Frank looked down at the box and was also mad. He stuck his tongue out at his dad (while his back was turned), knowing he'd be shouted at if he said anything.

'Jim, go and put your suit on. You've caused enough bother today,' said Helen, firmly.

'Yes, dear,' he replied sarcastically.

She picked up on his tone and wanted to throttle him, positioning her hands in the air like she was strangling him and acting out the deed.

***

Jamie was lying cosily with the puppies. He had been sceptical to begin with, when he'd been shoved into the dog kennel, but he was beginning to like it. He'd been a little bit hot, but had managed to pull his shorts and nappy off with the help of some of the puppies. Their fur was making his skin a little sensitive, but the puppies soon began to lick him all over and their loose fur stuck to his skin, which made him feel even cosier. The licking sensation actually felt really nice and, for a minute, he was so lost he felt like he might be in heaven.

This is way better than hanging out with those incompetent adults. I could stay here forever. Jamie pulled at his vest top with his arms and managed to pull it to a point that his face was covered. Brochan's head was next to him and her motherly instincts kicked in. She gripped the loose top with her teeth and pulled it right off with her mouth.

Yes. Can you be my mother now? At last I've found a decent family to live with.

Jamie snuggled right back into the puppies around him and they began to lick his torso and rub more of their red hair onto him. *Aah, bliss!*

***

Grant had poured forty glasses of Blue Nun into the fancier glasses. Helen had found these amber French wine glasses when her and Jim had hitchhiked to France the previous year (because it was all they could afford to do after buying the tea shop). They'd left Frank with May and Jimmy. She'd seen them lying outside an old restaurant and thought they'd be ideal for tea shop functions. Much to Jim's despair, she'd made him cart them around France and into each stranger's car. She'd refused to pay the cost of postage, but had to have them.

Next, Grant headed outside to the kennel area and was soon puffing his cigarette and enjoying the sunshine for five minutes, before he was needed to serve the wedding guests their drinks. He opened the outside door to let all the dogs and puppies out of the inside kennel as it was such a lovely day. He closed his eyes and took a long drag of his cigarette before blowing out a cloud of smoke. He wasn't passionate about too many things, but he loved smoking and considered himself a veteran of the habit as he'd started so young. He stubbed out his cigarette as he joyfully sniffed the air for a few moments, helping him prepare for the carnage inside the tea shop. Two of the puppies came bounding out and nearly knocked Grant off his feet.

'Careful there, you wee scamps!' said Grant as he tried to steady himself.

He took a long, laboured sigh before leaving the dog kennel. It was then that he decided it would be a brilliant idea to pick some flowers for the top table at the wedding. He loved to wind up his father and would deny any involvement when asked later about who had defiled Jimmy's border. He randomly picked about twelve different flowers, pulling them out from the root. This left the flower beds looking a little sparse and he giggled at his mischievous act, even though it was for a good cause. He carried the flowers back into the tea shop and went to look for a vase.

Jamie was lying comfortably surrounded by the puppies. He was now naked and covered in red fur. The dogs had all licked him so hard and rubbed themselves all over his face and body. He enjoyed the sensation of their tongues over his bare skin and hadn't tried to fight them off. There was a breeze coming from the outside through the open door and the puppies were gradually going to the exterior area, usually two by two. The room was stifling hot and the slow breeze had been welcome to the one human and all the dogs. Jamie felt like he was in heaven, a real place where he belonged. This all changed when the dogs began to leave the room – and when Brochan finally went outside, the remaining puppies followed her. Jamie was now lying by himself with his eyes closed. Tana was the only dog left in the inside kennel and you could tell she was relieved that they'd all gone. She was more than ready to not share her kennel space with the other dogs, especially the little, enthusiastic ones. She just lay in the corner like a big lump.

Jamie moved his arms around beside him and wasn't nearly as comfortable as he had been before. *What's going on? Where have they all gone?* He opened his eyes and turned his head, realising he was lying by himself. He turned around onto his front and could see Tana in the corner. *Gawd! It's just me and the lazy big fat one.* He decided he would crawl over to Tana and lay beside her – he felt separation anxiety from the dogs who had left and was desperate to snuggle. It was a feeling he'd yet to experience with any human before. Tana was on her side and her ten teats were on display. He cosied up to her, placing his tiny baby hands on her hairy red legs. She didn't seem to mind as she much preferred human contact to dogs. *Aah, bliss. This one's really comfortable. But it's so hot in here, though. And my mouth is really dry. I could do with some milk.*

He was torn by the feeling of loving the soft fur on his skin and an uncomfortable hotness all over his body. Jamie tried to move his tongue inside his mouth, but it was stuck on his inside top lip due to dryness. He was feeling a little dizzy when he stared towards Tana's stomach and noticed her ten teats for the first time. *Well, hello ladies. First time I've noticed you around these parts. Do you come here often? You're not quite as pretty as Laverne or Shirley, but beggars can't be choosers. There's bound to be some juicy goodness for baby to enjoy, especially in this clammy heat.*

Jamie moved his face in close proximity to Tana's stomach and looked directly at all her teats. *You. No you... no you. Who the fuck am I kidding. I'm just going to suck on the biggest one.* He garnered up all the saliva he could within his mouth and licked his lips with his tongue, then pressed his lips on Tana's biggest teat and sucked for dear life. *What a relief. Milk from a titty at last. It's a bit warm, but it'll do the job nicely.*

***

In the tea shop kitchen, Helen had made prawn cocktails for the wedding by taking leaves of iceberg lettuce and putting a good few spoonfuls of Marie Rose sauce on top of the lettuce with a wedge of lemon, sprinkled paprika and a slice of buttered bread, quartered. They were all laid out on plates ready for the wedding breakfast. The guests had all arrived and were sipping on their complimentary glasses of Blue Nun, waiting for the arrival of the brides and grooms. They were all in their allocated seats.

Jim was dressed smartly in his dinner suit – an outfit that had met with Helen's approval. He'd managed to do a swift turnaround and was now looking rather dapper, like an old-fashioned Hollywood film star. He was standing next to the top table, which was a table for four in the middle of the tea shop. Grant's vase of Jimmy's garden flowers was in the middle of the table and was the only distinguishable detail from all of the other tables. Grant opened the door to the outside and the two brides and their new husbands entered.

Jim spoke very loudly to address the room, 'Ladies and gentlemen, please welcome the newlyweds; Rona and John.'

Rona (who had a yellow frock on) and Dennis went to sit down.

'I'm Dennis. And I'm married to Rona now,' said Dennis as he went to sit.

Jim pulled back the chair for Rona. 'Rona and Dennis!' said Jim loudly, a bit confused.

The couple sat down and Jim announced the second couple as he read from his sheet, 'Margo and Den... John!'

Margo (who was wearing a red dress) smiled at Jim and winked. 'I'm married to John now,' she said.

John interjected, 'Aye, she's with me now. Not him.' He patted Dennis on the shoulder and laughed out loud.

Helen stood and watched Jim's awkward announcement. She tutted and shook her head, wondering how much more he could possibly mess up.

Jim stood between the two couples – who were now all seated. 'Please raise a glass for your happy couples, John and Dennis. And Margo and Rona.'

Jim didn't notice his oversight and nobody tried to correct him, but roaring laughter and merry applause filled up the room.

John leaned over and winked at Dennis. 'Hello, darling,' he said to Dennis, comically.

Helen had her hand over her face in absolute despair at how much her husband had blundered. She decided to start the food service to add a bit of professionalism to the day.

The guests were served their prawn cocktails and Helen began frying her steaks in two pans, making sure not to overcook them. She was holding the cooked ones in the oven at a lower temperature, but was aware they would still be cooking. She needed them not to be as chewy as a leather handbag. This was her first wedding and she wanted to impress the guests and hopefully pick up more of this high-end business. Jim stood and watched her.

Next, Helen stirred her pan of Diane sauce – she'd made it once before for her first wedding anniversary, but had added too much salt and it was inedible. She took a teaspoon and dipped it into the creamy sauce and tasted with her fingers crossed. There was no going back as she didn't have the time or enough ingredients to make another one. She screwed her face.

'I'm not sure, Jim,' she said as she took another spoon, dipped it into the sauce and handed it over the servery to Jim. He tasted it and half of the sauce went over his moustache. 'Well, what do you think?' she asked, impatiently waiting for an answer.

He semi-smiled at her. 'It's better than your last one,' said Jim with a wonky wince.

Helen threw her dishcloth at him and it landed over his face. 'Are you kidding me, Jim?' She lowered her voice so the customers couldn't hear her. 'The last one was disgusting.'

Jim removed the dishcloth from his face. 'It's nice, dear,' he said.

'Would you wipe that sauce from your moustache? You're an embarrassment,' said Helen and Jim wiped his mouth. 'Now, get the boys to clear the starter. I want to serve the wedding guests steak… not leather.' By now she was really feeling the pressure and was still really annoyed with her husband.

Jim went to check on the Irish lads, who were setting up for the bowlers outside and were also helping to serve the wedding guests, plus giving Frank the dictator a hand with the dishes – though they hadn't done much.

Grant had taken five minutes out the front of the tea shop while waiting for the guests to finish their prawn cocktails. Gail was on the jetty with Yvonne. He hadn't seen her for a few days and was feeling regretful about how he'd handled the relationship on the last day that they were together. Paddy had assured him that he was very much out of the picture, but he didn't have a clue what to say to her. He didn't even know if she still had feelings. Gail and Grant made eye contact across the road and this made him feel a mix of emotions again. He had to concentrate today, though; his life in Millport was in jeopardy, as Helen wouldn't give him a second chance if he messed up again.

Margo and John, one of the bride and groom pairs, came outside. He pushed her up against the wall and began to snog her. Grant spotted them and felt embarrassed and a little confused. He was sure that they were both married to the other bride and groom – Rona and Dennis. They didn't seem to care and were all over each other like a couple of teenagers. John was also acting extremely raunchy in a public area, as he squeezed one of Margo's breasts. Grant had to slide past them to go back inside and was thinking that this didn't seem like a very good start to a marriage, with instant infidelity.

From the other side of the road, Gail watched Grant go inside and felt rather empty. She was so love-struck she barely noticed the peep show that was taking place.

***

Jamie was lying next to Tana, sucking milk from her teat. He'd been doing this for half an hour and was very full, so pulled his mouth away. There was dog milk all around his face and dribbling down his chin. *Aw, plentiful sufficiency.*

Tana looked down at him with a sad look – like she'd just been violated by this creepy little human. She detested when her own puppies sucked on her teats, never mind a real human boy.

Jamie was still covered in fur and was roasting hot. He rolled over onto his back, placing his legs and hands in the air. He almost looked like one of the red hairy Setters and felt gleeful as he giggled away. *Why haven't I been in here before? Yes, she's a wee bit broken and the milk is warm, but there's plenty of it and it keeps my belly full. And there's enough titties of milk to feed the whole of Millport.*

***

Outside on the jetty, the three Irish lads were in the midst of table arrangements for the bowling club buffet. They had managed to find a load of old chairs and tables in the extra room. Jim had left them to their own devices with strict orders – the end sentence being, 'Keep Helen happy.' All the boys were scared of her and hadn't come across a woman who appeared to be the boss in the marriage before. It was one of Jim's tactics to keep harmony and he would quite often say, 'Yes, dear,' even though he would go off and do his own thing anyway. He was happy enough for other people to think he was a soft touch – until they crossed him and he would come down on them like a ton of bricks.

***

In the kitchen, Helen was tired as she had triple the food to cook and put out. There wasn't extra time to try and recruit more staff for the wedding. In her mind, she kept swearing about Jim and in some ways it made her feel better. She'd prepared all the steaks and had held them in the oven for warmth. Six of them had already been plated up and were on hot plates ready to serve. Her Diane sauce was on the cooker with the gas on low to keep it warm and she ladled enough sauce to pour over each steak. There were also side dishes of salad and new potatoes to put into the middle of the table.

Jim and Grant were the only ones serving and clearing, so they needed to work fast to keep up. Jim knew he had to work doubly hard as he'd been the one that messed up the day's events. The two guys picked up three plates each using dishcloths and served them out. Helen was roasting, having endured an awful lot of steam to her face and hands every time she'd opened the oven or taken a lid off a pot. She didn't have time to stop and just had to put up with whatever kitchen burn or cut came her way.

Frank was on his ladder at the sink. There were a couple of flies buzzing around the window and a glass of warm milk that had soapy suds around the outside of the glass, where his fingers had been. He wasn't happy as he'd been promised time off from dishes and was mad as the Irish boys were nowhere to be seen. He didn't understand why he was back doing the job he hated, as nobody had explained it to him. He kept turning around every time his dad came into the kitchen with more dishes to wash. When Jim's back was turned, Frank would scowl at him. He couldn't work out where all these extra dusty plates had come from – he'd never seen them before in all the time he'd worked there.

Sometimes he'd glance out the window at the sunshine and feel envious of any children who were down at the beach playing with sandcastles or others who'd had a delicious Ritz Cafe ice cream. He'd even have settled for helping his papa paint in the baking heat. Was this all life had to offer? A sink's worth of dirty dishes and a glass of warm milk?

He picked up his glass, which he hadn't had time to drink, and guzzled some down, leaving behind a white moustache. Before he managed to swallow the milk, he felt something move inside his mouth. He stuck his soapy fingers inside and pulled out a fly, who was still alive, and threw it towards the window and (in a rather over dramatic fashion) began to spit out the milk that was left inside his mouth. He then stupidly threw the glass into the soapy water. The remainder of the milk mixed with the water and he slapped his hands onto the contaminated water, annoyed he was going to have to empty the sink and refill it; meaning the piled up dishes would take even longer.

Freaked out by the fact the fly had been in his mouth, he put the cold tap on and pulled his head under it and supped up water in order to clean his mouth out. The fly was beginning to rouse on the windowsill where it had landed and Frank hit it with his hand to kill it, leaving a mushed puss and bloodied fly.

He looked toward his mother, who seemed like she was on another planet. There was food everywhere. Platters of sandwiches, scones, steaks, Black Forest gateau. He watched her multitask and move quite elegantly around the kitchen and he thought of her like that superhero character from the telly – "Wonder Woman". He'd seen it a couple of times and had quite enjoyed it, though his favourite superhero was the Incredible Hulk, who he wanted to be like one day – huge, strong and green.

***

Jamie had been lying on his back for a while as his stomach was full to the brim with dog milk. Tana had sneaked off and had gone outside to join the other dogs. Jamie hadn't noticed and must have nodded off at some point. He viewed his small arm out of the corner of his eye and could see it was totally covered in red hair. This reminded him of the comfort he had felt earlier when he was cuddled in with all the Irish Setters. He'd never felt such a wonderful feeling before and wanted to replicate the experience. He rolled onto his side, then his front and slowly began to crawl towards the exit to the outside kennel. *Fuck this.* Crawling was taking too long, so he decided he would stand up and walk out. He stood and staggered his way to the open door. He was like a drunk man trying to leave a pub after one too many drinks. Luckily, he didn't need to go back into the crawling position as he still wasn't taller than the dogs' door.

***

Grant had finished serving the main courses with Jim and was desperate for the toilet. He'd held it in for a few hours now and had worked hard all day, so decided he could treat himself to a pee. He went out to the corridor and there was a couple who were practically humping one another up against the wall.

Grant chuckled to himself and then noticed that it was one of the bride and groom pairs. This time, the couple in question were Dennis and Rona – the opposite couple to the one he'd spied outside earlier. He questioned whether his mind was playing tricks on him as he was sure that they were both now married to the other bride and groom. It was all a little mind-boggling and strange. He thought he should just mind his own business and went for his well-deserved pee. The guests would be finishing their main courses soon and he'd need to clear them for the dessert.

He took one last glance at the raunchy couple – who were oblivious to his presence – and shook his head. It made him think about Gail. He really wanted to see her as he missed her and now knew that he'd made a mistake.

***

The bowling club had finished their championship competition for the day and had begun to gather on the jetty opposite the tea shop for the prize-giving buffet. The Irish lads had done a decent job of setting up the tables and chairs. There was enough plates and cutlery. All they had to do was serve the buffet. Paddy took the lead and the other two were sent in to fetch pots of tea and sandwiches. It wasn't the easiest task as they had to walk across the busy road and – because it was a sunny day and the summer holidays – they had to squeeze past tourists who were everywhere and were also very inquisitive about the outside dining area. Some of them thought that they could just sit down and be served. This made Paddy's job extra tough as he had to differentiate between the bowlers and the general public. Luckily, the majority of bowlers were over sixty and wearing their bowling club jumpers.

Across the road from the jetty, an official van pulled up outside the tea shop. There was a male driver and a lady passenger. She was smartly dressed in a grey skirt and matching grey jacket. Her grey hair was tied in a bun on top of her head and she was a wearing a pair of clear glasses with grey rims. She slinked out of the vehicle, quickly glancing down at a clipboard that she was holding, and sashayed towards the tea shop entrance.

Seamus almost knocked the lady over when he came rushing out holding two pots of tea, which were filled to the brim. The hot tea was spilling over the pot onto his hands and was scolding him. The lady patted herself down with her free hand and went to open the door. That was when Pierce came bounding out while carrying a large platter of sandwiches. The lady was almost knocked to the ground. She held herself against the wall and watched the two Irish boys play chicken with the oncoming traffic, while holding onto the tea and sandwiches. After another frustrated pat-down, she eventually managed to enter the tea shop.

***

Inside the kitchen, Helen was still frantic. She'd just started to sort out the dessert course and really had to put her improvisation skills to the test, as she hadn't managed to find enough Black Forest gateau for forty guests. There was only about thirty portions – she'd managed to cut enough for forty, but they were still pretty small, so she had to use tins of pears, Black Forest fruits and extra ice cream to disguise the fact that she'd given them such a small serving. She didn't want the wedding guests to think the tea shop were mean with their portions. In between scooping ice cream into bowls, she filled up platters with scones and more sandwiches. Jim and Grant were doing their best to serve all the wedding guests to keep them happy, while directing the Irish boys to deal with the outside buffet.

The smartly dressed lady with the clipboard had walked to the reservations desk and payment area. She was standing there, waiting for someone to acknowledge her presence. Pierce and Seamus burst through the door, rushed down the restaurant floor and flew past the lady, who was now a little annoyed at them. They reached the servery.

'Boys, there's more sandwiches here and a platter of scones. Have you offered anyone coffee?' said Helen.

'No, but I've burnt my fecking hand. I spilt tea all over it,' said Seamus. He held his hand up to Helen.

'That's nothing!' Helen said as she dismissed his minor injury. 'Once you've taken out all the food, you can stick it under a cold tap. Seamus, you take the cold platters; Pierce, you take the coffee – but be careful this time.' Helen felt unsympathetic as she had way worse injuries than a wee burn.

The boys followed their orders and Jim came back over to take out more gateau for the wedding guests. The grey lady cleared her throat very loudly and Helen looked up and spotted her for the first time. The two Irish boys rushed past her once again without acknowledgement and she seemed very annoyed.

Helen looked at Jim, 'Who's that woman?'

Jim looked around and shrugged his shoulders. 'I don't know. Is she not a wedding guest?' asked Jim.

Helen hadn't stopped for a second and continued to plate her desserts. 'Well, you better go and see what she wants,' she said harshly.

Jim wandered over to the lady and stood in front of the desk and smiled with his usual Jim smile, which made his moustache tickle his nose – a sensation he quite liked. 'How may I help you madam?' he said, enthusiastically.

She held up a piece of paper and handed it over to Jim. 'Hello. Are you Mr Coyle?' she asked.

Jim glanced at the paper and then back at the lady. 'Yes,' he said.

'My name's Elizabeth Barclay,' she said in a very posh English accent and seemed like she expected Jim to know who she was. Jim was clueless as he read through the literature that she'd handed him and couldn't make head nor tail of it, so he smiled at her with his "Joker" smile. Pierce and Seamus rushed past and almost banged into Elizabeth again.

Jim shouted at them, using his favourite teacher voice. 'Slow down, boys,' he said very deeply. 'I'm so sorry about that.' He continued to smile at the mysterious woman.

'You have a very busy establishment,' said Elizabeth.

'Yes. There is a wedding on today and an outside buffet,' exclaimed Jim.

'Have I caught you at an inconvenient time? I spoke to Mrs Coyle last week and she informed me that Wednesday would be an ideal day for collection,' said Elizabeth.

Jim started to feel frustrated at the situation and the lack of clarity about what the lady was actually here for. He opened the bookings book in the hope that Helen had written something inside that provided a clue at least. 'Collection?' he asked.

'Yes. I'm a dog trainer, specifically for shows, and I'm here to collect four show-type Irish Setters,' she said.

Jim almost looked relieved. 'I see,' he replied. He leaned in closer to Elizabeth. 'Thank goodness. For a minute there, I thought you were a health inspector and, as you can see, it's absolute chaos in here today.' The very serious lady failed to see the funny side and had an awkward thirty seconds with Jim before he slowly backed away. 'I'll ask my wife, who knows more about this than I do,' added Jim.

At the kitchen servery, he interrupted Helen doing her work. 'Helen. Helen!'

She looked at him. 'Jim, I'm busy because you double-booked us today, remember?' Helen said, barely looking at him.

Jim was almost pleased with her response. 'Helen, I'm not the only one who has withheld important information today,' replied Jim a little smugly. 'Somebody else forgot to make a diary entry.'

'Jim, what are you talking about?' asked Helen impatiently.

'The little lady with all the grey over there is a dog trainer,' said Jim and Helen's face almost fell to the floor when she realised her own blunder.

'Oh shit!' said Helen loudly.

Frank's ears were burning over at the kitchen sink. 'You just swore, Mum,' he piped up.

'Not now, Frank,' Helen shouted back. She stopped all her tasks and froze for a minute, while she gathered herself together. 'Jim, we still don't know for sure which puppies are the pedigree ones.' She looked over at the lady, who now seemed impatient.

'You don't want her to know that. Isn't she paying fifty for each puppy?' asked Jim.

Helen shushed him, putting her middle finger against her mouth. 'She might hear you! I can't go because I've still got to finish the desserts and the buffet.'

'You've got a better chance of distinguishing between the pups, Helen. I know the one with the white stripe is Brochan's... or is it Tana's?' asked Jim, all confused.

A sudden loud cheer distracted Jim and Helen. The two wedding couples had stood on top of their chairs and were holding hands in a circle. The rest of the guests began to clap as all the wedding party dangerously moved around in a circle swapping chairs while standing on top of them. Every few seconds, they'd stop and the couples would kiss on the lips, but they kept changing partners.

Grant came back to the servery and looked puzzled. 'They're all a bit weird,' he said, using his thumb to point and gesture behind him.

Helen and Jim ignored him and continued their conversation. 'Jim, you take her out to the kennel and see if you can figure out which four puppies to sell her,' said Helen.

Grant overheard the conversation and butted in. 'I spend a lot of time out there and think I might know which pup belongs to which bitch,' said Grant.

'Do you?' asked Helen.

'Uncle Grant, you swore,' said Frank.

Shut it Frank!' they all said in perfect unison

***

In the tea shop, Seamus and Pierce once again rushed past Elizabeth. This time, Seamus had tripped over his shoelace and banged right into her and she'd finally raised her voice at him.

'Enough! Would you please be careful?' said Elizabeth loudly to the young Irish lad.

This caught the attention of Helen, Jim and Grant. Elizabeth decided to follow the boys towards the servery.

Helen smiled at her as she approached. 'I am so sorry, Ms Barclay,' she said, 'for keeping you waiting and bringing you into this chaos.'

One of the wedding guests approached the servery. 'Our table hasn't had any dessert yet,' said a man very loudly.

Jim smiled at him. 'Two seconds, sir. We're just plating them up now. If you'd like to sit back down, we'll be right over with them,' said Jim.

Helen had to think quick on her feet, knowing she couldn't stall the lady any longer, but that she also had to finish serving the wedding food and the bowlers' buffet, only half of which had been taken outside. 'Grant, would you show Ms Barclay outside to our kennel areas to see her four new pedigree Irish Setter puppies?' asked Helen. 'Grant has tended to the puppies' every need, along with their mothers, of course.' She gave Grant a knowing nod and he escorted Elizabeth outside. Helen then handed two platters to the two Irish lads, before she finished off plating the desserts.

***

Outside, Grant took Elizabeth Barclay into the garden area and led her to the outside kennel area. Fortunately, all the dogs were there. Most of them were lying on the ground rather lethargically – it was a relatively hot day and they didn't have a great deal of energy. Elizabeth stared towards her clipboard as she had to fill in forms for each puppy she was purchasing. Grant was fairly confident which puppies were Brochan's – or so he thought. He'd spent a lot of time in the kennel area as it was the ideal place to hide his cigarette addiction.

When he stared down at all of the dogs, he thought something was rather odd as one of the pups was under Brochan and was feeding from one of her teats. All the puppies had stopped feeding from their mother's quite a while back. He wasn't wearing his glasses and couldn't really focus properly, but something seemed off. The pup appeared to be fairly hairy, but there was also some pink skin on show as well and its shape seemed totally weird. Elizabeth was still filling in some details on her form and hadn't yet viewed the puppies.

Grant took his glasses out from the inside pocket of his work trousers and put them on, hoping to see much better. He looked as closely as possible through the chicken wire but still couldn't quite make out what he was looking at. In front of him lay a small red-haired body, but its face was hidden from view. Had the other pups attacked this poor wee soul and mauled it, and was Brochan just comforting her baby? Grant was mesmerised and almost forgot Elizabeth was behind him. He hadn't noticed her standing and staring.

'How very odd,' she said. 'I have never seen anything like this before.'

Inside the kennel, Jamie took his mouth off Brochan's teat and gasped quite loudly. His face was dripping with warm dog milk. *I think the fat one's milk is better than this skinny one's. And she's got way bigger tits. Much better for baby to munch on.*

Grant was in disbelief at seeing his nephew's face appear and suddenly remembered exactly who was behind him. He also knew the possible consequences of this scenario. This woman could call social services and have the baby taken away. He had to think quickly.

'I'm not sure that little one is even an Irish Setter,' said Elizabeth. Grant was relieved the old bird was as myopic as himself and knew he had to do something before she put her glasses on.

Grant choked really loudly as a way of distraction and began to pretend to hyperventilate. He turned to her while faking an asthma attack. His hand clutched onto the chicken wire of the fence and his gasps became even louder and more erratic. He was playing his part very well.

Helen stood at the window of the kitchen and stared out towards Grant and Elizabeth outside. She shouted over to Jim, 'Our Grant's almost lying on the ground and that woman is leaning over him. We better go out and see what's happening.'

Jim came and stood behind Helen. 'Something's definitely going on,' he said.

Frank was also curious and he stood on his ladder to try and see as well. Jim and Helen rushed outside. Frank clambered onto the sink and pressed his face against the glass, leaving smudges.

Helen and Jim arrived at the very dramatic scene of Grant lying on the ground with Elizabeth kneeling over him in a panic, not knowing what to do.

'Does your son not have an asthma inhaler?' Elizabeth asked Helen.

Jim looked down at him as Grant did a hand signal to look in the kennel. 'I didn't know he had asthma,' said Jim, naively.

'Look inside the kennel,' Grant mouthed to Jim.

"In all the commotion Jim was oblivious, but Helen had noticed and knew something was up. She glanced inside, while Elizabeth turned her focus back on Grant, who began to pant very loudly. Helen took a few seconds to see what he was talking about, but when she finally realised, she let out a scream. There was her own baby inside the dog kennel, completely naked, except for a thin covering of red dog hair. He smiled and giggled as dog milk dripped down his face.

Elizabeth heard Helen's scream and turned towards her.

Helen panicked and grabbed her toe and began to hop on her foot. '*Jim*! My toe... you stood on my toe,' she said. All of a sudden there were another two front runners in the 1979 Oscars race for best supporting actor and actress.

Jim was the one who should have won the award, though, as his performance was much more natural. He was yet to discover why his wife and brother-in-law were making such a fuss. He was used to Helen being over-dramatic, but Grant usually wasn't. Fortunately, Elizabeth just seemed concerned for them both and hadn't looked inside the kennel again. Helen pointed her finger at the kennel to try and get Jim's attention, so he could see the debacle for himself and help work out how to fix the problem. Every time Elizabeth's eye's veered towards the dogs, Helen would scream out, 'It hurts... it hurts!' or Grant would fake another asthma attack. Elizabeth had become rather panicky and didn't know how to help.

Jim finally looked inside the kennel and when he saw his son, his eyes nearly popped out of their sockets. He tried to work out how he'd ended up in there in the first place and how bad this would look to a complete stranger. He mumbled to himself as his eyes gawked at his hairy baby son, 'Why's he covered in milk?'

Helen and Grant both continued to fake their medical predicaments to distract Elizabeth. Helen nodded at Jim every time Elizabeth's head was turned away from her. Jim saw this as his opportunity to grab his son and take him inside. Luckily, Jamie had seen all the commotion and had begun to crawl over to the kennel gate for a closer inspection - or to get involved! Jim made sure to position his body to block Elizabeth's view of Jamie, as he didn't want her to see how grossly inappropriate the situation was. He swept Jamie off the ground, where he was as happy as a pig in mud. *Woolworths, no! This is my real family now!* Jamie wriggled in his dad's arms and extraordinarily managed to let out a couple of little dog barks. Jim turned to Helen while shaking his head incredulously. What had they done to their child?

Jim managed to escape into the inside kennel and this was Helen's opportunity to stop her Oscar-winning performance. She cleared her throat loudly at Grant and nodded towards the kennel. Grant could also see the coast was clear and miraculously his asthma attack suddenly disappeared without the help of an inhaler. Elizabeth looked strangely at them both – she had been rather stressed over the whole situation. She now looked at the brother/sister duo untrustingly. Who were these people? There was chaos and panic one minute, but now they both seemed as right as rain. Something very fishy was going on here.

Helen smiled nervously at Elizabeth. 'Let's gather up your four puppies, shall we?' she said, matter-of-factly, though inside she was a bag of nerves. This was Elizabeth's chance to view her Irish Setters, which she was paying top dollar for.

The newfound peace only lasted for a matter of seconds as Frank came outside, mimicking an act he'd seen one of the wedding guests perform. He skipped around all of them, while lifting his T-shirt over his head. 'Boobies, boobies!' he sang as he flashed his bare chest at his mother, then Grant and finally Elizabeth, who was flabbergasted.

Helen was also shocked, as she'd never seen him do anything like it before. 'Frank. Frank, love. What are you doing?' she said through gritted teeth.

Frank then went up to Elizabeth and did a moony at her. 'Bums, bums, bums!' he sang out loud. Elizabeth was completely overwhelmed and upset, not knowing what kind of place she'd come to. She was a woman of civility, of etiquette, of normalcy - she wasn't used to this type of barbaric behaviour.

Helen grabbed her son, lifted him in the air and tried to pull up his trousers to cover his bare bottom. 'Frank, what the hell are you doing?' she asked.

'I'm just copying the people that got married,' he said and couldn't understand why Helen was upset with him.

Helen carried him towards the door to take him back inside, but turned to Grant first. 'Grant, will you please show Elizabeth her puppies? I'll take Frank inside. I'm terribly sorry, Miss Bonkly,' she said, making a "May-ism".

Elizabeth was now on the verge of tears as nerves shot up her body.

Helen carried Frank inside and was almost knocked over by Jimmy, who barged outside, soaked from head to toe. 'Who's fucking idea was it to have our buffet on the jetty? Bert and Vera fell into the fucking sea, and I had to jump in after them. They're soaked to the fucking skin. Your mother's had to call a fucking ambulance,' shouted Jimmy, irate.

Elizabeth had had enough. This was the final straw. She shrilled, 'This is an absolute madhouse! I've never been so offended in all my life!'. She ran for the door as quickly as she could, flustered and upset.

Helen put Frank down, placed her back to the wall and slid down to the ground, while covering her face with her hands. She felt mentally and physically drained.

***

Shortly after, Helen and Jim stood outside and watched an ambulance cart off Vera and Bert, the two old folks who'd fallen in the sea due to an overcrowded jetty. Jimmy had a face like thunder and was wrapped in a large towel. Jim had managed to take most of the dog hair off Jamie and dressed him again, and was holding onto him to make sure he wouldn't end up somewhere else he shouldn't. Jamie smiled. *What a brilliant day. Best one I've ever had.*

Helen was really annoyed as £200 pound had just gone down the drain with Elizabeth Barclay disappearing off the island. She certainly wouldn't be back, which meant they'd have to sell the puppies to the general public and wouldn't make a fifth of the money. Helen was also confused about Frank's weird behaviour. Most of the wedding guests had gone home, but a couple now ran out of the tea shop front door, half naked. The woman had her bra and pants on and the man had just his Y-fronts on – their jangly bits were bouncing about. Helen and Jim were distracted by the ambulance and everything that was going on across the road and they didn't see them.

Only Frank spotted the couple and he pulled at his mother's apron to try and get her attention. 'See, Mum. I didn't make it up about the boobies and bums,' he said.

Helen made a face at him and by the time she looked, the couple had disappeared around Ritchie Street. 'Frank, what is the matter with you today?' she asked.

Frank pouted his lips and looked a bit like a duck. Why did nobody ever believe him?

Helen turned to Jim, 'We really need to sort ourselves out. Today was a complete disaster.'

Jim laughed out loud. 'Life certainly isn't boring, dear,' he replied.

Round the corner on Ritchie Street, the half-naked couple ran past Grant and Gail. The teenagers had rekindled their romantic relationship and were passionately snogging. They'd both decided to draw a line over their fall out and start again.

Chapter 14

Jim and Helen had ventured out to Kames Bay, where there were some very grand houses opposite the beach. The two couples who had held their wedding reception at the tea shop had invited them to their house for a cheese and wine night. They all lived together, which Jim and Helen thought was slightly strange, but their busy summer was now over and they had some extra time to socialise. Grant had been left on babysitting duties, as he was the only one of the family who was left in Millport. When they'd told him where they were going, he'd thought it was odd, as did Frank. They'd both witnessed how weird the couples had acted during the wedding. Jim and Helen had been too distracted with all the other mishaps of the day and just thought that they were a little eccentric, thinking they were in for a fun night. Grant decided not to question their decision as it was an ideal opportunity to have Gail around to the flat. They'd reconnected and were very much the loved-up couple once again.

Jim and Helen arrived at the lavish, traditional-looking house that belonged to the two couples. Helen turned around to face the sea and smell the air. This reminded her why she loved Millport, especially after such a stressful summer. 'I'd love to live in one of these houses,' she said to Jim.

He was away in his own world as he'd been to see a solicitor in Glasgow and had a brilliant surprise for Helen. In his head, it was a great opportunity – one that he should have discussed with her, but as was typical of Jim, he had forgotten to have the conversation out loud.

Rona answered the door and she was practically wearing underwear. She had on a very racy velvet red bra (an Ann Summers one), which could be viewed through her revealing red negligee.

Jim's jaw almost dropped at the sight of her and Helen slapped him on the back. 'Awl!' he said.

Helen was very apprehensive about going inside. 'Is it a themed party?' she asked.

'Oh no, I just like to be comfortable in the house. Hope you don't mind,' said Rona. Helen looked at her suspiciously. 'Do come inside,' she said and she escorted Helen into the house. As Jim passed her, she eyed him from head to toe with sexy eyes and gave him a flirty smile.

Inside the house, there were about six different couples, who were all scantily dressed. Helen, who was a bit of a prude, was beginning to regret coming along. She was wearing a long hippy dress and had her long blonde hair down at her shoulders. Jim was dressed in his casual suit and he was slightly curious as to why the men at the cheese and wine night were wearing tight short shorts that were more akin to one of his gym classes, except he'd never obviously seen ones made of leather! Helen looked at Jim worriedly.

John came over to them with a couple of glasses of pre-poured red wine and handed them over. Then, Margo brought over a cheese-and-onion hedgehog that she'd prepared.

'Aren't you sweltering in that long dress, Helen?' asked Margo.

Helen shook her head. 'No, I get cold easily,' she replied as she pretended to shiver - as she continued to scan the room.

Margo then picked a bit of cheese off one of the sticks on the hedgehog and placed it inside Jim's mouth, before she preceded to unbutton the top two buttons on his shirt.

Helen was speechless and downed her red wine, as she was feeling so uncomfortable and didn't know how else to react. John put his arm around Helen's shoulder and she flinched. He began to massage her shoulders and then filled up her red wine. Helen tried to make eye contact with Jim, but he was flanked by both Rona and Margo now. He was oblivious to their physical contact being anything more than friendliness.

***

In the upstairs flat of the tea shop, Grant and Gail were on the couch and were passionately snogging one another. Frank was in his bedroom and had been given a Scottish teams football stickers magazine and two packs of cards. Gail had bought them in the Newsagents earlier. She thought it was an ideal way to bond with Frank, as she knew young boys usually loved football – and even if that wasn't the case, it would introduce him to the game. Grant had suggested it to her when she'd mentioned wanting to buy him something small. He had an ulterior motive, though, as it meant Frank would be in the bedroom instead of sitting in front of the TV, which gave him more alone time with Gail.

Jamie was lying in his bouncing cradle in front of the TV. Grant had put him in it after he wouldn't stop crying in his cot. He'd outgrown the cradle a while back and barely fitted inside at all. Grant had to make a real effort to strap him in and his feet were hanging right out, onto the floor. *Artful Dodger, you think you can keep me prisoner in this thing so you can eat up that Wee Punk. I don't think so, as baby ain't fucking stupid. It's not the Wee Shrimp you're dealing with here, with his wee sticker books.*

Grant gently unlocked lips with Gail and smiled at her with an amorous grin, then pulled out a crumpled-up piece of paper from his pocket. She stared at him curiously as he unwrapped the paper to reveal a small pile of tiny mushrooms. A few small ones dropped onto the floor. He raised his eyebrows at her and gave a mischievous smile. Gail was absolutely clueless. *Uh huh. They don't call you the Artful Dodger for nothing. I see what you're doing, you very naughty boy. Baby likes what he sees.*

***

Helen and Jim had been escorted over to the seating area in the house. En route, Rona had whispered in Jim's ear, 'I hope you brought your car keys, Jim,' in a sexy voice.

'I'm having a drink so I didn't bother,' he'd naively replied.

Helen was on the opposite side from Jim and had been cosily squashed in between Dennis and another man who was attending the party, much to her dismay. She was beginning to feel very uncomfortable now. Although she was normally a tactile person, these people were very overly friendly. She was also beginning to feel light-headed as she'd downed two glasses of red wine and had forgotten to eat. Jim wasn't so bad as he'd been force-fed the cheddar cheese-and-pickled onion hedgehog from Rona, who seemed to be on a mission to seduce him. The man next to Helen stuck his arm around her shoulder and she suddenly sat forward, then stood up from the couch and stumbled a little onto the coffee table in front of her.

'Where's the bathroom please?' said Helen. She tried to make eye contact with Jim, who was blissfully unaware of the female attention and was just enjoying his wine and cheese – one of his passions in life. Helen shouted over to him, 'Jim! I'm going to the toilet.'

John sprang up from the couch and placed his arm on her shoulder again. This time, she squirmed and quickly batted his hand away.

'No, I'll manage,' she said. 'Just tell me where it is, please.'

'First on the right, down the corridor,' said John, before moving away and nonchalantly putting his arm around another lady.

***

Gail sat doe-eyed across from Grant, while holding hands. Jamie was still in his cradle. He was trying to release himself from the loose strap that was holding him in. *This stupid strap. The Artful Dodger thinks he can hold me prisoner.* The TV was on and the news was blaring out. There was a news story about a Harrier jet crashing into a house and killing three people.

Gail looked disappointedly at Grant. 'Why do you think I'd want to take these?'

Grant continued with enthusiasm. ''Cause it will be fun. You see all kinds of weird and wonderful things through the hallucinations.'

Jamie's ears pricked up for a second. *I'll have some. I've been bored shitless today.* The strap unclipped as Jamie forced his body against it with all the strength he had.

'No, Grant. It's really impulsive to take drugs. People die on magic mushrooms,' said Gail.

'I don't think so. They just have a really cool time,' said Grant in a groovy voice.

What a knob!

'And besides, you're in charge of your nephews tonight. What if something happens to them? It's just really irresponsible, even the suggestion of it,' said Gail, who was clearly annoyed with him. She stood up from her seat and grabbed her jacket. 'Sometimes I just don't really see where you're coming from, Grant. I'm going home.' She went out the door.

'Come on, Gail. Don't get your knickers in a twist,' shouted Grant as he ran after her.

There appears to be trouble in punk world. Wee Punk needs to loosen up a bit and stop being a wee prude. Now, let's go and find some scraps. Jamie climbed off his baby cradle, which he'd resented being put in in the first place. *Do those muppets think I'm a newborn? I can fucking walk.*

He stood up and walked towards the couch and held himself up with the cushion, before deliberately plonking himself on the floor. He felt around the haggard old carpet with his hands and looked for the two small wayward mushrooms that Grant had dropped. He knew he only had a short window to consume them, so picked one up and stuck it in his mouth as quickly as he could. *This better be good. 'Cause it tastes rank.* He tried to chew with his mouth open and used his little new teeth to bite into the mushroom, eventually managing to swallow some.

He eyed up the living room door that had been left open. *Good time to escape.* He decided he would be quicker to crawl towards it rather than walk, as he was much more confident on his hands and knees. Once out the room he could see the front door for the flat had also been left open. *The perfect opportunity. It's about time I escaped from this madhouse.* He crawled down the corridor and out of the front door, ending up on top of the landing where he was met by a set of stairs that spiraled downward. *Never been down these by myself before.*

Jamie placed his hands on the top stair and his feet a bit further down until he was lying on his front, fully stretched. He let go of his grip on the top step and slid down a few stairs fairly slowly. *Ye ha. It's like being at the showies on the helter-skelter.* He slid fairly slowly to start, but sped up and began to bang his limbs. *Awl, you fucking bastard!* Fortunately, he was wearing an all-in-one night-suit that covered most of his body, therefore the carpet burns were fairly minimal. He was beginning to feel a little light-headed as he tumbled down the stairs. On the last few, he rolled onto his side and went down more like a barrel. His body hit the deck after the last stair and he lay on his back, out of breath, a little bruised but still very much alive.

Phew. That was a close one. He gathered himself together and rolled onto his front and stared down the corridor. *The front door is shut, so an escape seems to be out of the question… Oh yes… ye wee beauty. The Artful Dodger has been very, very stupid. I see the light… Lots and lots… of beautiful swirling colours.*

***

Helen was in the downstairs cloakroom of the two wedding couples' house and was doing a pee. She felt really anxious and on edge, worried that Jim was having too much of a good time. What if he refused to leave with her? They had been each other's first time and only believed in monogamy – or at least she did. No, she was sure of the man she had married. He could be a little sexually innocent and probably wouldn't even pick up on any signals.

She wiped, pulled up her knickers, pulled down her dress and flushed the toilet, then went to wash her hands. While she rubbed soap on them, she noticed that there were a load of pictures of the two couples hanging on the bathroom wall, above the sink. It suddenly dawned on her. They had been married before to opposite partners and had swapped. There were pictures of Rona and John at their wedding, but also of Rona married to Dennis and the same with the other bride, Margo. Helen was shocked and knew she had to rescue oblivious Jim and leave as discretely as possible. She needed to find him ASAP before he was seduced by these two vixens. It was so typical; this had been her first night out all year... and now look - she had joined a sex cult! Helen took a deep breath and decided to just be her forthright self. These people's morals were on a different scale to anyone she'd ever met, she was sure of that. She opened the cloakroom door and made her way into the living room.

***

Jamie was outside in the garden of the tea shop. He'd managed to walk past the kennel area and the mud patch and made it to the gate, which was blowing and creaking in the wind. He closed his eyes and began to see a clear picture of the night sky – all the stars, the planets and the moon. It felt like he was in the midst of the universe – so beautiful and recognisable.

I've been here before. I know I have. This is where I'm meant to go. He felt a light glow around his entire body, but he no longer felt like a baby – he felt like he was more than one person. He felt like many people who had previously walked the earth. It felt really weird and strange and he began to question who he was. He opened his eyes and he could see a cluster of large glowing elevated arrows that pointed in one direction. This was definitely a sign. He realised he was six feet tall and was an adult. His body was strong and robust, and he knew he had to follow the arrows that would guide him.

***

Helen barged into the sitting room. She was going to be forthright and rescue Jim from the depths of depravity. She thought she'd see six hungry woman lying on top of her husband and would need to fight them off one by one. Fortunately, she'd only been gone for five minutes and he was just sitting forward and digging into the whole cheese-and-onion hedgehog while guzzling copious amounts of red wine. It was the good stuff, the kind you would get in France – the wine they couldn't afford.

The couples around him were being seriously raunchy with one another and there was a bowl in the middle of the table that had a load of car keys inside of it. Helen had heard about these parties. Full of debauchery, with everyone sleeping with anyone, swapping partners and having sex in the public eye. The idea of this made her sick in the stomach. She looked at her husband and felt safe and couldn't love him more – at how naive he was being. He was completely clueless to his surroundings.

Dennis stood up from the couch after spotting Helen. 'Helen, wonderful,' he said as he attempted to grab her hand. 'Just in time for the games to begin.' Helen edged herself away.

Jim seemed pleased – he was having a great time. All the things he loved – cheese, wine and now games – what a night this was.

Dennis shouted loudly, 'Who's first to pick?' He turned to Helen, 'Why don't you pick first, Helen. Seeing as you're the newbies.'

Helen pulled away harshly. 'I feel sick,' she blurted out.

She marched over to Jim and grabbed his hand, pulling him off the couch. 'Jim, we're leaving! Now!'

'But the fun and games are about to start,' said Jim, disappointed.

'It's not the kind of fun you think it is. These aren't the games we play at Christmas,' said Helen, determined to drag her husband out of the door.

Margo, who'd had her eye on Jim all night, stood up sexily and whispered in Jim's ear, 'But *we* play these games at Christmas, Jim.'

Helen had reached her limit. 'He's my husband and we're leaving,' she said, dragging Jim by the hand as much as she could.

***

Grant was outside the tea shop with Gail. He was begging her to stay. 'Look, Gail, I'm sorry – okay? I thought we could have a little fun together,' said Grant.

'You've got two small nephews upstairs who you're meant to be in charge of right now,' Gail replied. 'I know we're young, but I want the boy I fall in love with to be someone I could raise a family with.'

Grant's face looked like he was on a road and a truck was about to run him over in the next few seconds. Gail suddenly realised what she'd said, thinking she'd made a massive blunder. They'd talked over the fact that they were still very young and that the serious stuff could wait for at least a decade.

'This is what I mean, Gail. You're talking about marriage and kids. I just want us to be young and have fun,' said Grant. He hadn't thought negatively about their relationship since they'd got back together and here she was acting like they were in their mid-twenties. 'I need to go back inside to check on Jamie and Frank,' he said as he turned to leave Gail standing there.

Once again she'd messed up by being overly eager about their relationship. He was about to go back inside, but Gail – who'd previously held in her thoughts – said, 'I will do fun stuff, Grant, but tonight we need to make sure the boys are looked after. Imagine if anything happened to one of them. You'd feel guilty for the rest of your life.'

He turned to her and held out his hand. 'Will you come back inside and help me?' asked Grant.

Gail grabbed his hand. 'Yes, but no magic mushrooms tonight,' she said.

***

The birch tree was covered in glowing lights and looked like Santa had had a Christmas wank all over it. Six-foot Jamie stared towards the tree, which appeared to be growing faster than the speed of light. There was a small twister circling around the bottom of the tree and Jamie was being drawn towards it. He took a step closer and was sucked up by the wind and began to circle inside the twister himself, going higher up the tree. He felt happy and knew he was going to a better place. Jamie could see his family members as he flew up the tree, but they all seemed distorted.

Woolworths' moustache was in the shape of a motorbike handlebar, twirling around at the ends with the actual hairs all bright-coloured – every colour you could imagine: red, yellow, pink, blue, violet. The list was endless and the moustache kept growing and covering Woolworths' face.

Blondie was also there and just like Woolworths, her hair was changing rapidly. It was growing and changing colour. Her once blonde hair was becoming longer and whiter and now covered her entire face. She looked like an albino version of Thing from *The Addams Family*. The Wee Shrimp had shrunken down even more, if that was even possible. He had his little face, but his eyes were black and hard and stuck out from their sockets. His abdomen was a pink colour, hard-shelled and semi-transparent. He had extra limp legs and a fanlike tail. All three of them were there, but Jamie was flying away from them. He was going somewhere new.

***

Helen and Jim had just escaped from the house of ill repute.

'What was that all about, dear? I was really enjoying that lovely wine and cheese,' said Jim. Helen looked him up and down. 'And we were about to play some fun games,' he continued, genuinely a bit annoyed.

Helen shook her head. 'Why do you think all the men in there put their car keys in the bowl?' she asked.

'I don't know, but I'm sure Dennis was about to explain the rules,' said Jim.

'Seriously, Jim. I thought I was uneducated about sex until I met you,' said Helen as Jim looked on, puzzled.

'Well, I could see it was a "tarts and surfers" party. A new take on the old "vicars and tarts" parties,' said Jim.

'Yes, Jim. The women were dressed as tarts because they were tarts. And the men were also scantily clad, not because they were surfers, but...' said Helen to Jim, who was still trying to work it all out. 'But because we were at a sex swapping party and that is why the car keys were in the bowl,' continued Helen, pleased that she'd worked it out and Jim hadn't.

Jim's face suddenly dropped as he remembered something.

'Jim, what is it?' asked Helen, recognising the look on Jim's face.

'One of us better go back inside then,' said Jim, as he laughed out loud.

'Why, Jim? What have you done?' Helen replied, agitated.

''Cause I put the tea shop keys in the bowl. I didn't have my car keys,' he said as he snorted through his nose.

Helen lightly clipped him around the head - even she couldn't instantly think of a way to get out of this one.

***

Grant and Gail had just walked into the living room to discover that Jamie had disappeared from his cradle. Grant slapped himself on the forehead. 'Where's he gone?' he said in a panic.

Gail ran to the kitchen and looked there. 'He's not in here,' she shouted as she checked all the cupboards and even in the fridge, just in case.

Grant ran to Jim and Helen's bedroom and looked everywhere – including inside the wardrobe and under the bed. 'He's not in here either!' said Grant. He was sweating profusely and breathing heavily.

Gail went to Frank's room and popped her head in. Frank was sitting up on the bed – he'd opened the sticker book Gail had bought him and was in the middle of sticking the Steve Archibald sticker into the book next to the Aberdeen Football Club. 'Frank, have you seen your little brother? Did he come in here?' asked Gail.

Frank looked at her. 'No – and let's hope he's lost.' Gail looked at him suspiciously.

Grant came barging in the room. 'Frank. Where's Jamie?' he asked as he went down on the floor and checked under the beds and the wardrobe.

Frank stared at them. 'Maybe he's been buried in the garden,' he said, with a deadpan face.

Gail looked a bit creeped out – she hadn't really interacted with Frank too much before.

***

Helen barged back into the party like Queen Boudica - to retrieve the tea shop keys. She hadn't knocked on the door as she wanted little interaction from these sex-hungry perverts. She had to cover her eyes as the couples were now fornicating with one another and she didn't want to see their bits. Dennis, however, spotted Helen and looked pleased.

'Did you come back for some sexy fun, Helen?' he said and went to approach her.

She put her hand right out in front of him. 'Certainly not. I'm just here for our keys,' said Helen, dismissively. She grabbed them from the bowl and stuck them in her bag. On the table was a full bottle of red wine and a half-eaten cheese-and-onion hedgehog. Helen grabbed the wine and the hedgehog. 'I'm taking these,' she said to Dennis, who didn't seem to care. She side-stepped her way out the door and Dennis shouted to her as she was leaving, 'Helen, you'll always be the one who got away, with those lovely big bouncing boobs.'

Helen turned to them all. 'You're filthy – and your minds are in the gutter,' she shouted. 'I'm very happy with my boring one-positioned sex life in my monogamous relationship with the man I love.' She left and slammed the door.

Jim stood behind her and had heard her exit speech. He raised his eyebrows at his wife. 'And what position might that be?' he asked.

'The missionary,' replied Helen.

'What's that one?' asked Jim.

'The one we do all the time,' replied Helen.

Jim raised his head. 'Ah,' he said as he had a proper think.

***

Six-foot Jamie was at the top of the extended birch tree, with his arms and legs spread like he was sprawled out on a bed, but he was mid-air and appeared to be levitating. There was a shining bright light in the sky in front of him, which turned a maroon colour and changed to look like curtains on a stage.

'Jamie Coyle, why are you here so soon?' asked a voice behind the curtain. The voice was like candy floss, if you could imagine candy floss talking – soft, fluffy and very unusual.

Jamie's entire adult body was lit up with a bright white light. 'I've come to pass. I think I've been here long enough,' he said.

The curtain suddenly opened and there in front of Jamie was a very weird-looking creature. It had a cloud for a head; bright yellow pebbles for eyes; a gobstopper nose, that looked like it had been recently licked by a child; lips made from the hard, green skin of a watermelon - baring fleshy red watermelon-meat teeth; and long seaweed hair that awkwardly waggled in the wind. Its neck was the shaft of an upside-down, black umbrella - it's many legs being formed from the six spokes that protruded from its base - like an umbrella that had been inverted by a big gust of wind. At the end of each spoke then dangled a different animals foot; like a wind chime - a duck's, an ostrich's, a pig's, a human's, a horse's and a tortoise's. In between floated a body, made of pink parachute silk festooned in long, red, fur which seemed to flow as if underwater.

Jamie stared towards this creature, mesmerised by its weirdness. 'Who are you?' asked Jamie in a deep adult voice.

'Who am I? Why, I am Mae-mae, the gatekeeper for all that is beyond the sky,' said the voice in a very marshmallow voice – if a marshmallow could speak.

'And your name's not on the list,' Mae-mae continued.

Jamie was mad at this. 'But I've had enough! Think it's time for me to pass. I've been here so many times,' said angry older Jamie.

'No, no, no! You have a whole life ahead of you and I can't, won't, let you pass,' said Mae-mae.

'But the people you sent me to live with are total nutters,' Jamie replied.

'You fit in with them perfectly,' replied Mae-mae.

All of a sudden, Jamie began to fall from his levitating position and his body began to reverse age as he fell towards the ground. He went from being an adult, to a teenager, to a young kid, to a toddler, then back to a baby in seconds. Baby Jamie lay on the ground, below the tree. His eyes were closed as he lay still.

***

Helen and Jim were walking along the high street, swigging out of the red wine bottle that Helen had stolen from the sex party. They were also nibbling on bits of cheese and pickled onions. They decided to nip through the Garrison for a change of scene and felt a bit like teenagers again. They passed the paddling pool and Jim took off his socks and shoes, then jumped in for a paddle and began to splash about. There were a couple of teenagers up ahead who were skateboarding. Jim splashed and soaked Helen's dress as she polished off the red wine with a massive gulp, spilling some on her hippy dress. She was pretty drunk and spotted the skateboarders.

'I'm going to ask them for a shot,' said Helen in a drunken slur. She ran towards them and Jim looked on, not sure if it was a good idea.

'Gimme a go,' said Helen to one of the boys and he jumped off.

Jim was over at the pool and was now sitting down, putting his socks back on. Helen stepped onto the skateboard with one foot, pushed with the other foot and travelled for a few seconds before she suddenly lost her balance, flew up into the air and landed awkwardly on her leg. She screamed out, clearly in pain, and Jim ran towards her.

***

Grant and Gail were searching in the garden for Jamie. They'd searched everywhere else, but hadn't found him. Grant was in a full-on panic, knowing he'd have to tell his sister he'd lost her baby.

Gail was over at the birch tree. 'Grant! Grant! He's over here,' she shouted.

Jamie was lying flat on his back with his eyes open, staring up towards the top of the tree. Gail bent down and picked him up. Grant rushed over, took him off her and checked he was okay.

Ga… ga… goo… goo. Jamie stared towards his uncle blankly. 'Mae-mae,' he said and Grant was relieved. To his knowledge, he hadn't spoken out loud yet.

Gail became excited. 'Aw! He's trying to say Mamma,' she said.

'Glad we found him. Let's take him inside to warm him up,' replied Grant, relieved.

Jamie continued to stare towards his Uncle. *Ga… ga… goo… goo.*

Chapter 15

Helen was lying in bed in a hospital in Glasgow after her self-inflicted accident. The doctor in Millport had discovered she'd broken her leg at the femur and she'd had to be taken to Glasgow in an ambulance. She'd insisted that Jim go back and tend to the children, adamant that she'd go to the hospital by herself. She'd needed an operation, which had gone okay, but she now had six months of recovery ahead of her.

Once Jim had been home and had a sleep, he decided to take the kids for a visit to cheer her up. He also had an ulterior motive for taking them, as it would soften the blow for what he was about to tell her.

She was lying in bed with her leg elevated in a brace. Jim came into the room with Jamie and Frank. Frank ran over to his mother and went to hug her. Jamie, who was in Jim's arms, just stared goggle-eyed towards Helen.

'Is he alright?' Helen asked Jim. 'He seems different. Maybe it's just the bright lights in here.'

Frank made a smart face to his mum. 'What did you do, Mum?' he asked. 'Were you drunk?'

Jim snorted.

Helen looked scornfully at him. 'What did you tell him?'

'Nothing,' replied Jim.

'I may as well tell you myself then. Mum was not drunk, but she was very stupid as she had a shot at using a skateboard, then fell off it and broke her leg,' said Helen.

Jim thought that this could be a good time to break his news to her. He took out a large set of keys from his trouser pocket, held them up and jingled them in front of her.

Doctor Douglas came in the room and picked up the notes at the end of Helen's bed.

'Good news, Helen,' Jim said with a massive grin.

Helen looked at him suspiciously. 'What have you done, Jim Coyle?' she asked.

'Remember a while back when we went to view the Millerston Hotel round at West Bay?' asked Jim. Doctor Douglas pensively scanned the notes.

'And you said how great it would be to live there,' continued Jim.

'Yes, but we both agreed it was too expensive and wouldn't be the right time because of…' said Helen, as she nodded towards Jamie.

Ga… Ga… Goo… Goo. Jamie stared blankly back at her.

'We both must remember a different conversation entirely,' said Jim.

Helen glared at her husband. 'Jim! I swear—'

'Surprise! We're now hotel owners,' Jim interrupted, dangling the keys in front of her.

Helen looked daggers at Jim.

Doctor Douglas brought the notes over. 'Mrs Coyle. Fortunately, no harm has come to the baby, but in future I would advise that you are careful. Skateboarding—'

'I wasn't holding my baby when I was on the skateboard, Doctor. He was at home with his uncle,' said Helen.

'I'm talking about your *unborn* child.'

'My what?' asked Helen and Jim looked directly at his wife suspiciously.

Frank slapped his hands on his forehead. 'Not another one!' he said to himself and stared at Jamie, annoyed.

Ga… Ga…. Goo… Goo.

'Helen?' asked Jim, shrugging his free shoulder.

'You're approximately three months pregnant,' said Doctor Douglas.

'But I can't be, because he's had a vasectomy. Did you not get it done, Jim?' asked Helen.

'Have you slept with someone else, Helen?' Jim whispered.

'When did you have this vasectomy?' asked the doctor.

'He was meant to have it in May,' said Helen.

'Did you wait the three-month period to allow the sperm to clear in the tubes? Your doctor should have advised you of this,' said Doctor Douglas.

Helen looked at Jim and was absolutely livid. 'No, Doctor, we did not. *Did we, Jim?!*'

'I'm sure I told you that dear,' replied Jim